THE EIGHTH COMMANDMENT —Sinful pleasures and stolen treasures terminate the lifestyles of the rich and famous . . .

> "Exciting suspense!"—*Nashville Banner*

THE TENTH COMMANDMENT —A detective tracks a team of killers who have turned religion into a racket for revenge . . .

> "Sanders is a pro!"—*Los Angeles Times*

THE SIXTH COMMANDMENT —One doctor breaks all the laws of God and Man . . . and one investigator must put them back together again . . .

> "The work of a master!"—*The New Yorker*

CAPITAL CRIMES —A power-crazed holy man holds the White House enthralled in a stormy alliance between good and evil . . .

> "Fascinating!"—*Los Angeles Times*

STOLEN BLESSINGS —The private life of a Hollywood superstar explodes in a public scandal of sex and crime . . .

> "A master!"—*Richmond Times-Dispatch*

THE TIMOTHY FILES —The shocking bestseller that opens the private files of private investigator, Timothy Cone . . .

> "Sanders shines!"—*Houston Post*

TIMOTHY'S GAME —Timothy Cone returns, to the lowest depths of New York City's criminal underworld . . .

> "A winner!"—*New York Times*

CAPER—A mystery writer plans a make-believe caper that turns horribly and murderously real . . .

> "Fresh, entertaining, tough and sexy!"—*Washington Post*

THE ANDERSON TAPES —The nationwide bestseller that launched Sanders' career and introduced Edward X. Delaney, hero of the "Deadly Sins" books . . .

"Action and suspense!"—*New York Times*

THE FIRST DEADLY SIN —One of the greatest suspense novels of all time. Delaney tracks a pickax killer on New York's posh East Side . . .

"Breathtakingly exciting!"—*Newsday*

THE SECOND DEADLY SIN —Delaney tries to solve the murder that shocked New York's "unshockable" art world . . .

"Best of the year!"—*Barkham Reviews*

THE THIRD DEADLY SIN —A "Hotel Ripper" stalks the city with a Swiss Army knife, until retired cop Delaney checks in . . .

"First-rate!"—*New York Times*

THE FOURTH DEADLY SIN —The brutal murder of a psychiatrist provides Delaney with six suspects: the doctor's own patients . . .

"Provocative!"—*Buffalo News*

THE MARLOW CHRONICLES —A brilliant actor is cast in the most demanding role of his career: his own death . . .

"It's a sin not to enjoy Sanders!"—*Columbia State* (SC)

LOVE SONGS —The dark side of the music world erupts in a storm of sex, drugs and scandal . . .

"Breathtaking!"—*Boston Globe*

THE SEDUCTION OF PETER S. —The smash bestseller about a man who pursues woman's oldest profession, until the Mob steps in . . .

"Totally engrossing!"—*Kansas City Star*

Continued . . .

THE PASSION OF MOLLY T. —The shocking erotic thriller of the loves and hatreds that consume one extraordinary woman . . .

"Action and intrigue!" —*Buffalo Evening News*

THE CASE OF LUCY BENDING —On the dark side of Florida's Gold Coast, evil can be as innocent as an eight-year-old nymphet . . .

"Supersonic narrative!" —*Los Angeles Times*

THE LOVES OF HARRY DANCER —A desperate, hunted man must turn the tables on seduction, betrayal and murder . . .

"Remarkable talent!" —*Wichita Falls Times*

THE PLEASURES OF HELEN —The sensual and uncensored account of one woman searching for Mr. Right . . .

"Consistently satisfying!" —*Washington Post*

THE TANGENT OBJECTIVE —Black gold and white greed ignite a blood-red bonfire of international intrigue . . .

"Bristles with tension!" —*Chicago Sun-Times*

THE TANGENT FACTOR —A troubleshooter for an American oil company faces a ruthless power-player's desperate gamble . . .

"Sanders delivers!" —*Rolling Stone*

THE TOMORROW FILE —Sanders' most unusual thriller, set in a nightmare tomorrow of planned sex and casual terror . . .

"Brilliant, horrifying!" —Mario Puzo

THE DREAM LOVER —A dangerous obsession lures one haunted man into a Hollywood nightmare of betrayal . . .

"A masterful storyteller!" —*King Features Syndicate*

Available from Berkley Books

PRIVATE PLEASURES

Lawrence SANDERS

BERKLEY BOOKS, NEW YORK

PRIVATE PLEASURES

A Berkley Book/published by arrangement with
Lawrence A. Sanders, Inc.

PRINTING HISTORY
Berkley edition/January 1994

ISBN: 0-425-14031-8

BERKLEY®
Berkley Books are published by
The Berkley Publishing Group, 200 Madison Avenue,
New York, New York 10016.
BERKLEY and the "B" design are trademarks of
Berkley Publishing Corporation.

PRINTED IN THE UNITED STATES OF AMERICA

10   9   8

AUTHOR'S NOTE

The sex hormones testosterone and oxytocin actually do exist. But the uses to which they are put in this novel are fantasy.

L.S.

1

GREGORY BARROW

I am thirty-nine years old and have been married for almost ten years. My wife, Mabel, and I have one child, a nine-year-old named Chester. It is not a happy marriage, and Chester is not a happy boy.

For the past seven years I have been employed as a senior chemist at McWhortle Laboratory, Inc. McWhortle's was essentially a research lab, developing new products for a long list of pharmaceutical, industrial, and consumer-oriented companies. We obtained patents on our inventions and then licensed them to our clients for manufacture.

Our specialty was biochemical formulas, including sedatives, stimulants, and synthetic hormones. One research section was devoted solely to the blending of new scents and fragrances for the perfume industry. And we had developed several chemical products for the U.S. armed forces. Those cannot be described here.

After working for almost two years, I had succeeded in developing a new method of synthesizing testosterone, the male sex hormone. My process, for which a patent had been filed, was relatively inexpensive and could easily be adapted to mass production.

This research was financed by a company that made and marketed personal toiletries and nonprescription drugs. The client hoped we would be able to isolate the element in testosterone that was responsible for one of the secondary male sexual characteristics: the growth of body hair. It was believed that if the project was successful, eventually an oral medication or injection might be a cure for alopecia (baldness) in both men and women. The commercial possibilities were dazzling.

On the morning of April 27 I was summoned to the office of Mr. Marvin McWhortle, our founder and chief executive officer. He was seated in a high-backed swivel chair behind his massive desk. Alongside the desk, lounging in a leather armchair, was a tall, narrow gentleman whose age I guessed to be about fifty. He was nattily dressed in civilian clothes but was introduced to me as Colonel Henry Knacker. His branch of the service was not mentioned, nor was his official position.

"Greg," Mr. McWhortle said, "the colonel would like to know more about our synthetic testosterone. You may answer all his questions."

Without preliminaries, the officer began to query me as to the exact chemical formulation of our new product and the method of manufacture. It was obvious Colonel Knacker knew a great deal about testosterone.

Suddenly his interrogation ended, and he stared at me a moment in silence. "You've worked for us before, Barrow," Colonel Knacker said flatly: a statement, not a question. "You signed an oath of secrecy. You're aware, aren't you, that there's no time limit on that oath. It is still in force. Understood?"

"Yes, sir," I said.

"There is no doubt whatsoever about Greg's loyalty," Mr. McWhortle put in.

"Loyalty is one thing," the officer said. "Secrecy is another. This conversation never took place. Clear?"

I nodded.

"Good. Now let's get down to bedrock. Testosterone is what makes men aggressive. Agreed?"

"It is generally thought so," I said cautiously. "But behavioral research is continuing to determine if testosterone is the sole cause of aggression or if other factors may be involved. These might include heredity, education, social status, and so forth."

"I know all that cowflop," the colonel said impatiently. "But I also know that studies have linked high testosterone levels to men who are aggressive, intensely competitive, and seek to dominate. Correct?"

"Yes, sir," I said. "But women can also be aggressive, competitive, and seek to dominate, even though their testosterone levels are much lower than those in men."

"All to the good," Knacker said with a tight smile. "Since women now play an important role in the military and may soon find themselves in battle action. *Capisce*?"

Apparently Mr. McWhortle felt matters were not progressing rapidly enough, for he interrupted the dialogue between the officer and myself.

"What the colonel has in mind, Greg," he said

briskly, "is developing a testosterone diet additive—pill, powder, or liquid—that would increase the combat efficiency of the average soldier."

"Even if the effect is only temporary," Knacker said earnestly. "We'd like to give our boys—and girls, too, of course—an extra edge in a firefight. We call it the Strength-Action-Power pill."

I confess I did not immediately question the morality or ethicality of what he proposed. My first reaction was astonishment at the name of the product.

"Strength-Action-Power?" I repeated hesitantly. "Colonel, the acronym of what you suggest is SAP. If news ever does leak out about the program, I'm afraid it would arouse a great deal of amusement in the media. That might even result in the cancellation of the project."

"Good lord, colonel," Mr. McWhortle said. "I never thought of that. SAP just won't fly."

"Suppose you name the diet additive Zest-Action-Power," I suggested. "ZAP is easy to say, easy to remember, and it implies moving swiftly to attack."

The officer looked at me admiringly. "I like the way you think, Barrow," he said. "ZAP it is! Now tell me: Do you think a testosterone pill to improve battle performance can be developed?"

"Possibly," I said warily. "But it would require a great deal of research, including animal testing followed by trials on human volunteers. The dosage would have to be very carefully calculated, and even then the long-term side effects might prove dangerous. We're dealing with an extremely powerful hormone here, and the ways in which it affects human behavior are still not fully understood."

"But do you think ZAP is *possible*?" he repeated. "One little pill or maybe a tasteless powder mixed in field rations? It could mean the difference between victory and defeat. It could be of vital importance to your country, Barrow. Concur?"

"Yes, sir," I said. "I think such a diet additive could be developed. Not overnight, of course. It would require an enormous amount of work."

"And I might add," Mr. McWhortle said quickly, "an enormous budget."

"Let me worry about the expense," Colonel Knacker said. "You guys worry about inventing a pill that'll make every American line doggie eager to charge into the cannon's mouth. How soon can you get started?"

I looked at Mr. McWhortle.

"As soon as funds are made available," he said smoothly.

"They're available right now," the officer assured him. "Get cracking—and remember, this involves national security."

"Of course," Mr. McWhortle said. "No problem. The entire project will be conducted in total secrecy. Am I correct, Greg?"

"Yes, sir," I said.

And that's how it all began.

2

MARLEEN TODD

Greg was driving that week, and the moment I climbed into his old Volvo I knew he was in a down mood. He usually greets me with a cheery "Good morning!" But on that day, April 27, he barely mumbled a hello.

"Well, don't you smell nice," I said, hoping to give him a lift. "It's the new after-shave I asked you to try, isn't it?"

He nodded.

"Like it?"

"Yes," he said. "Woodsy."

"That it is," I said, "and the client loves it. They're going to call it Roughneck. Isn't that a hoot?"

He didn't reply, and I didn't say anything until we had left Rustling Palms Estates and were on Federal Highway, heading for the lab.

"How was your evening, Greg?" I asked him, thinking perhaps he and Mabel had had another run-in.

"Mercifully quiet," he said. "Chester went upstairs to do his homework, Mabel watched one of her travelogues on TV, and I worked in the den."

"Greg, do you have to bring work home every night?"

"It's preferable," he said, and I knew what he meant.

He didn't speak again until we were through town and out in the country. "And how was your night?" he asked. "Did Herman come home?"

"Eventually," I said as lightly as I could. "Smelling of Johnnie Walker. Black Label, I believe. He said he was at a sales meeting. He went directly to sleep, and Tania and I played a game of Chinese checkers. Then, after she went upstairs to bed, I finished my needle-point pillow. And that was my exciting evening."

"Is this all there is?" Greg said wonderingly, and I looked at him.

And that was the extent of our conversation until he pulled into the underground garage and parked in his numbered space. I started to get out of the car, but suddenly he said, "Chester called me a wimp this morning."

"Oh, Greg," I said, "that's awful. Why on earth did he say that?"

"It was a silly thing," he said, "but significant, I suppose. We finished breakfast, and I got up to leave for work. Mabel told me to take my umbrella. She said the radio had predicted possible showers. I explained as patiently as I could—not for the first time, I assure you—that I would enter the car in our garage, drive directly to the lab, park in an underground garage, eat lunch in the employees' cafeteria, and then drive home in the evening. I would not brave the elements a single moment during the day, so an umbrella seemed unnecessary. But she just said, 'Take it. You don't know what's best for you.' So to avoid an argument, I carried my stupid umbrella. I was leaving the house when my son called me a wimp."

He was silent then, obviously troubled, and I didn't know what to say.

"Marleen," he said, almost desperately, "you don't think I'm a wimp, do you?"

I put a hand on his arm. "Of course, I don't, Greg," I said. "I think you are a very sensitive, caring man with many, *many* fine qualities, and I hope you stay just the way you are."

I left him then because he looked so woebegone that I was afraid he might start weeping, and I didn't quite know how I'd handle it. I took the elevator up to my office, thinking of Greg's problems and thinking of mine. I wondered about the two of us, wondered if it was a case of misery loving company or if there was more to it than that.

I sat at my desk and reread my final report on the development of Roughneck. The client would be responsible for design of the bottle and label, so I was finished and could get to work on my next assignment.

It was a proposal from Darcy & Sons, one of our oldest clients, for a new perfume, cologne, and *eau de toilette*. As usual, the description of what they wanted was somewhat vague, but I was used to that. The saying in our trade is, "I'll know it when I smell it," and my job was to create a scent that would convince the client they had received exactly the product they had envisioned.

Darcy & Sons, believing that women's tastes and manner of living were returning to traditional ways, wanted a fragrance that gave the feeling of romance, intimacy, and warm understanding. They did *not* want anything too strong, spicy, or sexually aggressive. They were seeking a "quiet" fragrance that would recall a woman's first kiss, her wedding day, the birth of her first child. They wanted a "soft, sentimental, and nostalgic" scent that might bring back memories of happy days and enchanted nights. The key to the new product, Darcy's proposal stated, should be "love" and not "passion." And it had to be as attractive to men as it was to women.

They even had a name for this new perfume. It was to be called Cuddle.

I read this prospectus, then sat back and pondered how it might be converted into reality. In the art of blending perfumes, a good "nose" must be able to identify as many as two thousand different scents, to distinguish frangipani from ylang-ylang with one sniff. Even more important, a "nose" must remember the evocative characteristics of scents and how they meld or clash with others. An expert perfumer is not unlike a composer of music: disparate notes are combined to produce a melody.

I left my office and went into our aromatic lab where two other "noses" were already at work on their own projects. They were seated at individual tables, dipping small strips of blotter into vials of essences and then passing the sample beneath their nostrils for a quick initial sniff. The scented strip was then clamped to a rack to dry, for a dry scent is often quite different from a wet. Neither of the "noses" looked up as I entered the lab.

I went directly to our "library": rack after rack of corked bottles, jars, and flacons holding oils, resins, and liquids containing the condensed scents of plants, flowers, tree bark, herbs, nuts, fruits, and a few rare animal products. No one had actually counted but it was believed we had more than ten thousand different smells in the library.

I walked slowly along the rack holding flower fragrances, glancing at labels. After reading the Darcy proposal, it seemed to me that a meld of lavender, lilac, and violet might be desirable. Or would that be *too* old-fashioned for a modern woman who yearned for a return to traditional values? I returned to my office intending to scribble possible formulas that might fit the required specifications.

A small stack of trade magazines had been left on my desk. All McWhortle employees were expected to keep up with the most recent advances in chemical research, but few of us had time to do more than flip the pages of these technical journals, reading only those articles that might affect one's own specialty.

My eye was caught by an article in a periodical devoted to behavioral neuroscience. The title was "The Cuddle Hormone," and I remember smiling because Cuddle was the name Darcy & Sons had selected for their new perfume. I began reading.

On the drive home that evening, I asked Greg, "Do hormones smell?"

He treated my question seriously. Greg very rarely laughed.

"I doubt if there is one hormonal scent, but I know my synthetic testosterone has an odor. It smells faintly of walnuts. Why do you ask?"

"Just wondering," I said. "Are you still working on the baldness remedy?"

"No," he said. "I was taken off today. It's been turned over to Steve Cohen."

"Oh? And what are you doing now?"

"Something else," he said shortly, and I knew better than to ask for details. Greg sometimes works on classified projects for the government. Hush-hush stuff. But it's not poison gas or anything deadly. Greg would never do that, I know.

"Would you and Mabel like to come over tonight for bridge?" I asked.

"Thanks, Marleen," he said, "but I'm afraid we'll have to pass. I'm bringing a lot of work home. Some other time."

"Of course," I said, knowing there would never be another time.

We came off Federal Highway, and he slowed before turning into Hibiscus Drive, the curving access road that led to our adjoining homes.

"You know what I'd like to do," he said in a low voice. "Just keep driving. Anywhere."

"With me?" I said, half-teasing.

"Yes," he said, and I could hardly hear him. "With you."

3

MABEL BARROW

On April 27, Thursday morning, I had a session with Dr. Cherry Noble. It was only my third, and I still wasn't sure she was going to do me any good. But she was a female therapist, and I didn't want to Confess All to a man. Greg made no objection when I told him I was going to a shrink. He just looked at me.

I had the wrong idea. I thought I could ask questions, and Dr. Noble would give me the answers. Not bloody likely. She'd ask questions, I'd answer, and she'd say, "Mmm."

For instance, I told her I liked to watch travelogues on TV. Other women watched sitcoms and soap operas; I enjoyed looking at Patagonia and Swaziland. Why was that?

"Why do you think it is?" Dr. Noble asked.

"I don't know," I said. "I guess I want to see foreign places. Learn how other people live. Do you think it's like, you know, I'm trying to escape?"

"Mmm," she said.

Silence.

"Sometimes I do strange things," I confessed. "I know they're weird, but I can't help doing them. Like this morning. I told Gregory to take his umbrella. The radio did say possible showers, but he never goes outside during the day. I knew that, but I insisted he carry an umbrella."

"Why do you think you did that?"

"Because he makes me feel so goddamned stupid, that's why. I had to assert myself. My husband is a very educated man, but he never talks to me about his work. I know he thinks I'm brainless. Believe me, I've got a brain. Maybe I'm not a research chemist, but I've got a brain. He ignores me. So I told him to take his umbrella."

"And did he?"

"Oh, sure. He'll do anything to avoid an argument. Because if we argued, that would make us equal, you see. I think he hates me."

"Why do you say that?"

"He brings work home almost every night so he won't have to talk to me."

"What do you want to talk about, Mabel?"

"Dopey little things. Like what the butcher said to me or how Chester is doing in spelling or silly stories in the news. Anything. But there's no communication. I'll bet he talks to Marleen."

"Who is Marleen?"

"Marleen Todd. She lives next door. She's married to Herman. He sells insurance. They have a little girl, Tania. She's one year younger than Chester. They take the bus to school together."

"Chester and Tania?"

"Yes. Marleen is a chemist at the lab. Like Greg. She makes perfumes. Greg drives one week, and then Marleen drives the next. They alternate. So they spend a lot of time together."

Silence.

"I don't believe there's anything going on there, doctor, if that's what you're thinking. Marleen is okay, very pleasant, but she's plain. No tits, no ass. I'm sure there's nothing going on there. They probably just talk shop. Besides, Greg isn't really interested in sex."

"Not at all?"

"Only occasionally. Like it's a duty. And if I turn him down, I think he's relieved. Once I gave him a funny birthday card that said, 'Use it or lose it,' but he didn't think it was funny. He hardly ever laughs. Herman is always laughing."

"Herman? Marleen's husband?"

"Yes. I think maybe he's got eyes for me."

"Why do you think that?"

"Sometimes, after Greg and Marleen have left for the lab and the kids have gone to school, Herman will stop by for a cup of coffee before he goes to his office."

"Are you attracted to him?"

"He's okay. No matinee idol, you understand, but he knows how to talk to a woman. He seems really interested in what I think and the things I say. You suppose he wants to start something?"

"Mmm."

Silence.

"When Greg and I were dating, I knew he was a serious man. The other guys I was seeing were mostly studs. One-night stands and so forth. But Greg was serious. Maybe a little dull, I knew that, but he had a good job and a good future. I figured that after I married him, I could lighten him up. Wrong! Maybe I shouldn't complain. He makes a nice living, I drive a Buick Roadmaster, and he doesn't say anything about my charge accounts. A lot of women I know are worse off. But still . . . Do you think I'm bored? Do you think that's why I'm so depressed all the time? Oh, and I forgot to tell you—he's a heavy drinker."

"Your husband?"

"Oh, God, no. Herman Todd. When he comes over in the morning, it's usually for black coffee and an aspirin for his hangover. He's not happy either. It's Marleen, his wife. She doesn't drink at all. Or smoke. She says it's because of her job with perfumes. Herman is a sport, always kidding around. The Todds came over for dinner last month, and Marleen and Greg kept talking shop. That's all they talked about, and finally Herman said, 'You know the difference between a vitamin and a hormone? You can't hear a vitamin.' They didn't laugh, but I thought it was hilarious. Don't you?"

"Mmm."

"Maybe he really does want to start something with me. I know for a fact he plays around. Do you think I should?"

"How do you feel about it?"

"I don't know how I feel. But I've got to do *something*. My life is empty, empty, empty. I mean there comes a time in every woman's life when she has to ask herself, is this all there is? That's where I'm at right now. I've even thought of getting a divorce. But getting a divorce just because you're bored is stupid, isn't it? And there's Chester to consider, of course."

"What about your husband? What would his reaction be?"

"If I asked for a divorce? He probably wouldn't care one way or the other. Greg doesn't love me."

"Surely he loved you enough to marry you."

"That was then, this is now. Maybe he loved me when he proposed. He said he did. But every Sunday night Greg makes out a list of things to do during the week: Get haircut. Take in drycleaning. Rotate tires on Volvo. Maybe I was just a note on his list: Marry Mabel. Oh God, I feel so miserable. I think I'm going to cry. May I have a Kleenex?"

"Help yourself."

Silence.

"What do you think I should do, doctor? About my life?"

"We've just begun. This is our third session—correct? I suggest you not make any major changes in your life until we have the opportunity to explore in greater detail exactly what it is that's troubling you. I think our time is up, Mabel."

"So soon? All right, I'll see you next Tuesday. I feel a lot better. Maybe all I need is someone to talk to."

"Mmm."

I left Dr. Noble's office and walked over to Hashbeam's Bo-teek, in the same mall. I went in to look around, and Laura, who always waits on me, showed me a new teddy they just got in: black lace cut high on the hips. Very racy.

"It's beautiful," I said, "but when would I ever wear it?"

"Put it in your hope chest," Laura said, laughing. So I bought it.

4

HERMAN TODD

I woke up late Thursday morning with a Godzilla of a hangover. Marleen had left for work, and Tania had gone to school, so I had the house to myself. That was just as well; I didn't want them to see the shape I was in. Although I doubt if they'd have been shocked; they've seen me before when I've had the meemies.

I drank about a quart of water, showered, and used my electric shaver with a trembling hand. Then I dressed and went next door to bum aspirin and black coffee from Mabel Barrow. (I've never figured out how to work that Italian coffee-maker my wife bought.) But Mabel wasn't home, so I had no choice but to drive to my office in the Town Center Circle.

Goldie was at her desk in the reception room, took one look at me, and shook her head sorrowfully.

"Save me," I pleaded.

She went down to the Dally-Deli and brought back a big container of black coffee and a prune Danish. Goldie is a sweet kid—great boobs—and I'd make a play there, but she's married to a police sergeant, and who needs trouble like that?

I gave Goldie the Danish, took the coffee into my private office, shut the door, and locked it. All my salesmen were out on calls, but I didn't want any of them returning unexpectedly, busting in on the boss, and catching him adding a double of California brandy to his morning coffee, which is what I did. After I got half of it down, I decided I might as well live, lighted a cigar, and started reviewing a million-dollar whole life insurance policy I had recently sold to Marvin McWhortle, who owns the place where Marleen works.

Around eleven o'clock I went out to the reception room and drew a cup of water from the cooler.

"Feeling better?" Goldie asked.

"Ready for a fight or a frolic," I assured her.

Back in my sanctum I added another shot of brandy to the water. That did the trick. I held out my hands, and they were steady enough to do brain surgery. By the time I was ready to leave, about noon, I was in fine fettle—whatever a fettle is. I told Goldie I'd be back in a couple of hours. She nodded; she knew I always had lunch with my brother on Thursday.

I stopped at the Dally-Deli and picked up two humongous corned beef sandwiches on rye, side orders of cole slaw, and an extra order of kosher dills, which Chas dearly loves. I went next to Ye Olde Reserve Fine Spirits & Liquors Shoppe (it opened last year) and bought a liter of Jack Daniels. Then I boarded my new Lincoln Towncar and started out.

I took my usual route: south to the Palmetto Park Road, then far west to the Fleecy Road turnoff, then north on Fleecy to a nameless dirt lane, and then west on that. Way back in the boondocks on five acres of what used to be hardscrabble farmland is where my brother lives and works. He calls it a studio; I call it a barn.

My brother—seven years older than I am—left two legs in Vietnam. The government wanted to fit him with prostheses and elbow canes, but Chas opted for a motorized wheelchair. He had a rough couple of years after he was shipped back—his mind was messed up—but he had psychotherapy and got it all together again. Now he writes children's books. He's not getting rich, but with his disability pension he does okay and won't take a cent from me. He's twice the man I'll ever be.

"Hello, shithead," he greeted me.

"Hi, asshole," I said. "You look beat. Been running the four-forty again?"

"I could take you any day," he said. "You're in great shape; your ass is dragging and your eyes are bleeding. You been dipping your wick around town again?"

"And I'm going to keep doing it," I said, "until I get it right." I displayed my purchases. "How does sour mash go with corned beef?"

"Let's find out," he said. "Pull up a chair."

It was more of a counter than a desk: a sheet of heavy plywood across two sawhorses, high enough so he could wheel his chair partly underneath and get close to his word processor. That's where I spread out our lunch and poured Jack Daniels into the jelly jars he used for glasses.

"How's Tania?" Chas asked.

"Okay."

"And Marleen?"

"She's fine."

"You're a lucky man," my brother said. "And a foursquare bastard for cheating on her."

"I can't help it," I said. "It's a terrible habit—like picking your nose."

He laughed. "I hope she nails you, sues for divorce, and takes you to the cleaners."

"She won't," I told him. "Marleen knows I tomcat around. She doesn't care who I boff—as long as it isn't her."

Chas looked at me. "Sonny boy," he said, "when it comes to women you're a total illiterate. Who you shagging these days? Anyone special?"

"Not really. I've got my eye on the butterball who lives next door. Great ass. But her husband works in the same lab as Marleen, and we visit back and forth occasionally. It would be hard to manage."

"You'll find a way," he said.

His questions about my love life were not just idle curiosity. When I said that Chas had straightened out his brain, it wasn't the complete truth. Since coming home legless from Nam, I don't think he had even tried making it with a woman. He said he just wasn't interested, but he sure as hell was interested in my extramarital feats.

I asked Dr. Cherry Noble about Chas. She was the shrink who pulled him out of his funk.

"He's a lot better," I told her, "but I don't think he's functioning in the sex department. He lost his legs, but he's still got all the necessary machinery. What gives?"

"He feels he's an incomplete man," Dr. Noble explained. "He's lost a part of himself. He's convinced women could be turned off by what he thinks is an ugly deformity. He's afraid that if he tries, he'll be rejected, or he won't be able to perform. So he doesn't try."

"How long will that last? For the rest of his life?"

"It could. But I'll try to bring him out of it. Chas is a fine man, and if anyone deserves a little joy, he does."

"Don't tell him," I said, "but send me your bills."

"There won't be any bills," she said.

I had one jelly jar of sour mash, but Chas was starting on his third when I left to go back to the office. He gave me an autographed copy of his new book to give to Tania. It was called *The Adventures of Tommy Termite*.

I was outside, unlocking the Lincoln, when Dr. Cherry Noble pulled up in her white Jag. She got out and came over to me.

"Herman!" she said. "What a pleasant surprise. I haven't seen you in ages—but I was thinking about you this morning. How are you?"

"If I felt any better, I'd be unconscious," I said. "And you?"

"Fine, thank you. You visited Chas?"

"For lunch. Every Thursday."

"Oh, that's right; I forgot. How is he feeling?"

"Fine, I think," I said. "Is he making any progress, doc?"

"Mmm," she said.

"Well, keep trying," I urged her. "I really appreciate it."

She nodded, and I watched her walk toward the barn. She was wearing a short pink linen sheath.

Great legs.

5

DR. CHERRY NOBLE

Chas Todd was the only Vietnam veteran I ever treated. I read all the literature on the subject I could find, but nothing I read prepared me for the severity of his problems. Fortunately, they proved as short-lived as they were intense. Still, it was almost two years before daily sessions could be gradually reduced.

I make no claim that it was my skills as a therapist that led to the disappearance of his horrendous nightmares, deep depression, and sudden onslaughts of uncontrollable weeping. I believe that with no assistance whatsoever he would eventually have recovered by himself. Chas Todd is a strong man.

During the course of his therapy I found myself attracted to him. At first he was profane with a penchant for scatological humor. But after he found I was unshockable, his speech became more conventional; he revealed a tender and vulnerable persona that I was convinced was the *real* Chas and not just a role he was playing.

I was aware of his atrophied libido, and our failure

23

to resolve that problem made his recovery less than
complete. I hoped that in time his rejection of sex
would fade. Doctors treat; nature heals. But it had
now been several years since his therapy ended and,
during my visits, I found no improvement.

He had locked the door after his brother left, but
when I knocked, I heard the hum of his motorized
wheelchair. A moment later he unlocked the door,
looked up at me, and smiled.

"My lucky day," he said. "And aren't you elegant!
Pink is definitely *your* color. Come on in."

His studio was in disarray. The remains of his lunch
with Herman were still scattered on his desk. I began
cleaning up.

"Forget it, Cherry," he said. "I'll get to it eventually. Would you like a dill pickle? There's one left."

"No, thanks," I said, laughing.

"How about a Jack Daniels?"

"A very small one with lots of water and lots of
ice. I'll mix it."

"Help yourself."

It was a ramshackle home, but he did have a small
kitchenette kept reasonably clean. I made my drink
and sat on a spindly ladder-back chair facing him.

"I met Herman outside," I said. "Did you have a
nice visit?"

"As usual. I'm always glad to see Herm—once a
week. I love my brother, but a little of him goes a
long way."

"Why do you say that, Chas?"

"He's such a lecher. That's all he thinks about—
chasing women. What makes a man act like that,
doc?"

"It could be a number of things. You say he continually chases women. Does he catch them?"

"Continually," he said, laughing. "If you can believe him. Then it's on to another conquest. What do you call a male nymphomaniac?"

"I call him a fool. But the term you want is probably satyr: a male who suffers from excessive sexual craving."

"Hermb doesn't seem to suffer." He gave me an ironic smile. "Just the opposite from me—right?"

"Mmm," I said.

"Hey," he said, "you promised to cut the 'Mmm' shit. I know that in your work you've got to be noncommittal. But not with me. Okay?"

"Mmm," I said, and we both giggled. "All right, Chas, I won't be noncommittal with you. How is your work coming along?"

"It doesn't get any easier. I thought it would, but it doesn't."

"Do you ever wonder why you write books for children?"

"Because I'm a kid at heart, that's why."

"Be serious."

"Of course, I've wondered why I write these fairy tales. You know what I decided? That they're an escape from reality."

"I thought you and I agreed there is no such thing as reality. There are only perceptions."

"Uh-huh. Well, let's just say I perceive reality as a world I don't particularly admire. So I created the world of Tommy Termite."

He poured more liquor into his jar. I've never met anyone who could drink as much as Chas and show no obvious effects. What his liver must look like I didn't care to imagine.

"How are you feeling?" I asked quietly. "Any nightmares?"

"Nope. Most of my sleep is dreamless."

"Depressed?"

"Only when my writing isn't going well. Don't worry abut me, doc; I've adjusted."

"No regrets?"

"About what?"

"And I thought *you* promised not to play games with me. Regrets for your lack of sexual desire, of course."

"Oh . . . that." He took a gulp of his drink. "I can live with it."

"I'm sure you can. But do you want to?"

"I don't have any choice," he said in a low voice.

"Of course you do," I said angrily. "I saw you change from a helpless wreck to an alert, functioning individual able to make a new life for himself. Therapy didn't do that. I didn't do it. You accomplished that because you *wanted* to change."

He shook his head. "I know I've got a hang-up," he said. "And I know the reasons for it as well as you do."

"Chas, would you like to start regular sessions again? Perhaps twice a week. I can come out here; you won't have to come to my office. Maybe we can work it out together."

"No," he said. "Thanks, but no."

I stared at him but he looked away. The upper part of his body had become heavily muscled. Grips and railings had been installed in his studio so he could lift himself into bed, onto the toilet, into the shower stall. It was vitally important to him to be absolutely independent—another reason he shunned my offer of assistance.

"You know what you're sacrificing, don't you?" I asked.

"I don't want to talk about it," he said.

I nodded, finished my drink, and rose to leave. He let me kiss his cheek. I was at the door when he called, "Cherry," and I turned.

"If I change my mind," he said with a wolfish grin, "you'll be the first to know."

I went outside and sat on the hot cushions of the Jaguar a few moments. I lighted a cigarette. I smoke infrequently, but at the moment I needed it.

I still felt there was more than a doctor-patient relationship between Chas and me. I knew how I felt about Chas, and I thought I knew how he felt about me.

That could be wishful thinking, of course. Let me say merely that I hoped my sense of his desire was correct. Not only did it hold out the possibility of his eventual happiness, it kept alive the possibility of mine.

6

CHAS TODD

I was ashamed of myself. That last thing I said to Cherry—"If I change my mind, you'll be the first to know"—that was stupid, macho posturing. As if my love was a great boon, to be bestowed if I felt like it.

Dr. Noble is a brainy lady; she knew very well the causes of my self-imposed celibacy. What she might not realize is what a stubborn man I am. Obstinacy has been my curse; I've always insisted on doing things my way—even when I know the suggestions of others make sense. There's no explaining it; I'm just pigheaded.

The studio seemed awfully empty after Cherry left. I wasn't able to pace, of course, but I could gun my chair back and forth, running down the battery and finding no tranquillity whatsoever. So I finished my jar of whiskey and capped the bottle. Not much left, but there were full bottles under the sink and under the bed. My 80-proof muse.

I believed that if I tried to make it with Dr. Noble, she'd go along. But I'd never know if she really *wanted* to, or if she intended it as part of my therapy.

And because I wasn't certain of what her motive might be, it seemed best to abstain and stew in my own juice.

Once, after I had been in therapy a year or so, Cherry asked me: "Why have you never married, Chas? I'm sure you have a dirty joke in answer to that, but I'd prefer the truth. Are you afraid of marriage? Don't want the responsibility? Don't want to lose your independence?"

"Oh, no," I told her, "nothing like that. As a matter of fact, I was engaged once. The date hadn't yet been set, but I was looking forward to marriage. Lucy was a marvelous woman. She was beautiful and she had a great sense of humor. I was happy with the idea of spending the rest of my life with her. She knew all my moods, and I don't think we ever had a serious disagreement. Then one day she was driving home from work and some drunken asshole in a pickup plowed into her car. That was the end of Lucy and the end of my dream of marriage."

"Oh, Chas," Cherry said softly, "I'm so sorry. What a shocking thing to happen."

What was really shocking was that the whole story was bullshit. There was never any Lucy. I was never engaged to be married. I just made up the whole thing on the spur of the moment. Don't ask me why. And Dr. Noble believed me because she later referred to it a few times. I think that's what helped me finally decide to try my hand at writing children's books. I figured if I could con a professional like Cherry with an impromptu fantasy, I should be able to spin believable yarns for kids.

And that's the way it worked out. I wasn't getting rich turning out kiddie shit—the illustrators made more money than I did—but my stuff sold well and didn't take long to write. It gave me a profession and kept me from crawling into a bottle of sour mash. That's what happened to my father. He died a lush from cirrhosis. Herman and I were both heavy drinkers, but neither of us was an alky. Not yet at least.

Now here's the cream of the jest: After writing children's books for a couple of years, my stories began to seem more real to me, *truer*, than my own life and the world around me. I started out scamming Dr. Noble with my Lucy fiction and succeeded in swindling myself. How's that for an O. Henry ending?

I stopped racing around the studio in my wheelchair and pulled up in front of my word processor. I switched it on and retrieved the few pages of a new book I had started. It seemed flat and lifeless, and I erased everything. Then I sat back and tried to dream up a fresh approach. But I couldn't concentrate. All I could think of was Cherry Noble in her short pink dress.

Once I asked her, "Why aren't you married?"

"I was," she said. "I'm divorced."

"Oh?" I said. "What happened?"

"It just didn't work out."

"Was he a shrink, too?"

"Yes," she said.

I didn't want to pry further. "Well, you don't act like a divorced woman," I told her.

She was amused. "How does a divorced woman act?"

"You know," I said. "Eager."

She considered that quite seriously. "I don't believe I'm eager, Chas," she said finally. "If you mean eager to marry again. It really doesn't seem all that important to me. Perhaps one day it will, but not now."

"So there's nothing doing in the romance department?"

She smiled. "I didn't say that."

Recalling that conversation gave me an idea for my new book. My New York editor had loved *The Adventures of Tommy Termite*. She had written, "You've made Tommy so *real*! How about a sequel?"

Now it occurred to me that I could do something with *The Romance of Tommy Termite*. I could create a girl termite called, say, Lucy. Tommy could be injured—maybe a shingle he's been gnawing falls on him or something like that. And Lucy comes along and nurses him back to health.

I liked it: a real "boy meets girl, boy loses girl, boy gets girl" story. I'd have to work out the details, but I thought the basic idea was a winner. There would be misunderstandings, of course, perhaps even arguments, but eventually Tommy and Lucy would get together and live happily ever after.

But that finish, I realized, didn't have to be the end of Tommy Termite. He and Lucy could marry, have children, and future books could be about the termite family, their tribulations and victories. I began to see it as a Termite Saga that went on for generations.

"No children?" I had once asked Cherry Noble.

"No," she said stiffly. "Not yet."

"You have time," I assured her.

She looked at me strangely. "Do I?" she said.

7

MARVIN MCWHORTLE

It was a wasted weekend—Gertrude insisted on visiting her dull family in West Palm Beach. Those people are *antiques*, and all they talk about are friends who fell and broke their hips and how slow Medicare payments are. It was enough to drive a man to drink—which it did.

But the new week brought a lovely spring morning. After I made a few phone calls and dictated a few letters, I went outside to the private practice putting green I had installed behind the laboratory. I spent an hour there and didn't do too badly. I sunk one 18-footer that was a lulu.

I went back inside, and Mrs. Collins told me Gregory Barrow had asked if he could see me for a few minutes.

I glanced at my watch. "Tell Barrow to come up now," I said. "If he stays more than ten minutes, you barge in and remind me of some appointment I'm supposed to have."

"Yes, Mr. McWhortle," she said.

I settled down behind my desk and lighted my first cigar. The company doctor wants to limit me to two a day, and I rarely smoke more than four.

Barrow came in, and I knew immediately he had a problem. The man is a world-class chemist but a real worrywart. He gets these two vertical lines between his eyebrows, and that means something is bothering him.

"Mr. McWhortle," he started, "it's about this ZAP project for the government."

"I'm glad you reminded me, Greg," I said. "I had a phone call from Colonel Knacker. He said from now on ZAP should not be called a diet additive but always referred to as a diet enrichment."

"Yes, sir," Greg said, "but what I wanted to speak to you about were the moral and ethical implications of the project. I've been doing a lot of thinking about it, and it seems to me we're treading on dangerous ground here."

"How so?"

"First of all, Colonel Knacker never explicitly stated that the combat soldiers will be told they're receiving a drug to make them more aggressive. I think informed consent is absolutely necessary if the government wants to avoid a scandal if ZAP becomes a matter of public knowledge."

"I see what you mean," I said, "and you're probably right. I think the best solution would be to announce the existence of ZAP, if it proves successful. Then put on a big public relations campaign to sell it to the enlisted men and women and to the American people as a harmless diet enrichment that will give our soldiers an edge in combat."

I could see he was not totally convinced.

"No one is going to be fed a drug without his or her knowledge, Greg," I said softly. "I'd never allow that to happen. But, believe me, when soldiers are told about the aggressive spirit ZAP will give them, they'll be happy to gulp it down because it will increase their chances of survival."

"I guess you're right, Mr. McWhortle," he said finally.

"Was that all you wanted to talk about?" I asked him, knowing it wasn't.

"One other thing," he said. "If soldiers are fed testosterone before going into battle, isn't there a danger that in addition to attacking the enemy they may also turn to slaughter, mutilation, rape, and other excessive forms of violent behavior?"

"Why, Greg," I said gently, "that depends on the strength of the dosage, does it not? And that's your job. The product you develop must be strong enough to achieve the result we want but not so powerful that it results in those horrendous acts of savage brutality you mentioned. If I didn't think you could do it, I wouldn't have handed you the assignment. You're the best chemist in the house, Greg. I know that, and I'm depending on you."

"Yes, sir," he said, standing. "Thank you, Mr. McWhortle."

Those worry lines were gone from his face. He was *such* an innocent.

"And remember," I cautioned him, "absolute secrecy is a must. Not a word of this to anyone."

The moment he was out of the office, I looked at my watch again and picked up my private phone.

The line doesn't go through our switchboard. I called Jessica Fiddler. She picked up on the second ring.

"Hello, Jess honey," I said. "It's Mac. Got time for me?"

"Oh, daddy," she said huskily, "I was hoping you'd call. I'm out at the pool in my new bikini. Bright red! You'll love it. Can you come over now?"

"On my way," I said, and hung up.

"Got a golf date, Mrs. Collins," I told my secretary. "If anything important comes up, you can leave a message at the club."

"Yes, Mr. McWhortle," she said.

Life can be beautiful.

I had bought the house for Jessica. It was in her name: the best investment I ever made. It wasn't a mansion, but it was a comfortable two-bedroom ranch with a patio and pool that faced south. Jess kept the fridge filled with my favorite snacks and the wet bar supplied with potions I preferred. Jess was twenty-one, looked sixteen, and was on the McWhortle Laboratory payroll as a consultant. I consulted her frequently.

I sat on the patio in the shade, sipping a Michelob Dark, while Jessica lolled in a chaise in the sunlight, her top off. Her body was the stuff of dreams. She had an apricot suntan, and she just gleamed. I loved everything about her. And if I was three times as old as she, so what?

"Have you been working hard?" she asked lazily.

"Too hard," I said. "But I've got to make a lot of money. Baby needs new shoes."

"You better believe it," she said, laughing. "What are you working on now?"

I enjoyed discussing business with Jessica. My wife

couldn't care less. Gertrude wants to talk about her garden and when are we going to buy a summer place in North Carolina. But Jess was really interested in the work being done at the lab. I had warned her never to repeat what I told her, and I figured she was smart enough to know that her income depended on her discretion.

"We landed a big government research contract," I told her, and explained how we hoped to develop a testosterone pill that would increase a soldier's aggressiveness.

She listened, fascinated. "You think it will really work?"

"It may or it may not. But we get paid either way—so how can we lose?"

She rose and came over to stand close to me. I put an arm about her and leaned close to kiss her flat stomach. She ran a palm over my bald head.

"Well, if that ZAP pill works," she said, "I don't want you trying it. You're powerful enough for me just the way you are."

"Let's go inside," I said.

I was a decamillionaire, I lived in a nineteen-room beachfront home, I drove a white Mercedes-Benz 560 SEL, but nothing I owned gave me as much pleasure as Jessica Fiddler. Holding that young, springy body in my arms made *me* young again; I could forget my hairless scalp, dentures, a ticker that keeps acting up. Making love to Jess was turning back the clock, to a time when I thought I'd live forever.

I liked to think I gave her something, too. I don't mean just the house, the salary, the gifts. I mean understanding companionship: a real interest in her health, her feelings, her hurts and her dreams. I also liked to think she enjoyed my lovemaking. She continually said she did, and if actions speak louder than words, she was telling the truth; she would do anything I asked her to do.

If you want to believe it was more obsession than love on my part, you may be right. But love *is* an obsession, is it not? All I knew was that if I could no longer hold that tight, fervid body in my arms, feel it, kiss it, I would suddenly become an old man.

8

MARLEEN TODD

Cuddle seemed to me a cornball name for a new perfume, but the client pays the piper and calls the tune. So when I saw that article, "The Cuddle Hormone," naturally I was interested and read it again on Monday morning to make certain I fully understood what the author was writing about.

Briefly, his subject was oxytocin, a hormone secreted by the pituitary gland, which stimulates uterine contractions during childbirth. It has been synthesized and for years women in labor have been given the synthetic form to ease pains and speed up birth.

But recent research indicated a more important role for oxytocin. It was found that it aided sexual arousal and, after intercourse, contributed to a feeling of satisfied relaxation. More curiously, in animal tests it seemed to result in increased affection, including stroking, grooming, and nuzzling.

Although for a long time oxytocin was studied for its physiological effects on women, it had now been discovered that heightened levels of the hormone were present in a man's blood during copulation and ejaculation. In fact, experiments were underway to see if added doses of oxytocin might help impotent men.

But it was the hormone's ability to foster feelings of pleasure and satisfaction that interested me, especially after I read that an aerosolized form of synthetic oxytocin had been developed. It seemed possible that such a spray might be used in a dilute amount in the new perfume.

If it succeeded, the hormone-enhanced fragrance would give women who wore it a desire for close affection and warm intimacy, and would arouse the same feelings in men who sniffed the scent. The effects of oxytocin on human behavior mentioned in the article seemed to indicate "love" rather than "passion"—exactly what the proposal from Darcy & Sons had stated was to be the leitmotiv of Cuddle.

Mulling all this, I wandered to my office window, looked down and saw morning sunlight glinting off the bald pate of Mr. McWhortle. He was practicing on his putting green, and even as I watched, he missed a shot that couldn't have been more than six inches. I laughed and went back to my desk. I wrote out a requisition to the supply department asking them to obtain what I estimated would be an ample supply of the aerosolized form of synthetic oxytocin.

It was quite possible, of course, that the addition of a hormone would have no effect whatsoever on the new perfume. So I spent the remainder of the morning jotting down several combinations of conventional scents I thought might serve for Cuddle if oxytocin proved a failure.

I like to lunch early in the employees' cafeteria, and so does Greg. We usually sit together at a table in a far corner, where we are away from the crush and have a small measure of privacy.

Greg was already seated when I filled my tray. We had both selected the same items: chef's salad, iced tea, key lime pie. He helped me unload my tray and gave me one of his buttered rolls because I had neglected to pick up my own at the serving counter.

"I don't know how I could have forgotten," I said.

"Probably too much on your mind," he said. "How is the new perfume coming along?"

"Slowly," I said. "And your project?"

"Even more slowly," he said, and we both smiled. Greg is notorious for his meticulous research. Then, not looking at me, he asked in a low voice, "And how are things at home?"

I hesitated a long moment before I replied. "Greg, I'm going to tell you something, and I know you won't repeat it to anyone. I'm thinking seriously of divorce."

Then he looked at me but said nothing.

"I want to avoid it," I said. "Because of Tania. But now I wonder which is worse for her: being a child of divorced parents or living in a home where all she sees and feels is coldness between Herman and me. It's such an unhappy situation for her."

"Marriage counselor?" he suggested quietly.

I shook my head. "I mentioned it, and Herman became absolutely livid. He refuses to discuss it. I think he's deliberately trying to make my life so miserable that I'll walk out on him. Then he'll be the aggrieved party, and if there's a divorce, he'll hold all the cards."

"Oh, Marleen," Greg said sorrowfully. He glanced around. The cafeteria was filling up. "Let's talk more about it on the drive home. This isn't the place."

I nodded, and we finished our lunch without saying anything more.

I went back to my office wondering if I had done the right thing to confide in Greg. But then I realized I had no other option. My parents are deceased, I'm an only child, and I have no close women friends. I had to talk to *someone*, and Greg is a thoughtful, serious man. And I knew he'd be understanding; his married life is as wretched as mine.

I was driving that week, and on the ride home that evening Greg and I resumed our luncheon discussion. I recited the whole sad litany about Herman's heavy drinking, his constant philandering.

"I thought he was a diamond in the rough when I married him," I said ruefully. "He turned out to be a zircon in the rough, and he's getting progressively worse."

"You've spoken to him about how you feel?"

"Many, many times. All he does is laugh and then give his awful imitation of John Wayne: 'A man's gotta do what a man's gotta do.' But what am *I* going to do, Greg?"

He was silent a long time. Then: "It's such a personal decision, Marleen, and so difficult that I hesitate to offer advice."

"You're not offering," I said, "I'm *asking*. I value your opinion. What do you think?"

"It seems to me," he said carefully, "that if you find your situation completely unendurable, then you must take steps to change it."

"That means divorce," I said determinedly. "There's no other way."

"Would you consider a trial separation?"

"For what purpose?" I demanded. "He's not going to change."

"Perhaps he might. After he's been away from you awhile and misses you and Tania."

"Never!" I said. "Herman is a self-centered oaf who thinks only of his own pleasures, which, in his case, mean whiskey and women. I blame myself. Marrying him was the worst mistake I've ever made in my life. I just didn't recognize him for the lout he is."

Greg moved uncomfortably in the passenger seat, and I realized my confession was embarrassing him.

"I'm sorry to dump all this on you, Greg," I said, "but you're really the only one I can talk to."

"I wish I could suggest some solution," he said despairingly. "But I'm no good at personal relations. Human behavior just mystifies me. I suppose that's why I turned to science."

"I think you're too hard on yourself," I said. "You're a sympathetic man, always willing to listen to other people's problems."

"Perhaps I'm willing to listen," he said forlornly, "but I don't seem capable of *doing* anything about them. And that includes my own problems."

I turned my Honda into our driveway and stopped. Greg started to get out of the car, then stopped and turned to me.

"Please don't do anything at the moment, Marleen," he said earnestly. "It may prove to be rash. Let me think about it awhile. All right?"

I nodded and watched him trudge across the lawn to his own home, to a marital misery that matched mine.

I had told him that I did not think him a wimp, and that was the truth. But I did wish he would be more assertive. He simply would not argue or even disagree. Not because he was weak and ineffectual, but because he was a sensitive man who abhorred crude, loud, and violent behavior. I believe it almost made him physically ill.

It wasn't timidity on his part. He just wanted everyone to be civil—a vain hope, as well I knew.

9

JESSICA FIDDLER

I'm a liar. I've lied all my life; I admit it. Not because I enjoyed it, but I *had* to lie if I wanted to survive.

Let me give you a for-instance. I told Marvin McWhortle I was twenty-one when actually I am twenty-six. Thank God I've got the body to get away with it. Besides, men are such shlubs about women's ages; ask them to guess, and they probably won't hit within five years.

Why did I lie to McWhortle? To make myself more attractive to him. I knew porking a twenty-one-year-old would give the geezer's ego a real charge, and that's how it worked out. Also, I call him daddy. He likes that.

If I had had a good education and learned to do something like run a computer or be a nurse, maybe I wouldn't have had to lie. But putting out for him a couple of times a week sure as hell beats selling pantyhose at K Mart. The house is in my name; he can't take that away from me. And the salary I get is

44

walking-around money. So I'm not complaining.

Marvin picked me up in a Miami hotel bar. He never asked me what I was doing there. Looking for a fish like him, that's what. But let me say this: After he set me up in his town, I never cheated on him once—and that's no lie.

I had been living in my house about six months when a guy came to the door and wanted to talk to me. He was well-dressed and all, and his silver Infiniti Q45 was parked at the curb, but I made him for a grifter right away, and believe me I've met a lot of them. It's their cool way, hard eyes, and the way they never blink that tip me off.

"What's it about?" I asked him. "You selling something?"

He handed me a card. He was William K. Brevoort, or claimed to be. No company name, no address; just the name and a phone number, engraved yet.

"Okay," I said, "now I know who you say you are and your phone number. But you haven't answered my question: What do you want to talk to me about?"

"About the Snakepit," he said.

I sighed. The Snakepit is a nude dance joint in Miami, and I worked there for almost a year. I quit after the place got busted for the fourth time. That's when I hit the convention circuit, which was how I happened to meet McWhortle.

"All right, Mr. William K. Brevoort," I said. "What's the game—a shakedown?"

"Far from it," he said. "You don't pay me; I pay you."

The guy looked like a weasel—a long, pointy nose, you know—but he didn't look like a mad rapist or even a strongarm, so I let him in the house. We sat in the living room, and he looked around.

"Nice," he said.

"Is that what you wanted to talk about?" I asked. "My interior decoration?"

He took a notebook from his jacket pocket and began flipping pages and reading out loud: "Jessica Mae Fiddler. Born in Macon, Georgia. Father deserted family when you were six. One brother in the navy, killed in a fire at sea. Mother died of cancer. Raised by your Aunt Matilda. You were kicked out of high school as incorrigible. Pot and moonshine. Lied about your age and married Bobbie Lee Sturgeon, a gas jockey. Marriage annulled. Moved to Atlanta. Busted for loitering for the purpose of prostitution. A fine but no jail time. Moved to Miami. Busted with the other girls at the Snakepit. No convictions. Now you're here in this nice house. Paid for by Marvin McWhortle, owner of McWhortle Laboratory. Have I got it all correct?"

"Close," I said, "but no cigar. You missed the time I got a ticket in Fort Lauderdale for double-parking. How much did it cost you to find out all that stuff?"

"Not much," he said. "It's easy when you know how."

"Why did you go to the trouble?"

"How about offering me a drink?"

"Talk first," I said. "What's on your mind? I know you're not law; your suit is too elegant."

"Nice," he said, stroking his lapel. "Italian gabardine. You like?"

"Cut the bullshit," I told him, "and make your pitch. If it's blackmail, McWhortle is the one you should be talking to."

He shook his head. "Not blackmail," he said. "Not my style. I buy and sell information. Buy from people who know and sell to people who want to know."

"So? What's that got to do with me?"

"Does McWhortle ever talk to you about his business?"

"Sure he does."

"About new products his lab is working on?"

"Yeah, sometimes he talks about those."

Brevoort stared at me. "Well?" he said.

"What would you like to drink?" I asked him.

And that's how it started. Whenever McWhortle told me about a new project at the lab, or brought me a sample of a new perfume or maybe a new headache pill, laxative, or whatever, I'd give Willie the Weasel a call, and he'd come over to get it. He always paid in cash and he wasn't a tightwad, I'll say that for him.

I never did learn where his office was, if he had one, and I never asked who his customers were. I figured the less I knew, the better—in case he ever got busted for stealing business secrets, you know. I don't think he was spying for Russia or anything like that. His clients were probably competitors of the companies that paid McWhortle Laboratory to develop new products, and I imagined they paid Willie mucho dinero for the information and samples I passed along to him. I got a thousand dollars a pop.

So now I had the house, I was a salaried employee with a Social Security number and paying withholding taxes and all, and in addition I had a safe deposit box that was filling up with the cash Brevoort paid me.

After McWhortle left me on that Monday afternoon, I waited a half-hour to make sure he wasn't coming back because he forgot something or wanted an instant replay of our roll in the hay. Then I called Willie. Most of the times I phoned I'd get his answering machine, but this time he was in. I said I had something for him, and he said he'd be right over. He was there in fifteen minutes—which meant his office or home was nearby, right?

As usual, he looked spiffy. I'll say this for him: He never made a move on me. Of course, he could have been gay, but I don't think so. I figured he didn't want to start anything because that would give me an edge on him, and he wanted to keep it strictly a business deal. As long as those hundred-dollar bills he handed out were good, I was satisfied.

I had a vodka martini and he had a club soda, while I told him about the big research contract the government had given McWhortle Laboratory to develop a pill that was supposed to make soldiers more aggressive.

"Nice," Brevoort said—his favorite word. "Did he happen to mention any of the ingredients?"

"Testo something."

"Testosterone?"

"Yeah, that's it. They call it the ZAP pill."

"Uh-huh," he said. "Keep asking him about it, Jess. Here's a grand. If they actually produce ZAP and you can get a sample, there'll be another two big ones for you."

"Oh-ho," I said. "That important, is it?"

"You have no idea," he said.

After he left, I had another drink and wondered if I had been wrong; maybe he really was selling my information to Russia or some other foreign place. But what the hell did I care.

It's all about survival. And survival means money. I knew that at the age of four. And believe me, only people with money can afford morals—even if a lot of richniks haven't got any to speak of. But when you're poor, dirt-poor like I've been, morals are a joke. You scratch, claw, and do a lot of things you'd rather not do just to survive.

I had nothing against Marvin McWhortle personally. He was getting what he wanted, and I was getting what I wanted. It was strictly business. Just like my deal with Willie the Weasel.

10

CHESTER BARROW

S ometimes I could kill them. Like tonight at supper, Mom is picking on Dad about buttered carrots. He don't like them, and she knows he don't like them. But she dumps a big spoonful on his plate and says, "Eat them."

He don't say a word but he eats the carrots. Some of them. Sort of pushing them around. What a wimp he is. Then they didn't talk at all anymore. So I got up and left the table.

"Where do you think you're going?" my mom yelled, but I just slammed out.

I went over to Ernie's, but his house was dark. Then I remembered they were going to the movies that night. My parents never take me to the movies. I don't care.

There were a lot of stars out, and I wondered what to do. I had a book report to write ("Tom Sawyer") but I didn't want to go back to my house. Dad would be working in the den with the door closed, and Mom would be watching one of her dopey travel shows on TV. They wouldn't even know I was home. They don't care.

I went through backyards, and Tania Todd was sitting on her back steps. She's a year younger than me but she's a good kid. We take the school bus together almost every morning, but I'm a grade ahead of her, so we don't have the same classes. But we both belong to the Nature Club.

"Hi, Tania," I said, and sat down next to her.

"Hi, Chet," she said.

My name is really Chester but I like to be called Chet. It sounds better.

"Why are you sitting out here?" I asked her.

"Just because," she said. Then she added, "Family matters."

"Yeah, well, I got the same thing," I said. "Sometimes grown-ups can act dopey."

She didn't say anything, and when I looked sideways at her, I saw she was crying. She wasn't making any sounds, but her face was all wet.

"Hey," I said, "you shouldn't be doing that."

"I can't help it," she said. "Why do they have to be that way—like they hate each other."

"I know," I said. "Mine, too. It makes you wonder why the hell they got married."

"You shouldn't swear," Tania said.

" 'Hell' isn't swearing," I told her. "It's just a plain word. I know some real swear words."

"Well, I don't want to hear them. My father says them sometimes, and I cover my ears."

"At least he talks," I said. "My dad don't even do that."

"Doesn't," she said.

The back door opened. Mrs. Todd came out and saw us. "What are you guys doing out here?" she asked,

"Just sitting," Tania said, not looking at her.

"That's nice," her mother said. "I have chocolate chip cookies. Would you like some, Chet?"

"Okay," I said, and she brought us a plate of them. They were still warm, so I guess she had just made them. "Thank you, Mrs. Todd," I said.

She went back inside and Tania and I had a cookie. They had a lot of chocolate bits in them, which I like. My mom gets the store-boughten kind that come in a plastic bag and they don't have enough chocolate in them.

"Sometimes I wish I had never been born," Tania said.

"Yeah, well," I said, "I feel like that sometimes, too. But we were. Born, I mean. So there's nothing we can do about it."

"Then I wish I had different parents. Like Sylvia Gottbaum. She and her brother and her mother and her father are always doing things together. Like this summer they're all going to Paris, France. I never get to go anywhere with my parents."

"And look at Ernie Hamilton," I pointed out. "He went to the movies tonight with his mom and dad. You know how many times my folks have taken me to the movies? Maybe three times; that's all. There's one cookie left. You want it?"

"You can have it, Chet."

"Thanks. Your mom is a good cook."

"I wish my father thought so. Maybe he'd come home for dinner more often."

"He doesn't come home? Where does he eat?"

"Oh, he always has business meetings and things like that. Anyway, that's what he says." She leaned close and whispered in my ear. "But I don't think so. I think he eats with other women."

"What other women?" I said in a low voice.

"I don't know," she whispered. "But I heard Mother tell him he smelled of *Passion*. That's a perfume. My mother knows all about perfumes. She makes them."

"But why would your dad want to have dinner with other women when your mother is such a good cook?"

"I don't know," she said. "But it makes Mother unhappy."

"Because he won't eat her cooking?"

"I guess. They're always being nasty about it. It scares me. I'm afraid they'll get in a real fight, and something awful will happen."

We were quiet a long time. It really was a super night with the stars and all. There was a half-moon and it lighted up the whole sky. It made everything seem big.

"You know," I said to Tania, "I've been thinking. Maybe I'll leave."

"Leave where?"

"Home. Maybe I'll leave home."

She turned to look at me. "But where would you go?"

"I don't know. But I'd like to go somewhere. Away from here."

"But how would you do it?" she asked. "I mean how would you travel?"

"I've got some money," I said. "Not very much, but maybe it's enough for a bus ticket somewhere. Or I could hitch a ride. Like on a truck going up north or anywhere. I don't care."

She was silent awhile. Then: "When are you going to go?"

"I don't know. I haven't decided yet. But I don't want to live at home anymore. I want to be someplace else. Maybe I'll meet some people who'll take me in. Nice people."

"Chet," Tania said, "can I go with you? When you decide to go, can I go along with you?"

"I don't know," I said. "It might be dangerous. I've never been away from home before. Ernie Hamilton, he went to camp."

"I don't care. If you go away, I want to go with you. Okay?"

"I'll have to think about it," I told her. "It's very important."

"I know it is. If you leave home, promise me I can go with you. Promise me, Chet. Cross your heart and hope to die."

"I'll think about it," I said, and that's all I said. After a while I got up and went home. Just like I knew, my father was in the den with the door closed, and Mom was watching TV.

I went upstairs to my bedroom, locked the door, and counted my money. I had four dollars and sixty-seven cents. I didn't know how much bus tickets cost, but I thought it would be more than that. But if Tania came with me, maybe she could get some money. I thought it would be great if we were just walking along and found a wallet someone had lost, and it had a lot of money in it. That would really be neat.

I'll tell you one thing: When I grow up and get married and have a kid, I won't be like my dad. I'll talk to my wife, as much as she wants, and I'll do things with my kid. Like I'll take him to the movies, and we'll go fishing. I've never been fishing. Also, I will play catch with him and things like that.

I felt like crying, but of course I didn't. It was okay for Tania to cry, she's a girl, but I couldn't cry. That's for girls and babies. Although once I saw my mom cry. I went into her bedroom without knocking, and she was sitting on the bed hunched over, and she was crying. I don't know what for. I just went away.

I never saw my father cry, but I never really heard him laugh either. Sometimes he smiles, but not very often.

After I run away, I'm going to laugh all the time. That shows you're happy, don't it? Well, I'm going to be happy. And Tania will laugh, too. We'll be happy together.

11

GREGORY BARROW

"I don't want to lean on you, Greg," Mr. McWhortle said to me, "but you know what the military is like: They want everything tomorrow. So requisition whatever you need and don't worry about the expense. We have a cost-plus contract; Uncle Sam is picking up the tab."

Actually, there wasn't a great deal I needed in the way of new hardware and supplies. My private research lab at McWhortle's is fully equipped and our own supply department could provide from stock most of the additional items I required.

I had two small video cameras on tripods moved in along with an eighteen-inch TV monitor and VCR. Stacks of small wire cages were arranged along one wall. They held thirty mice—ten males, twenty females of a normal strain. And I had a new lock affixed to the lab door. It could be opened only with a magnetic card. I kept one; the other was held by our security department.

After these arrangements were completed, I settled down in front of my PC and consulted the database I have found to be of most value in chemical research. I had done a great deal of reading on testosterone prior to developing the new synthetic formulation. Now I concentrated on the behavioral aspects of the sex hormone.

The information I gleaned was for the most part conjectural and, in some cases, contradictory. But I learned that it was generally believed that high testosterone levels were indeed linked to aggression. Apparently this was true of all the primates, not just humans.

Several studies concluded that high testosterone levels did not exist solely in muggers and football players but were also present in dominant and successful individuals in business, the professions, and the arts. There were some oddities noted: actors, for instance, were found to have a plenitude of the sex hormone, while ministers and academics usually had low levels. I wondered idly what my own testosterone level might be.

I found nothing in my research that indicated or even suggested that the ingestion of additional testosterone would heighten the aggressive behavior of human males. But neither did I find anything that flatly refuted such a possibility. So, in a sense, I would be venturing into terra incognita.

I wish I could tell you that I was completely engrossed by the ZAP Project and thought of nothing else. But I must confess my personal problems had assumed such size and complexity that they interfered with my concentration on the task assigned me. I admit it.

My confusion and indecision were compounded

when Marleen Todd told me she was contemplating divorce as her only means of escaping an unhappy marriage. My immediate reaction—which I didn't voice to her—was that it might serve me just as well: ending a marriage I found arid and mean.

There is something else I should disclose: I had long harbored suspicion that Chester was not my natural son. I married Mabel because she told me she was pregnant and refused to have an abortion. Marrying her seemed the proper thing to do.

It is true that I had sexual relations with her (once) prior to the time she discovered her pregnancy. But it is also true that at the time she was seeing other men, and I had little doubt that she had granted them the same favors she had granted me (once).

I suspected it was quite possible she didn't know precisely who the father of her child really was, and she had picked me because my income and career prospects were the best of all the men with whom she had been intimate. I had been selected as a victim, the one man who would pay for the indiscretions of several.

My reconstruction of what happened may or may not be accurate. But the uncertainty had soured my marriage from the start. Mabel and I—and eventually Chester—observed an armed truce, and what should have been a warm, loving relationship was spoiled by caution, inattention, and even rancor.

Despite all this—and here's the part I truly did not understand—I could not hate Mabel, even if my suspicion was correct. She had acted in her own best interest, and to blame a human being for doing that is akin to blaming them for breathing.

In truth, I believe I felt an odd affection for her, even though I rarely revealed it in word or deed. She was not an ill-natured woman. Prior to our marriage I had found her jolly, outgoing, and generous. Her present surliness, I knew, was due more to my chilly unresponsiveness than to her essential nature.

She had put on weight in the past several years—she was now quite chubby—but I still found her physically attractive, and I knew other men did as well. She was an immaculate woman, and I could not justly complain of her skills as a homemaker.

Recognizing all that, I suppose it was inevitable that my feelings toward her should be edged with guilt. She may have tricked me into marriage, but I bore some, if not most, of the fault for our failure to achieve a reasonably happy family life.

My feeling of guilt was even sharper in my relationship with Chester. To be honest, I loved the boy and yet could not express or display my love. I thought him handsome, alert, and possessing a delightful curiosity and innate intelligence. Why I could not communicate to him how I felt, I just don't know.

Finally I took up my pen again and resumed planning the ZAP project. It was a relief. Everything involved would be finite and determinable.

But human relations are infinite, are they not? There is nothing concrete to measure, nothing to weigh. And too often what you conclude from your observations is tainted by your own ignorance and prejudice.

I could study my caged mice, experiment with them, and record the results on videotape. But you can't do that with humans.

Can you?

On the ride home that evening I expressed to Marleen Todd some of my feelings about Chester.

"I know I'm not a good father," I confessed. "And yet I love the boy. I wish I knew how to get closer to him."

She asked if the two of us had ever done things together. For instance, had I ever taught him to ride a bike.

"No."

"Taken him to a football game? Any kind of a sporting event? A rock concert?"

"No," I said. "I really don't enjoy those things."

"*He* might," Marleen said gently. "You could ask."

"Yes, of course. But I have so much work. . . . Oh, Lord, I'm using that as an excuse again."

"Yes," she said, "you are."

"I'm good with *things*," I said angrily. "I know I am. But with people I'm an absolute klutz."

"Recognizing that is the first step," Marleen said. "Resolving to change is the next."

"Change," I repeated. "I'm not sure I can."

We were silent a long time. Then: "Will you help me?" I asked her.

"Yes," she said, "I will."

12

DR. CHERRY NOBLE

After I was divorced, I moved back into my parents' home—at their invitation—and resumed my maiden name. I had refused to accept alimony from Tom, a rather quixotic gesture, so the offer of a large bedroom, study, and bath in a comfortable two-story town house was welcome. The drive to my office took less than ten minutes.

My mother and father were in their late seventies and in excellent health, for which I was thankful. They were careful to respect my privacy, but always ready to provide companionship and counsel when asked. It really was a delightful household, and I considered myself fortunate.

"Would you like to visit my home?" I once asked Chas Todd. "I think you'll like it. A nice view of the ocean. I can borrow my father's old station wagon; your wheelchair will fit into that."

"No," he said. "Thanks, but no."

I told him that after listening to eight or more hours of human pain, it was a relief to drive home to the

61

peace and security of my parents' home. I could only wish all my patients had similar sanctuaries.

"I do," he said, but I didn't believe him.

My work was going well, my income was increasing, I was able to keep up with recent research in my field—so why wasn't I content?

Please notice that I use the word "content" rather than "happy." I have always felt that contentment is a more feasible aim than happiness. To be contented is to be satisfied with one's life. Happiness is something else.

"Physician, heal thyself." But in my case it was: Psychiatrist, analyze yourself. I did, frequently, and the reason for my discontent was not difficult to recognize. I lacked a man in my life.

I know there are those, including women, who will scoff at such a lament. Indeed, there are many women who lead productive and *contented* lives without men. But I am not one of them. I felt the absence of a man as a hunger.

Some of it was physical, of course. That was part of the craving I felt: the need for a naked male body pressed to mine. The other part was an emotional need: I wanted desperately to love and be loved in return. Not affection, not devotion, but *love*, mutual and complete. A romantic psychiatrist, you smile? Well, why not?

And so, on a Saturday afternoon, I drove out to visit Chas Todd.

He unlocked the door for me, then wheeled over to switch off his word processor. His housekeeper had obviously been there that morning; the barny studio was as clean and ordered as it could ever be.

"Were you working, Chas?" I asked. "Sorry to interrupt."

"That's okay," he said gruffly. "I wasn't really working; just reading over what I wrote last night."

"How is it coming?"

"I like it," he said, and laughed. "And I think you will, too. It's a love story, Cherry."

"I like it already," I told him.

"Between a boy termite and a girl termite. My God, you look great today. A luscious bouquet!"

I was wearing a flowered sundress. The back was wholly straps. I twirled in front of him. "You approve, Chas?"

"What's not to approve? How about a gin and tonic?"

"Only if you'll let me make them," I said and went into his tiny kitchenette. "I know what I'll get you for your birthday: a set of decent highball glasses. I'm tired of drinking out of jelly jars. When *is* your birthday?"

"You've got it in your records, doctor," he said.

There was an edge to his voice, but I let it pass. I handed him his drink and sat in one of his spindly kitchen chairs. We raised glasses to each other but made no toast. He took a deep gulp, then grinned at me. What a handsome hulk he was! A damaged hulk.

"Feeling all right?" I asked him. "No nightmares? No depression?"

"Nothing I can't handle," he assured me. "I'm fine. What have you been up to?"

"Work mostly. Plus an hour on the beach this morning and maybe another hour or two this afternoon."

"Yeah, you're getting a glam tan. But no serious mischief?"

"No," I said. "No mischief. How about you?" I saw his expression and added hastily, "I'm asking as your friend, not your shrink."

He shrugged. "Friend or shrink, no mischief to report."

"Drinking?"

"Of course I'm drinking," he said testily. "And smoking up a storm. And thinking lewd, lascivious thoughts. Okay?"

"The last part is," I said.

"You never give up, do you?" he said, shaking his head.

"No," I said, "I never do. Tell me more about the boy termite and the girl termite."

"He meets her, loses her, finally gets her. And they live HEA. That's trade talk for happily ever after."

"How does he lose her?"

Chas gave me a crooked smile. "Because the poor schlumpf can't get it up. Even termites have problems."

"But you said that eventually he gets the girl. How did he solve his problem?"

"Did you put any gin in this?" he demanded, holding out his empty glass. "I couldn't taste it."

I mixed a fresh drink and brought it to him. "Chas, you didn't answer my question: How did the boy termite solve his problem?"

"I was kidding, for chrissake," he said. "Let's just drop it."

"All right," I said.

He looked at me. "You never argue, do you?"

"Would it do any good?"

"No," he said, "it wouldn't. Tell me something, doc: Why do you waste your time with me?"

"I don't consider it a waste. I enjoy being with you."

"You do?" he said, sounding surprised. "I can't think why. I don't particularly enjoy being with myself."

I regarded him thoughtfully. For some time I had been wondering if shock therapy might cure his impotence, which, I was certain, was psychic in origin. I decided, at that moment, to try it. But it would have to be framed as a request rather than a question he could kill with an explosive "No!"

"Chas," I said quietly, "I'd like to make love to you."

It was the first time I had ever seen him blush. His naturally ruddy face took on a deeper hue, and I saw how shaken he was.

"What the hell is this?" he blustered. "Is this a new kind of treatment? Something you provide all your hung-up patients?"

"You know better than that. This is something for me."

"I don't believe it."

"Believe it," I said, confused by my own motives.

"It's impossible," he said hoarsely.

"Let's find out," I suggested.

"No!" he cried. "I don't want your pity."

"I want yours," I told him. "Please."

He sat there, face twisted, and I could see how this struggle was roiling him.

"No," he repeated in a softer voice. "I can't. I'm afraid."

"Of what?"

"Failure. Leave me alone, doc."

I finished my drink and rose. "You'll think about it after I go," I said. "I know you will."

"You think you know everything," he said furiously. "Get the hell out of here and don't come back."

I left, wondering if that line from *Hamlet* could be correct. "I must be cruel, only to be kind."

That evening a florist's box was delivered to my home. Inside was a luscious bouquet and a brief card from Chas: "Come back."

13

WILLIAM K. BREVOORT

I don't care how smart you are or how rich you are, if you haven't got The Luck you've got nothing, zip, zilch.

Now take me; I've always had The Luck. All my life.

Like I was running a small crib out in Denver. Nothing flashy, but clean. I had four girls—three white, one black—and a boy. None of them dopers. I also had a police sergeant on the pad, a nice enough guy who was as straight as a crooked cop can be.

One night Phil comes up to my place and I poured him a Chivas which was all he drank.

"Willie," he says, "I think you better get out of town."

That was all he had to say. I closed up shop and caught a plane the next morning. My kids got away, too. I read later the Denver vice cops had made a sweep the afternoon I was flying east. All the skin peddlers I knew got cuffed, and some of them ended up doing time.

See what I mean by having The Luck?

I went to Miami and looked up some wiseguys I knew to see if I could work a deal. But they were all in heavy stuff like drugs and guns. Not my style. So I went to Fort Lauderdale and located Big Bobby Gurk who was my cell mate once when I did a little bitty stretch in a Frisco clink.

Big Bobby had a good thing going. He was a bookies' bookie. Like if a street bookie had a real heavy play on a horse or a football team, he could lay off some of his bets with Bobby. For a fee, of course. Gurk was like a reinsurer and doing okay. But he had no place for me in his organization.

"But I heard of something you might like, Willie," he said to me. "I got a client and his brother-in-law is in the tile business. Floor and wall tiles. It's Italian stuff and expensive. This guy has got a competitor who sells the same tiles at a discount and it's killing him. The same importer sells to both of them and swears he charges both the same, but my client's brother-in-law don't believe him. He wants someone to crash his competitor's office and swipe the guy's invoices so he can find out what the guy is paying the importer for the tiles. Know what I mean?"

"I follow, Bobby," I said. "I'm no B-and-E guy but there may be another way to work it. What's he offering?"

"He says he'll pay a grand, but I think he'll spring for two."

"What's his name and where do I find him?"

It took me a week to cozy up to the competitor's secretary. She was a spacey broad who was saving up to put the down payment on a white Caddy convertiblé (used). For five yards she delivered to me photocopies of all her boss's recent billings from the importer of Italian tiles. I delivered them to my client and collected my two grand.

The Luck again.

Anyway, that was my first caper in what I learned later was called industrial espionage. It was like spying but no one got hurt, and the take was so good I bought myself a condo, a new Infiniti, and more clothes than I had ever owned before—suits and dresses.

If that stops you, I might as well confess I've been into cross-dressing most of my life. Now, in the bucks, I've got women's shoes, silk stockings, pantyhose, lingerie, evening gowns, sweaters and skirts, even a mink stole.

There are a lot of guys with the same hobby, and I stay in touch with some I've met all over the country. We mail each other Polaroids of ourselves all dolled up. There are cross-dressing clubs in every city I've ever been, and we have cocktail parties and fashion shows with prizes for the most attractive outfits.

You're probably not going to believe this, but none of us are gay or have had sex-change operations. We're just normal, average guys who happen to enjoy wearing women's clothes. Hey, it's not a crime; there are no victims.

I've met several good clients at cross-dressing soirées, and one I met about a year ago—wearing an absolutely stunning strapless silver lamé sheath—was the CEO of a company that sold cosmetics, grooming aids, suntan lotions, and stuff like that. I told him I was in the commercial information business, and he was *very* interested in what his competitors were having developed at the McWhortle Laboratory. He asked me to find out.

The Luck!

I tailed Marvin McWhortle for a week and discovered he was keeping a bunny named Jessica Fiddler. I ran a trace on her, and she had the specs of a sharp hustler. I figured she'd play ball, and she did. She sold me so many McWhortle secrets, including samples of new products, that I had three different clients buying information on perfumes, pharmaceuticals, and personal care products.

But when she told me about the ZAP Project to produce a testosterone pill that would make soldiers more aggressive, I knew immediately I was on to something that was too good to sell to a client for five or even ten big ones. Instead, I went back to Big Bobby Gurk and treated him to a twenty-four-ounce steak dinner.

"Bobby," I said, "years ago you steered me into a new career, and I appreciate it. I owe you one, and now I'm going to pay you back."

"Yeah?" he said, chomping away. "How?"

I told him about the ZAP pill and how, if it worked, it would make a Rambo out of a Milquetoast.

He stopped scarfing for a moment. "Hey," he said, "that's inarresting. But what's it got to do with me?"

"Look," I said, "you're in the gambling biz. Maybe you don't book bets yourself, but your clients do, and everyone says you're the best man in Florida on odds, points, and spreads."

"Maybe not the *best*," he said modestly. "Harry Finkle in Sarasota is pretty good."

"And you got connections all over the country," I went on. "Right?"

"Yeah," he admitted cautiously, "I got a few contacts."

"Well, how about this . . . ? Suppose, just suppose, the ZAP pill works, and I can glom on to a sample. We take it to a private chemist and he does an analysis. That's how we find out what's in the stuff. Once we know what's in it, we can have the chemist make up a supply."

"I still don't get it," Gurk said.

"Look, say there's a heavyweight title fight in Vegas. We go to the challenger's manager and tell him we got a pill that will make his boy a tiger. The manager wants to win, his boy wants to win, and we want to win—especially if the champ is heavily favored and we've bet a bundle on the challenger who gulps a ZAP pill."

"Now I get it," Bobby said slowly. "Or like there's a football team, a bunch of palookas with the odds against them. We play them heavy all over the country, and then we get the pills into their pizzas."

"Right," I said approvingly. "Or grind the pills into powder and sprinkle it into their water bucket. What do you think, Bobby?"

"Yeah," he said, pushing his empty plate away, "it might fly. Providing the pill works, of course. When can you get one?"

"I don't know. It's just being developed. I'm telling you about it now to see if you'd be interested if it's a success."

He looked at me. "And if it is, how much you asking?"

I shook my head. "This isn't a one-shot deal, Bobby. I want a piece of the action."

"Uh-huh," he said, "that makes sense. I think we could work something out along those lines. Listen, I gotta get back to my office. Let me know when you got the pill."

Later that night I attended a Rumba Dansant at my private club. I wore a dress that had been purchased at a West Palm Beach shop specializing in slightly used haute couture, designer gowns. Mine was a really gorgeous Galanos: a black lace chemise over a stretch body stocking. I had applied makeup, of course, and was wearing my new blond wig with short bangs and a chignon.

After the dance a fashion competition was held and I won first prize: a bottle of Dom Perignon.

The Luck was still with me.

14

TANIA TODD

Chet Barrow was just the handsomest boy I ever met in my whole life. And he was nice. I mean he never punched my arm or pushed me like that icky Ernie Hamilton does sometimes.

So when Chet told me he was thinking about running away I decided to go with him because in the first place I liked him and in the second place things were getting so nasty at my house that I just didn't want to live there anymore.

Like Daddy came home late one night, and you could tell he had been drinking alcohol. He and Mother got in a terrible fight. I was upstairs doing my homework but I could hear them. Then I heard a loud slap and Mom came rushing upstairs. She came into my room and locked the door. One side of her face was all red, and she was crying.

She sat on my bed and I went over and hugged her and she hugged me, and then I started to cry.

"Don't cry, darling," she said, trying to smile. "Please don't."

"You're crying," I said, "so I can, too." I touched her cheek. "Does it hurt?"

She shook her head but went into my bathroom and washed her face in cold water. Then she came out.

"May I sleep with you tonight, Tania?" she asked me.

"All right," I told her. "But try not to snore. The last time you slept with me, you snored and I couldn't sleep."

She laughed and hugged me again. "I promise not to snore," she said.

Well, she didn't but I couldn't sleep anyway because I was afraid Daddy might break down the door and come in and kill us or something. I just didn't know what to do, and then I decided I would talk to him and tell him how he was making me and Mother feel.

I didn't get a chance until Saturday when she went shopping. Daddy got up late and came downstairs acting grouchy. I made him some coffee and he said it was good coffee and drank three cups. He also ate a sticky bun. I ate one also and sat at the kitchen table with him.

"Daddy," I said, "I don't think you should drink so much alcohol."

"I don't drink so much, baby," he said. "Just enough to make me feel good."

"I am not a baby," I told him. "I'll be nine next year, and maybe alcohol makes you feel good, but it doesn't make Mother feel good or me either. And you slapped her. You shouldn't have done that."

He sighed. "I know I shouldn't, baby, and I'm going to apologize to her. Everything will be all right."

"Well, I don't see why you don't like her cooking. Mother is a very good cook; everyone says so."

He looked at me. "What makes you think I don't like her cooking?"

"Well, a lot of times you don't come home for dinner, and you smell of perfume, so I guess you had dinner with some other woman because you like her cooking better."

His face got all twisty. "Who told you I smell of perfume? Your mother?"

I didn't want to get her in trouble. "No," I said, "I smelled it myself. I know what perfume smells like."

"Listen, baby," he said, "sometimes you get too bossy. Maybe I do things that you and your mother don't like but that doesn't mean I don't love you. When you grow up, you'll discover that at times you do things that seem wrong to other people, but you just don't change because of other people's opinions. Either because you can't or because you don't want to. It's your own life. Do you understand what I'm saying?"

"Well, I don't understand why you drink so much alcohol when it makes Mother and me so unhappy, and you say you love us and all."

He stood up. "I've got to go, baby; I'm late for a golf date. Tell your mother not to expect me for dinner."

Then I knew he was just going to keep on doing like he was and nothing was going to be different. So I decided I better run away with Chet Barrow.

Chet didn't have much money and neither did I, but I thought that maybe if I left home my parents would be worried and Daddy would be so sorry for the way he had treated us that he really would change. Then even if the police found me and brought me back, Mother and Daddy would be so glad that everything would be better.

It was like a book I read that my uncle wrote. It was called *The Adventures of Tommy Termite*. It was about this boy termite who runs away because he thinks his parents don't love him and sometimes they are mean to him. A lot of things happen to him, some good and some bad, but finally he decides to go home and he finds his folks were worried sick about him, and now they love him and treat him nice.

I went looking for Chet, and he was in their garage. He was sitting on an old wooden box and looking at a folding map of the entire country. I sat down on the box next to him.

"What are you doing, Chet?" I asked him.

"I've been thinking," he said. "Look at how big the country is. See here—this dot? That's our town. Just look at all the places I've never been—the whole rest of the map."

"Are you looking for a place you want to go when you run away?"

"Not so loud," he said. "My dad went to the lab, but Mom's still in the house. Your father's in there, too."

"He is? He told me he had a golf date."

"Maybe he does. I heard him say he just stopped by to bum a cigarette. Hey, look here—this is the Intracoastal Waterway. You know where that is, don't you?"

"Of course. It's near Federal Highway."

"That's right. And it goes all the way up the coast. You get on a boat down here and you can go all the way up to Maine. Isn't that neat?"

"Uh-huh. Is that what you're going to do?"

"I haven't decided yet. I'm just planning things."

"Did you do what you promised?"

"What did I promise?"

"That you'd think about letting me go with you."

"Yeah, I been thinking about it. But I don't know . . . It could be dangerous. You might get hurt."

"I don't care. I want to go."

"Well, I'll keep planning about it. That don't mean I'm leaving tomorrow."

"Doesn't. I don't care how long it takes to decide. I talked to my father this morning, and nothing is going to change in my house so I might as well go."

"Your mother will cry."

"She cries now, Chet, and I'm still there."

He tried to fold up his map but he made a mess of it so I took it from him and folded it up right. We sat there awhile without talking. Chet scratched his ankle.

"You know," he said, "grown-ups are supposed to be so smart. I don't think they're so smart, do you?"

"Sometimes they can be dumb," I said. "Like this morning my father told me he couldn't stop drinking alcohol. You know that film we had at school about taking dope? It was like that, like he was addicted and couldn't stop."

"Maybe he is. Addicted, I mean."

"He could stop if he wanted to. Like I used to eat candy bars all the time. I got so fat. Remember that?"

"Yeah, I remember."

"Well, I decided I'd just quit and I did. Once I make up my mind to do something, I do it."

"But that's you. People are different."

"Well, I don't see why my father can't just decide to quit, and then he would."

"I don't know," Chet said. "Ernie Hamilton wants to stop picking at his zits and he's still doing it."

"Because he's a stupid boy."

"You really think so?"

"Yes. I do."

"Do you think I'm stupid, Tania?"

"Of course not. I think you're very smart. You get all good marks, don't you?"

"Well, maybe not *all*, but a lot of them. You're smart, too."

"Thank you," I said.

He turned to face me. Suddenly he leaned forward and kissed me right on the mouth. It was the first time a boy had ever kissed me. I pulled back.

"You shouldn't have done that," I told him.

"Sure I should," he said. "Did you like it?"

"Yes," I said.

15

MABEL BARROW

Greg went in to work on Saturday—he does that a lot—and Chester was outside when Herman Todd stopped by to ask if I could spare a cigarette. He looked sharp in a plaid sport jacket and lime green slacks. He said he had a golf date but he didn't seem to be in any hurry.

I was in the kitchen making a meat loaf we were going to have for dinner that night. And I was watching a travelogue about Baluchistan on the little portable TV I keep on the counter. But I turned it off when Herman came in and gave him a cigarette.

"You look very snazzy this morning," I told him.

"And you don't look like Mother Hubbard yourself," he said, grinning. "Now those are really *short* shorts."

"I like to be comfortable around the house," I said. "There's no point in dressing up to make a meat loaf or run a vacuum."

"It's a wonder Greg can get any work done if you dress like that," he said. "Is he around?"

"No, he went to the lab."

"All work and no play," he said. "Doesn't he ever relax?"

"Not very often."

"Too bad. He doesn't know what he's missing. How about you, Mabel? What do you do for kicks?"

"Watch Baluchistan on television."

"That sounds tame. Don't you ever get an urge to take a walk on the wild side?"

I was working at the sink and didn't look at him. "Such as?" I asked.

"Oh, this and that," he said. "There's a big, wonderful world out there, Mabel. A lot of fun, a lot of laughs. You should be getting your share."

"Someday," I said. "Maybe."

He came up close behind me and put a hand on my fanny. "Don't wait too long, sweetie," he whispered in my ear. "You and I could have a great scene together."

"Yeah?" I said. "How could we do that?" I don't know why I said it.

"It could be worked," he said, stroking my can. "Trust me. It would take some finagling, but it could be done. Will you think about it?"

I nodded, still not looking at him. He gave my butt a final pat and then he left. I held the edge of the sink because I was shaking. It was the first time a man had come on to me since my marriage, and I was all bollixed up. I decided I better tell Dr. Noble about it. That's what I was paying her for, wasn't it—advice.

I had a session with Cherry on Tuesday and told her how I had been propositioned. I didn't say who it was, but I had already mentioned Herman Todd so she probably guessed.

"How do you feel about it?" she asked me.

"Shaky," I said. "I want to and I don't want to. Oh, shit, I don't know how I feel. Tickled in a way because I can still turn a man on. What do you think I should do?"

She looked at me a moment, not saying anything. Then: "Mabel, how often do you and your husband have sex?"

"Infrequently," I said. "And that's one word, not two."

She didn't even smile. "Were you sexually active before your marriage?"

"Very. And I do mean *very*."

"What made you decide to get married?"

"Oh, I just figured it was time to settle down."

"Were you in love with Gregory?"

"Oh sure, I liked him. But to tell you the truth, doc, I liked all the men I dated, one way or another. I like men. That's no sin, is it?"

"Of course not. But of all the men you liked, you picked Gregory. Was there something special about him?"

I laughed. "Sure there was. He had a good job and good chances for promotion. You can't blame a girl for being practical, can you?"

"Mmm. Do you want to save your marriage, Mabel?"

"Of course I do. If it can be saved. I'm willing to do anything I can, but I'm not sure Greg is going to change. He's so cold and distant."

"Have you ever told him how you feel?"

"I've tried to. He just doesn't want to talk about it. To talk about *us*."

"Do you think he'd be willing to talk to me? I could see the two of you separately and then, if progress is made, the two of you together."

"Greg would never go for it. A lot of the work he does at the lab is secret; he never says a word about it. And gradually his life has become secret, too. He just won't reveal anything about himself. He won't talk about personal things. Not to me anyway. Sometimes I think he must hate me."

"Why would he hate you, Mabel?"

"Who the hell knows. I've never hurt him."

"Never?"

I found it hard to tell her. Listen, it's not easy to confess private things to a stranger. She may have been my therapist but she was still a stranger. I mean I liked her and all, but I wouldn't strip myself naked in front of her. And what she was asking was a lot harder than taking your clothes off.

But then I figured what was I paying her for and then holding back things that might help her to help me. That didn't make any sense at all. So I decided to tell her. I was sure she had heard worse things from some of her screwed-up customers.

"Actually, I did something," I told Dr. Noble, "but it couldn't have hurt Greg because he doesn't know the truth about it."

"What was it, Mabel?"

"Well, before I was married, I got pregnant. I told Greg it was his. Look, it might have been; I wasn't really telling a lie. But it also could have been four or five other guys. I was playing a big field and I just didn't know for sure."

"But you selected Gregory?"

I nodded.

"Why him?"

"I told you. He was smart and making a good living. The other guys weren't serious. If I had told them I was pregnant by them, maybe they'd have offered to pay for an abortion but probably they'd have said, 'Ta-ta, Mabel; lots of luck.' "

"Why didn't you have an abortion?"

I figured I better level with her. I had already confessed so much, it seemed silly to stop now.

"At the time I was working in a bakery. It was just walking-around money but I didn't need much. I was dating almost every night, so my food bills were nothing. And sometimes the guys would give me gifts. Costume jewelry or maybe a sweater. Nothing really expensive. I never took cash. Never! I had a great body in those days. Everyone said so. But the fun and games went on and on, and I began to get scared. I still had the bod, but I was getting a little long in the tooth. You know what South Florida is like—a new crop of centerfolds every year. I wasn't ancient or anything like that but I began to wonder what was going to happen to me. I'd see a bag lady rooting through a garbage can and I'd get the chills. I figured I better make a permanent connection real soon. And then I got knocked up. I know I'm not the brainiest woman in the world—you've probably discovered that for yourself—but I saw that pregnancy as leverage. You know? To get what I wanted: a steady husband and a home. So I picked Greg. I suppose you think I'm a stinker for doing that."

"No, I don't think you're a stinker, Mabel," Dr. Noble said. She really did have a nice smile. "I think you reacted to your circumstances in a remarkably sensible way. What you did solved your immediate problems—but it resulted in the new problems you have today. Do you think that's a fair assessment?"

"I guess."

"Mabel, I previously urged that until we can get your life straightened out I would prefer your not making any major changes. That includes having relations with the man you say propositioned you. I can't tell you what to do, of course; it's your decision. But I believe that if you start a new intimate relationship at this time, it will only add to your problems and make a solution more difficult. Will you think long and carefully before you decide?"

"Oh sure, doc, I'll do that."

"And now I think our time is up. See you on Thursday?"

"I'll be here."

I left Dr. Noble's office realizing she hadn't really told me what to do. I guess she didn't want to be blamed if what she told me to do turned sour. Like she said, it was my decision. The way I saw it, it was a no-win situation.

Laura at Hashbeam's had sent me a postcard saying they had a new shipment of sequined T-shirts she thought I might like. So I walked over there to take a look. I was feeling so miserable I had to buy *something*. Just for a lift, you know.

16

HERMAN TODD

I've played the fool all my life. And I've discovered you can know it and not do a damned thing about it. I mean you can be stone-cold sober and still act the fool. You do something stupid and you say to yourself, "This is stupid," but you keep right on doing it. I've decided a man is really a slave to his glands. At least I am.

"You're an erotomaniac," Chas once said to me. "When the hell are you going to grow up?"

"Never," I said. "What's the point, big brother?"

Wednesday was a rough one at the office. Most of my days are rough, but this was superrough: a lot of unexpected claims, two big deals that fell through, and a nutsy client who stormed into my office screaming his policy was paid up but he just got another premium notice. It took me an hour to calm him down and send him on his way. He was wrong, of course.

By four in the afternoon I'd had it and told Goldie I was going out to the club and she could reach me there if the office burned down or one of our agents dropped dead.

"In other words," she said, "you don't want to be bothered."

"Good thinking," I said.

This golf and tennis club I belong to is a great place. Marleen hates it but I love it. She'll only go out there for the New Year's Eve bash, but I'm there three or four times a week. I run up some humongous tabs, but the company hasn't complained yet since I've done a lot of business on the back nine or at the bar.

It's an unusual country club for Florida because it has absolutely no restrictions. Blacks, Jews, Cubans—we take anyone who can afford the fees. No prejudices whatsoever. My God, we even have members who don't drink.

One of the best things about the place is that a lot of women go there: wives, mistresses, girlfriends, or just wannabes. They go for golf or tennis, to have lunch, or to enjoy the free buffet during the Happy Hour. Usually there are more women than men in the bar.

By the time I got out there on that Wednesday, the Happy Hour was in full swing, and there were many, many gorgeous heads, not all of them with escorts. I exchanged greetings with several pals, male and female, and was finally able to belly up to the crowded bar and order a double vodka-rocks. By the time I got that down (ten minutes tops) my rough day at the office was a dim memory and I was looking around for company: something tasteful and friendly.

I didn't find her, she found me; asked me to light her long, brown cigarillo, and that was that. Her name was Laura, and she was a funky lady with marvelous lungs and a raspy voice she used to tell jokes usually heard only in the men's locker room. She was divorced, she said, and had just canceled her boyfriend.

Well, to make a long story short—if it isn't too late—we had more drinks, a lobster dinner at the club, and by midnight we were bouncing together on her king-size waterbed in a ground-floor condo in Boca.

"Pull the drapes, for God's sake," I said. "Or turn off the light."

"Nah," she said. "This place is totally inhabited by retirees. They take their Fiberall and they're asleep by nine. No one's going to peek in on us."

What a scrimmage that was! I staggered out of there around three A.M., wondering if I should head for the nearest Intensive Care Unit.

I was crossing the parking lot to my Lincoln when a guy who looked like a sumo wrestler stepped from the shadow of a bottle palm and fed me a knuckle sandwich that dumped me on my ass.

"You son of a bitch," he growled. "I see you around here again, you're dead meat."

He stalked toward Laura's apartment, and I had no desire to stop him. Would an injured hummingbird challenge a rabid rhino? I figured he was the "canceled" boyfriend, and dear, sweet Laura had left the drapes open, the light on, and had used me to raise his jealousy level.

Well, what the hell. I learned a long time ago that if you're going to drink and cruise, sooner or later you're going to get hurt.

I dragged my split lip and loosened bicuspid home to Rustling Palms Estates. Marleen and Tania were asleep, of course, so I stumbled into the guest bedroom and got most of my clothes off before I fell into the sack.

I awoke a little after eleven on Thursday morning, and naturally I had the house to myself. I phoned Goldie and told her I'd be late.

"I already know that," she said.

I tossed down an ounce of cognac, took a hot shower, and then put an icebag on my puffed lip. It didn't look too bad, but my loose tooth was throbbing. I used my electric shaver, dressed, and went over to the Barrows. I hoped Mabel would make me a cup of coffee, and while she was doing that, I could take up where I had left off Saturday morning.

But she wasn't home, so I got in my car and headed toward my brother's studio for our weekly lunch. I stopped on the way to pick up a big pepperoni pizza and a cold six-pack of Bud.

Chas took one look at my face and said, "I bet the other guy hasn't got a mark on him."

"You'd win your bet," I said. "I was overmatched."

We ate warm pizza and drank cold beer. I didn't feel much like talking, but Chas did.

"One of these days," he said, "you're going to get into serious trouble. Did you ever think of that?"

"It'll never happen," I told him. "God looks after fools and drunks, and I qualify on both counts."

"Why do you do it?" he asked me. "Drunk almost every night and whoring around. If you want to destroy yourself, that's your business. But you're also hurting your wife and daughter."

"Don't try laying a guilt trip on me, Chas," I said. "I get enough of that at home. Hey, remember my telling you about the dumpling who lives next door? I think I'm making progress there. I got a feeling she's ready."

But he wouldn't let me change the subject.

"Do you really enjoy the way you're living?" he demanded, and I got miffed.

"Damned right I enjoy it," I said. "Look, pal, you're born, you live a little while, and you die. What's the big deal? It's all bullshit, and you know it."

"What is?"

"Life is, that's what. So I grab what pleasure I can."

"Don't you believe in anything?"

"Sure I do," I said. "I believe in gathering ye rosebuds while ye may. And I'm going to gather as many goddamn rosebuds as I can before I kick off."

He shook his head. "Your lousy rosebuds are booze and broads. Did it ever occur to that tiny, tiny brain of yours that there are other things that might give you more pleasure?"

"Such as?"

"Love, for one."

"Spare me," I said. "As far as I'm concerned love is just another four-letter word."

"You've got a lot of learning to do, sonny," he said.

"I don't want to learn," I said. "I'm selfish and I know it. But everyone's selfish. Did you ever know anyone who didn't act out of self-interest?"

"Yeah," he said. "Me."

"That's right," I said. "And look what it got you."

"Have you ever heard me complain?" he asked quietly.

"No, I haven't," I admitted. "And I admire you for it. But I don't admire you for volunteering to have your ass shot off. That was just stupid."

"For you maybe," he said. "Not for me."

I sighed, finished my second beer and stood up. "I've got to get back to the office," I told Chas. "You and I are never going to agree on what it's all about."

He crushed his empty beer can in his heavy paws and looked down at it. "I worry about you," he said in a low voice.

"Not to worry, big brother; I'm fine." Then I bent suddenly to kiss his cheek. I couldn't remember ever having done that before. "Take care," I said huskily.

I drove back toward town thinking of what he had said and what I had said. He had shaken me up; I admit it. I've always known Chas was smarter than I was, and it bothered me when we disagreed; I'd get an antsy feeling that the deep sonofabitch might be right. So I turned north and headed for the club to get hammered.

Maybe Laura would show up.

17

GREGORY BARROW

It was obvious to me from the start that I had two vital and interrelated problems on the ZAP Project: correct dosage and behavioral results. Since I could find no record of similar research that could be used as a guide, my only option was raw experimentation.

When all the specialized equipment was in place in my private lab, I prepared what I considered a weak solution of the synthetic testosterone I had developed. I made careful notes of the amount of the hormone used and the volume of the inert carrier in which it was suspended.

I then donned heavy rubber gloves, removed a male white mouse from its cage, injected it, and returned it to the cage. I removed my gloves and positioned a TV camera to record results, if any. When I turned back to the cage, the injected mouse was dead, lying on its back with all four paws in the air.

I then weakened the solution progressively with small subtractions of the quantity of testosterone, and the sixth injected mouse lived, scampering about the cage energetically and exhibiting no apparent ill effects. I captured this reaction on videotape and updated my notes.

I then obtained a larger wire cage from the supply department. I injected another male mouse with the weakened hormone solution and put a dot on its back with a black Magic Marker. I put it into the large cage, then focused and started the TV camera. I put an untreated mouse into the large cage with the injected mouse and stood back to observe the results, stopwatch in hand.

The untreated mouse was killed in less than thirty seconds. After the killing, the dotted mouse continued to bite and worry the corpse for several minutes. I repeated this experiment twice more with identical results.

I then put *two* untreated mice in the cage with the injected and marked mouse. Both were killed almost instantly. I tried three mice, and then four. It was a remarkable and disturbing thing to witness: The untreated mice were totally incapable of defending themselves against the savage attacks of the mouse with a heightened testosterone level.

Because I work slowly and precisely (and keep copious notes) these experiments took the better part of two weeks. Then Marvin McWhortle came down to my lab and asked for a progress report.

I reported what I had accomplished so far, and I ran videotapes of the murderous activities in the big cage. Mr. McWhortle watched intently, fascinated.

"Incredible," he said, shaking his head. "But are you certain the killings were the result of the testosterone injections and not due to some other factor?"

"Naturally I ran control experiments," I replied, somewhat offended that he imagined I might have neglected such an important discipline. "When untreated males were placed together in the same cage, there was no overt display of aggression. In fact, they spent much of their time playing with each other."

"So you feel the aggression was definitely the result of the added testosterone?"

"Preliminary results would seem to indicate it," I said cautiously. "But there is much work still to be done."

"What comes next?"

"I want to place two, three, and then several injected male mice in the same cage and observe what happens. Then I intend to repeat all my experiments with female mice placed in the same cage with an injected male. I think it important to establish if the male's murderous frenzy occurs in the presence of ovulating females or if his aggression is converted to an increased sex drive."

"That should be interesting," Mr. McWhortle said, grinning at me. "Be sure you make tapes. I've got to see that."

That evening, on the drive back to Rustling Palms Estates, I asked Marleen Todd, "Do you admire strong men?"

She laughed. "What a question! If you mean weight lifters and bodybuilders, the answer is no, emphatically no! I think they're grotesque."

"I phrased the question awkwardly," I said. "I meant vigorous men, aggressive men, men who want to dominate."

"The answer is still no. I've always suspected that men like that are trying to conceal an inner feeling of inferiority. And so they overcompensate."

"Do you think most women feel the way you do?"

She considered that a few moments. "I really can't say," she said finally. "I know there *are* women who admire forceful men and respond to them. Why do you ask, Greg?"

"Just curiosity," I said. "I told you I'm a klutz when it comes to human relations. I usually know how research animals will react, but I can't predict people. I just don't understand why they do the things they do, what their motives are, what drives them."

"I think most people have a very basic drive," she said. "Self-preservation. That may be the fundamental instinct, but then it gets complicated. For instance, I'd die for Tania. I'd sacrifice myself if it meant her survival."

"And these women you mentioned who respond to forceful men, are they also motivated by self-preservation?"

"They may be," she said warily. "Perhaps it's atavistic: the cavewoman wanting a strong, aggressive caveman because he can kill a saber-toothed tiger and bring home meat."

"Probably," I said, smiling. "So the females who admire aggressive males are really trying to insure their own survival?"

"That's one possibility," Marleen said. "Another is that they're instinctively seeking strong genes for their offspring. And that leads to the survival of the family, the tribe, the nation, and ultimately the human race."

I groaned. "No wonder I'm confused. We start with women responding to strong men and end with the immortality of the species. Well, I suppose that's what evolution is all about."

"Greg, does this have anything to do with the project you're working on?"

"Only indirectly," I said cautiously. I couldn't reveal more. "And speaking of projects, how is yours coming along?"

"I'm going to be just as secretive as you," she said. "But I will tell you it's a new perfume, and if it works the way I hope, it will revolutionize the fragrance industry."

"That sounds exciting," I said, although I didn't think it did. "What makes it so revolutionary?"

"Well, I don't want to go into details, but you know that scientists still don't understand exactly how the sense of smell works. They do know that certain scents can recall emotions and awaken memories or—and this is iffy—inspire emotions and awaken appetites. That allegedly includes sexual desire. But my new perfume, if it succeeds, takes a totally different approach. It aims at behavior modification. Greg, why are you looking at me so strangely?"

"You mean," I said, "your new perfume might work the way nitrous oxide makes people laugh and acts as an anesthetic?"

"Not precisely like that," Marleen said. "But its effects would cause people to act differently from the way they normally act."

"And this modification or change in their behavior, would it be pleasurable?"

"Oh yes."

"But could your new fragrance result in any ill effects? For instance, antisocial conduct by the women wearing it or by anyone sniffing it?"

"Good heavens, no!" Marleen said decisively. "If I thought that might happen, I'd drop the whole project immediately."

I was about to say, "I wish I could say the same," but I remained silent. Still, her forthright statement stirred up all my original doubts about the moral and ethical proprieties of what I was doing. I had no desire to create a new crop of killers and rapists. It seemed to me there were enough of that breed without encouragement from the McWhortle Laboratory.

"A penny for your thoughts," Marleen said.

"Haven't you heard of inflation?" I asked. "Now they're worth at least a nickel."

And we both laughed.

18

JESSICA FIDDLER

McWhortle called me from his office one morning, a Friday it was, and said he was feeling horny and would be over at noon. That was a pain because I had an appointment to get my nails done. Naturally I told him to come ahead, and then I phoned the beauty shop to cancel. I had a good thing going with the old man, and I wasn't about to make waves.

He showed up hot to trot and started undressing right away. He always wore boxer shorts that almost came to his knees—real droopy drawers. One pair even had little bunnies printed on them. I never laughed of course. I just said, "Oh daddy, you look so cute!"

He told me from the beginning that his ticker was on the fritz—it speeded up sometimes—so when we had sex, I did most of the work. I always told him what a great lover he was, and he liked that. Note to wives everywhere: If your man doesn't get that bullshit at home, he'll get it somewhere else.

Afterward I brought him a cold bottle of the dark beer he liked, and got a diet cola for myself because

I had put on a few pounds recently and my tush was getting pillowy.

He had brought me a big jar of a new moisturizing creme his laboratory had developed. It had a bronzer in it so you could get a tan without going out in the sun.

"Thank you, daddy," I said. "It will be great for rainy days. How are you coming along on that crazy pill you told me about—the one that's supposed to make every soldier into Superman?"

"Coming along fine. Greg is making progress."

"Who's Greg?"

"Gregory Barrow, our top research chemist. He's handling the project. The man is a genius."

"I've never met a genius. What's he like?"

"A mousy kind of guy but all brain. I know he's married and has a kid, but his job is his whole life. I mean he doesn't play golf or anything like that. A real workaholic. I wish I had twenty more like him."

"You think the ZAP stuff is going to be a success?"

"Well, Greg has it in liquid form now, and when he injects it into mice, it turns them into pit bulls. I don't see any reason why it shouldn't work with humans if we can get it into pill or powder form."

"Maybe the government will give you a medal."

He laughed. "If they pay their bills on time, I'll be satisfied. Listen, Jess, I've got to get back to the office. A client's coming in who wants to talk about a new product: a suntan lotion combined with an insect repellent."

"Hey," I said, "that's a great idea. The last time I went to the beach I almost got eaten up alive by sand fleas."

"Lucky fleas," McWhortle said, grinning at me.

He gave me my salary check before he left. What a sweet hustle I had going.

I showered and dressed, then phoned William K. Brevoort. He wasn't in, so I left a message on his answering machine. I watched a soap opera on TV for a while, but then Willie got back to me. I told him I had something for him, and he said he could come over that evening around nine o'clock, and I said okay.

I phoned Laura Gunther at Hashbeam's Bo-teek and asked her if she'd like to have an early dinner at a rib joint we both liked. She said sure, and we made arrangements to meet there at six-thirty.

Laura was the only close woman friend I had made in town since I moved up from Miami. She worked at Hashbeam's, and I stopped by one day to look around and we got to talking. It turned out she had been in the game herself but had gone straight and married a real-estate broker. That lasted all of two years and now she was divorced. She wasn't exactly hurting for bucks but had taken the job at the Bo-teek to keep from hitting the convention circuit again.

She was a wild one: a big, heavy broad who smoked long, skinny cigars and had the voice and vocabulary of a trucker. Her current boyfriend was a guy named Bobby Gurk. I think he was in the rackets in Lauderdale, but I never asked questions.

We had a great dinner at the rib joint. Laura told me about the problem she was having with Gurk. He wanted her to stay home every night in case he suddenly decided to drop by. She told him to get lost, and they were always fighting about it.

"That elephant thinks he owns me," Laura said. "He doesn't pay enough to own; he just rents."

"Why don't you dump him," I suggested. "You should be able to do better."

"I'm working on it," she said. "I met a guy out at the club the other night who thinks he's God's gift to women. Married, of course, but he's got deep pockets. I gave him a freebie. The next time he comes sniffing around I'll tell him the facts of life: no pay, no play."

Then we started talking about new summer fashions, what was in and what was out. After a while it was time for me to leave. We split the check and made plans to go to the beach on Sunday. I got home around eight-thirty. My six-year-old Pontiac was making funny noises, and I decided I needed new wheels. I figured I'd drop a few hints to McWhortle. He knew all about no pay, no play.

Willie the Weasel showed up right on time, looking as nifty as ever. That guy sure knew how to dress. All he wanted to drink was a glass of club soda, so I brought him that.

I told Willie about McWhortle's visit that morning. I didn't want to give him the whole jar of the new moisturing creme with bronzer in it, so I dug out a tablespoonful and wrapped it in aluminum foil. He said that would be enough for analysis. I also told him about McWhortle's client who wanted the lab to develop a suntan lotion combined with an insect repellent.

"Sounds good," he said. "See if you can get me a sample when it's finished."

He took the foil-wrapped moisturizer and gave me a

white envelope containing my payoff. I guess handing me bare cash just wasn't his style; it had to be in a clean white envelope.

He started to leave, then suddenly stopped. "Oh, by the way," he said casually, as if he had just remembered, "anything new on that testosterone pill?"

It was a great performance, but it didn't fool me one bit. I mean the guy was slick but I was slicker; I knew immediately that he was *really* interested in the ZAP thing, which meant big bucks were involved.

"Yeah," I said, "McWhortle talked about it some."

"What did he say?"

"Tell you what," I said, "I figure that project is something special. Very important. Top Secret stuff."

He stared at me. "I told you there'd be an extra two big ones if you can get me a sample."

"So you did," I said. "But I prefer a pay-as-you-go plan. How about an extra grand right now?"

His expression froze up. "You wouldn't be getting greedy on me, would you, Jess?"

"Nah, Willie," I said, "not me. I'm just doing what you do. You told me you buy information from people who know and sell to people who want to know. Right? Well, I know and you want to know. Greed isn't involved. It's just business."

His face was still set, but he dug out his wallet and this time he handed over the cold cash, his hand to mine, no white envelope. I thanked him and told him what McWhortle had said about the injections making pit bulls out of mice.

"And does he think it's going to work on men?" the Weasel asked.

"He said he doesn't see why it shouldn't if they can

make it into a pill or powder."

"Did he happen to mention the name of the chemist who's working on it?"

The schmuck wanted me to show him my hole card? What did he take me for—a total twerp? I was going to feed him information all right: a little bit at a time. Cash on delivery.

"No," I said, "he didn't mention any name."

Brevoort nodded, tucked his wallet away, and started out. He paused at the door.

"That's a very attractive frock you're wearing tonight, Jess," he said.

"Thank you," I said.

After the door closed behind him, I stood there a moment, still startled.

How many times have you heard a man use the word "frock"? I wondered: What's *with* this guy?

19

MARLEEN TODD

I must confess I had high hopes for a perfume based on oxytocin, the "cuddle hormone." If it succeeded, the wearer and anyone who sniffed it would become emotionally warmer, more affectionate, more *caring*. It seemed to me that in today's world such a scent would be of inestimable value to both sexes, but especially to men.

But Cuddle might have an even wider application. I was aware of the exciting things the Japanese were doing with what are called home fragrances or area fragrances. Perfumers were releasing scents through the ventilation ducts of homes, offices, and factories. It was claimed that certain tailored fragrances reduced stress, calmed anxieties, and improved the morale of workers assigned to boring routine jobs.

In other words, mood and behavior modification via the sense of smell!

It was fascinating to imagine what effect Cuddle might have on a large gathering in an enclosed area. It was possible that such a mollifying scent, released through air conditioning vents, could be used to control prison riots. And sprayed in the hall of a diplomatic conference it might result in quick and friendly agreements.

Our supply department had to order the aerosolized form of synthetic oxytocin from Europe, and while awaiting its arrival I busied myself experimenting with top and central notes for the new perfume. Top notes are usually of the citrus family. They give the scent a fresh, tangy odor when first sniffed, but rarely last long. Central notes are the body of the fragrance, giving it richness and "heart." They are customarily floral scents.

The base or bottom note in the final meld is the longest lasting and gives each perfume its unique personality.

I started blending a lemony extract as a top note with lavender for the central. The oxytocin, if its scent was acceptable or if it had an objectionable odor that could be neutralized or masked, would be the distinctive foundation of Cuddle.

When the containers of the aerosolized synthetic hormone finally arrived, I carried them into the lab and organized my private worktable. There were two other "noses" in the lab at the time, but they were intent on their own projects and paid no attention to what I was doing.

I prepared several strips of blotting paper and set up a drying rack. Then, donning thin latex gloves, I held a strip of paper with wooden tongs and dampened the lower half with oxytocin spray. I passed the strip quickly beneath my nostrils and sniffed. I smelled nothing.

Then I brought the strip closer and inhaled deeply. I caught an odor that was neither pleasant nor unpleasant. I tried again. The faint scent puzzled me. There was nothing in my experience as a perfumer that was even remotely similar. It was not citrus, floral, resinous, oily, or of animal origin. It really had no relation to any scent that I could recall.

I clipped the dampened paper strip to the rack to dry. Then I slowly walked along the shelves of bottled fragrances and extracts, reading labels and hoping to find one that might jog my olfactory memory and provide a clue to which family of scents the hormone belonged. I found nothing that could be compared. The oxytocin seemed to have a unique fragrance.

I returned to my table and sniffed my test strip again. This time the distinctive odor was more pronounced, as it naturally would be since the liquid carrier was evaporating. Now the drying scent was more pleasing and triggered a vague association in my mind I could not define. I sniffed once again and was convinced the scent was stirring a sensory memory. But I couldn't pin it down.

I took the test strip from the drying rack with tongs and carried it across the lab to the worktable of Mary Goodbody. If there was ever a misnamed woman it was Mary, for the poor dear was terribly obese. But she was sweet-tempered and an absolutely first-rate "nose." She looked up as I came near.

"Mary," I said, "I hate to interrupt, but would you take a sniff of this and tell me if it reminds you of anything."

"Sure," she said cheerfully. "Hand it over."

She took the tongs and passed the strip quickly beneath her nostrils, taking a small sniff. "Odd," she said.

She brought the strip closer to her nose and inhaled deeply. She was obviously as puzzled as I had been because she stared at the stained blotting paper a moment, shaking her head.

"Does it recall *anything* to you?" I asked.

She took another whiff of the diluted hormone, and her eyes closed. She was silent for almost a minute. Then her eyes popped open.

"Got it!" she said triumphantly.

"What is it?" I said excitedly. "What does the scent recall?"

"Mauve," she said.

You know, she was completely correct. The smell of oxytocin produced a memory of mauve. It was the first time in my professional life that a scent had called up a recollection of a color.

I bent to kiss Mary's cheek. "You're wonderful," I told her, "and right, as usual. Thank you so very much."

"What is that stuff?" she asked curiously, handing back my sample.

"Something new," I said, and sailed back to my worktable considerably elated. The recalled memory of mauve fit Darcy & Sons' prospectus perfectly. They wanted Cuddle to be a "soft, sentimental, and nostalgic" fragrance. What color fit those specifications better than mauve?

I wasn't yet ready to test the aerosolized oxytocin on my skin. I first had to determine its effects on mood and behavior. If it proved to have none or had deleterious effects, it would simply have to be discarded.

Our most recent company newsletter had reported the pharmaceutical division was working on a new nasal decongestant to be packaged in an inhaler. I took the elevator up to their enormous lab and asked one of the chemists, Tony Siddons, if I could have any empty plastic inhalers. He gave me three of them.

I returned to my own lab and spent the remainder of the afternoon carefully packing one of the inhalers with sterile cotton batting that had been saturated with synthetic oxytocin. Finished, I plugged the inhaler into my nose, once in each nostril, and inhaled deeply. I had an almost instantaneous physical reaction. I was flooded with warmth, a condition somewhat akin to a hot flash. And I felt a mild tingling in my extremities. But these symptoms lasted no more than a minute or two. Then I went down to the garage to drive Greg Barrow back to Rustling Palms Estates.

We were almost home, chatting of inconsequential things, when Greg said, "Would you drop me at the Seven-Eleven, please, Marleen. Mabel phoned and wants me to pick up a quart of milk. I'll walk home from there."

"Of course, darling," I said. "But there's no need for you to walk home; I'll wait for you, sweetheart."

He turned slowly to look at me. "There's really no need for you to wait," he said. "I'm sure you're anxious to get home."

"No problem," I said gaily. "Herman is taking a client to dinner tonight, and Tania and I are just having a salad. No cooking to do, so I'll be delighted to wait for you, dear."

He said nothing more until I pulled into our drive-way. Before he could get out of the car, I grabbed his arm, yanked him close and kissed his cheek.

"Have a wonderful, wonderful evening," I said. "And sleep well. I love you, Greg."

"Thank you," he said faintly, and hastened away.

Tania was downstairs, setting the table in the dining nook.

"Hello, you beautiful thing!" I caroled. "You look so charming in your jeans and T-shirt. Give Mother a great big kiss."

She complied but then drew away to stare at me. "You okay?" she asked.

"Never felt better in my life," I said, laughing. "Give me another hug."

Herman came downstairs, showered, shaved, and dressed for his dinner.

"Well, don't you look handsome!" I cried, embracing him. "I married a movie star!"

He pulled away to inspect me. "If I didn't know better," he said, "I'd say you had a few."

"Love your jokes!" I said. "Just *love* them! Oh, honey, hurry home as soon as you can." I looked around to make certain Tania couldn't hear. "Sweetie," I whispered, "you and I are going to have *such* fun tonight. It's been a long, long time, but tonight we'll make up for it. I love you, Herm."

"Yeah," he said. "Sure." And he left hastily.

I heard myself chattering nonstop during dinner. But before it was finished, I became so sleepy I knew I had to get to bed before I collapsed into the salad bowl.

"Mommy is going to take a nap," I said brightly to

Tania. "Now you finish your dinner like the angel you are, and I'll come down later and clean up. I love you, sweetheart. Love you, love you, love you!"

I managed to get upstairs but I was too sleepy to undress. I fell atop the bed fully clothed and was instantly asleep. I never did go downstairs to clean up the kitchen, and I wasn't aware of my husband coming home. I slept for twelve hours.

All my dreams were colored mauve.

20

CHAS TODD

I got maybe ten phone calls a month, at the most, and three or four of them were usually wrong numbers. Late in May my phone rang one evening, and I couldn't imagine who it might be unless the cops were calling to tell me my nutsy brother was in the hoosegow and needed bail.

But it turned out to be my niece, Tania, and I laughed.

"Hiya, honey," I said. "It's good to hear from you. Behaving yourself?"

"Of course I am," she said, very primly. "I called to thank you for that book you gave me which you autographed."

"My pleasure," I said. "Did you read it?"

"Yes, I did. I liked Tommy Termite—he was funny—and I think you should write another book about him."

"I'm happy you said that, Tania, because that's exactly what I'm doing. In the new book Tommy meets a girl termite and falls in love."

"That's very nice," she said approvingly, and then she was silent. I began to get a little uneasy.

"Everything all right?" I asked.

"Uncle Chas," she said finally, "will you do me a favor? A big favor?"

"Of course I will, honey. What is it?"

"Could you send me some money?"

I was startled. I was sure the kid got an allowance, and I wasn't certain if Marleen would approve of my giving cash to her daughter.

"How much do you want, Tania?"

"A lot."

"How much is a lot?"

"A hundred dollars?" she said hopefully. "I really need it."

That was a stun. "Can you tell me what you need it for?"

"It's a secret," she said.

At first I thought she might want to buy her mother or father an expensive birthday present, but then I recalled both their birthdays were in November.

"A secret?" I said. "Well, you can tell me. I promise not to repeat it."

"Not to anyone?"

"Not to a soul. Scout's honor."

"Well," she said slowly, "I want to give it to a friend."

"Oh?" I said. "Boy or girl?"

A long silence, then: "Boy."

"What boy?"

"Just a boy," she said.

Now I was really concerned. If she had said she wanted to buy a birthday present for a boy, that would have been okay I guess. But I didn't like the idea of her giving a hundred bucks to some nameless boy. I had visions of some kiddie extortion racket going on here.

"I'm not asking you to *give* me the money, Uncle Chas," she said earnestly. "I want to borrow it. I'll pay you back, really I will."

"You don't want to ask your mother or father for it?"

"I can't," she said miserably. "You're the only one I can ask."

I hate dilemmas like that. I mean I loved Tania and thought she loved me. More important, I thought she *trusted* me. I couldn't betray her secret, not even to her parents. Especially not to her parents. That would, I knew, be the end of my niece's love and trust.

"Tell you what, honey," I said, "I'll give you the money but—"

"Lend," she repeated. "*Lend* me the money."

"Okay, I'll lend you the money, but I don't want to mail it because it might get lost or your parents might open the envelope. Why don't you tell your mother I phoned and invited you to have lunch with me on Saturday. Tell her it will be like a party, just you and me. She can drive you out here and then go shopping or something, and then pick you up later. And while she's gone, I'll give you the money personally. How does that sound?"

"I don't know," she said doubtfully. "Maybe she'll want to stay for lunch, too."

"Nothing doing," I said. "This party is just for the two of us. If she gives you a hard time, have her phone me. Okay?"

"All right, Uncle Chas," she said. "I'll call you back and tell you if I can come."

I hung up, not certain I was doing the right thing. But I had the definite feeling that something was troubling Tania, and I didn't want to risk compounding the problem with no questions asked and her parents kept in the dark.

I used to be a man of action—a *brainless* man of action. I loved track and swimming, fancied myself a world-class miler, and didn't do too badly in the freestyle. I was a real jock and even had dreams of the Olympics. But, of course, all that was when I had legs.

While I was in the hospital and after I got out, I acquired the habit of thinking—something I had never done much before. And this may sound screwy to you, but I discovered thinking can be as addictive as alcohol or nicotine. You can just surrender to pondering, and time passes before you know it and you lose all sense of where you are and what's happening around you. Talk about reverie!

Thinking can be very seductive. You can dream, fantasize, create all sorts of wild and wonderful scenarios. A lot of my thinking had no relation to reality or—according to Cherry—to what I perceived as reality. But I found it pleasurable. It was still a new world for me, and I never ceased to wonder at the depths of thought. I hadn't yet gotten to the bottom.

Now I spent at least a half hour thinking about Tania's request for a hundred dollars and envisioning a dozen different plots that might account for it. You may say I was wasting time, but I didn't think so. I believed there was a crisis of sorts in that kid's life, and my actions might help solve it or make it worse.

I'm not such a heavy thinker that I don't recognize my own limitations; after all, I came to the habit of reasoning late in life. So I phoned Dr. Noble, hoping for reassurance that I was acting sensibly.

She was home, and after some small talk I told her about Tania's call, her request for money, and the Saturday luncheon I planned so I could have a heart-to-heart with the kid.

"What do you think, Cherry?" I asked.

"She's how old?"

"Eight."

"Chas, I don't like the sound of it. It could be something completely innocent, but I doubt it. I don't know how eight-year-olds feel about money these days, but when I was that age a hundred dollars seemed to me an unimaginable fortune. I think the child may have a serious problem."

"That's my reaction."

"But I'm not sure you should have promised to give her the money. You did promise, didn't you?"

"Yes, but I figured it was the only way I could get her to come to lunch. If I had said to her, 'Let's talk about it,' I think she would take that as a rejection and drop me. Listen, Tania is no dummy; she's not going to tell me in advance why she wants the money because she's afraid if she tells me I won't give it to her."

"You're probably right. I'd like to know what it's all about, Chas. I hope you'll tell me."

"I will. I'll phone you after I talk to her."

"Can't I come out and visit you? You can tell me then."

I hesitated longer than I should have. "All right, Cherry."

"See you then," she said lightly.

We hung up, and I went back to thinking. I told you it was addictive.

But this time I wasn't thinking about Tania's problem; the subject, as usual, was my problem and the solution so kindly offered by Dr. Cherry Noble. I don't mean to put her down with a smartass remark like that. Believe me, I had nothing but gratitude and admiration for that brainy lady.

But she wanted something from me I wasn't ready to give. I wanted to, but I couldn't. I told you that when I was young and had a whole body, I was a pretty fair swimmer.

But I never had the nerve to go off the high board.

21

LAURA GUNTHER

Bobby Gurk was the biggest man I've ever known—and I've known a mob. He said he weighed two-fifty, but I figured he was closer to two-eighty, maybe more. It wasn't *all* fat; he was just a tall, wide, humongous man. I'm no petite but he made me feel like Mrs. Tom Thumb.

Big guys like that can be fun, if you know what I mean. What wasn't fun was the guy's stinginess. I mean he was in the rackets and probably pulling down zillions. But he drove a ten-year-old clunker, lived in a fleabag motel, and dressed like Bozo the Clown. He took me out to dinner once—just once. It was a cheapie joint, but he almost fainted when the check came. He left a whole dollar for a tip. I told him never to eat there again or the waiter would spit in his soup.

Finally I got sick and tired trying to pry some decent funds out of Gurk. So I started looking around for a new fish who didn't carry his roll with Scotch tape around it. I thought I found one at the club: a heavy drinker named Herman who was in the insurance business and seemed to be well-heeled.

I gave him a freebie, just as a come-on, you know, to prove my talent. But the second time I met him at the club I laid it on him straight, and he got sore.

"Listen, kiddo," he said, "the day I have to start paying for it is the day I take up shuffleboard."

What a jerk! I mean he was probably taking women to ritzy restaurants and buying them clothes and expensive gifts, but he didn't consider that payment. A lot of guys are like that. They'll buy a digger a mink coat but handing over cash offends them. Go figure it.

So there I was, stuck with Big Bobby Gurk, a world-class tightwad. I was getting a mingy alimony check every month and with what I was making (and boosting) at Hashbeam's Bo-teek, I was getting by. But my bank account was so flimsy I couldn't even afford to get sick. So I kept cruising and hoping.

Now take my girlfriend Jessica Fiddler. She has to take care of a rich geezer a couple of times a week, and for that she got her own home, a weekly salary, and lots of perfumes and cosmetics. I'd be okay if I could find a mark like that.

Then something happened that turned my whole life around.

Bobby Gurk came over one night, but it wasn't for fun and games.

"I got a job for you, babe," he said.

"Great," I said. "How much does it pay?"

"Hey," he said, "don't you want to know what it is first?"

"I didn't figure you'd want me to rob a bank."

"Nah, it's nothing like that. This is something right up your alley."

"I've got a big alley," I said. "Okay, what is it?"

"There's this hustler I know who's got an in at a place that invents all kinds of medicines and stuff. An inside guy, on the take, sneaks the hustler new things they come up with. Then my pal peddles the new things to other people who rip them off and make a mint. Get the picture? Right now they're working on a pill that a guy takes and it puts lead in his pencil."

"You don't need it, Bobby," I told him, and that was the truth.

"It ain't for me, dummy," he said. "But if I can get hold of this pill I can have it copied, bootleg it, and make a nice couple of bucks."

I stared at him. "So?" I said. "Buy the pill from your hustler pal."

"He's going to hold me up," Gurk said. "I know he is."

"Oh-ho," I said. "Now I get it. You want to cut the hustler out of the deal."

"That's right. But to do that, I got to know who the inside guy is who's going to sneak him a sample pill. You follow?"

"Way ahead of you," I said. "You want me to cozy up to this hustler and pump him. You want me to ball him?"

"I don't care how you do it."

"Okay," I said. "A grand in advance."

"A grand?" he cried. "You nuts or something? A hundred now. Another five hundred when you get me what I want."

"A thousand now," I insisted. "Another thousand when I get the stuff. Or no deal."

Well, we went back and forth with a lot of yelling and screaming. Finally, he gave me five yards in advance and promised another grand when and if I found out who the hustler's inside man was.

"It's called the ZAP pill," Gurk said. "And it's being made at a place called McWhortle Laboratory."

"I'll remember," I said. "Now how do I get to meet this pal you're going to shaft?"

We talked about several ways to arrange a meet so the guy wouldn't suspect a setup. But none of the scams we dreamed up seemed even halfway legit.

"Look," I said finally to Gurk, "honesty is the best policy. What's this guy's name?"

"Willie Brevoort."

"Well, you tell Willie you know this roundheel who puts out at a moment's notice just for kicks. If he's interested, bring him around, introduce him, and then you take off."

"But what if he ain't inarrested?"

"Then the whole deal is dead, isn't it? If I can't be nice to him, how am I going to squeeze him?"

"Yeah," Bobby, the great brain, said slowly, "I see what you mean. Okay, we'll do it. If it doesn't work, I'll try another way."

But it worked out just fine. Two nights later Gurk showed up with the hustler in tow. This Willie Brevoort was a slim, elegant guy with a long, pointy face. And dressed? Right out of *GQ*. I made his suit for a black-label Armani, and his suede loafers had those little tassels on them. What a dude he was!

The three of us had a drink, traded a few jokes, and

then Bobby said he had to get back to his office and took off. I poured Willie and me another drink—if you can call club soda a drink. That's all he was having. I stuck to something with more vitamins: Absolut on the rocks.

"You got wheels, Willie?" I asked him. "Or did Bobby drive you here in that bucket of his?"

"No," he said, "I drove my own car."

"Smart," I said. "What do you drive?"

"A silver Infiniti."

"Love it," I said. "Listen, why don't we both get more comfortable."

"Suits me."

"I got a waterbed," I said. "I hope that suits you."

He didn't answer that, but he asked a question of his own.

"Are you a lady of leisure, Laura?"

"Hell, no," I said. "Wish I was. I'm the manager of a boutique." I wasn't, of course; just a salesclerk. But what's the dif?

"A boutique?" he said, and he seemed to come alive, smiling and leaning forward. "That must be a fascinating job. I suppose you're getting advance info on the fall fashions."

"Some," I said. "Skirts are down and prices are up. But with me, prices are down and skirts are up."

He laughed, and we both started undressing. He was wearing aqua silk briefs. That figured. I stripped down and went to my walk-in closet. Willie followed and looked over my shoulder.

"You have a lovely wardrobe, Laura," he said. "Unless I'm mistaken, there's a lot of Donna Karan. You like her designs?"

"Love them," I said. "They make me look smaller."

"Yes," he said, "you are a rather large lady. I imagine you and I might wear the same size."

"Wouldn't doubt it," I said.

We were both needle-naked. I yanked a plum-colored chiffon robe off a hanger, and Willie grabbed it.

"What a gorgeous peignoir," he said. He looked at me. "Do you mind if I try it on?"

I wasn't shocked. Listen, if you've been in the game like I have, nothing men do surprises you. I once had a john who liked to play a ukulele while I was blowing him.

"Go ahead," I said to Willie Brevoort. "Slip it on."

It fitted him perfectly.

22

MARVIN MCWHORTLE

I've been in the manufacture and marketing of pharmaceuticals most of my adult life, and I knew from
the git-go that the ZAP Project was a no-brainer. It
wasn't that a testosterone pill couldn't be developed—
Gregory Barrow was a dynamite research chemist, and
he might just do it—it was the public reaction that
would condemn it to become just a chemical curiosity.

Listen, I served in the Quartermaster Corps in World
War II, and the rumor got around that we were putting
saltpeter in the GIs' food to reduce their sexual desire.
It was all bullshit, of course, but it caused a big flap,
and the brass had to assure the mothers and fathers
of America that their boys weren't being drugged by
Uncle Sam.

So despite what I had told Colonel Knacker and Greg
Barrow, I knew damn well the ZAP Project would never get off the ground. Even if the pill did what it was
supposed to do, there'd be no way to keep it secret,
and there'd be such a public stink that no amount

of slick PR would convince John Q. Public that the armed forces weren't force-feeding a dangerous drug to the troops to make them into snarling killers.

But what the hell, it was a juicy contract, and I wasn't about to say no to the Pentagon. If they wanted a ZAP pill, I'd do my best to provide it. The resulting brannigan with the public and the media was a problem for the Department of Defense, not for McWhortle Laboratory.

I think it was about the middle of June when Greg Barrow phoned me one morning and asked if I could come down to his lab; he had something to show me. I wanted to know how long it would take, and he said no more than an hour. That was okay. I had alerted Jessica Fiddler to expect me at noon, and I wasn't about to postpone it. I needed some of her TLC.

Greg was waiting for me at the opened door of his private lab. After I entered, he closed and locked the door carefully—he does *everything* carefully—and got me seated in front of a TV set.

"The first recording," he said, "shows the results of placing two or more male mice injected with the testosterone compound in the same cage."

The tape was murder—literally. I've never seen such bloody carnage in my life. Whether it was two, three, or four mice, they attacked one another with a brutal ferocity that was hard to believe. In all cases, one victor remained alive, but so badly wounded I knew he'd never recover. Greg confirmed that there were no survivors of these savage contests.

"The final moments of the tape," he said, "show several untreated male mice together in the same cage. Notice there is no sign of violent behavior."

The tape ended, and he rewound and then switched cassettes.

"I think," he said tonelessly, "that from what you have just seen we can conclude that the murderous frenzy was the result of the testosterone and no other factor. This next tape shows the behavior of an injected male placed in a cage with a single ovulating female, and then with several females."

What I saw made it obvious that the injected male had no desire to kill the female mouse—unless he intended to fuck her to death. I've never seen such enthusiastic animal copulation. The same held true when the male was placed in a cage with five females. The little bugger went wild. He just couldn't seem to get enough, but mounted the nearest female first, went on to the others, then started over again. Finally he flopped over on his side and lay still.

"Is he dead?" I asked, awed by the sexual prowess of the injected male.

"No," Barrow said, "just exhausted. After he revived, he started in again. Apparently the testosterone increases physical aggression against males and sexual aggression against females. It's a very disturbing result that makes me wonder—as I did before, if you'll recall—if a human diet enrichment of testosterone might not have the same results."

"What are you saying, Greg?"

"That it may prove impossible to encourage the kind of behavior we desire without also encouraging the kind we wish to avoid. We're hoping to make soldiers more aggressive in combat. We certainly don't want to create an army of rapists."

"Yes," I said, nodding, "I can see why you might

be concerned, and I am, too. Have you considered a weaker dosage?"

"I've tried it," Barrow said. "The results are the same."

I thought a moment, then I told Greg about the saltpeter fuss during World War II.

"Look," I said to him, "I'm no chemist; I don't even know what saltpeter is. But there must be *some* chemical you could add to the injection that has a proven taming effect. You follow? It would increase male aggressiveness toward other males but would dull their sexual appetite, or at least keep it at normal levels."

I could see Barrow was intrigued. "That's an interesting concept, Mr. McWhortle," he said. "It's just possible that such a compound could be formulated. I'll do some research on it. What we're looking for is a sexual tranquilizer that might be combined with testosterone."

"Exactly," I said, standing up. "See if you can find something like that. It could be the answer to our problem."

I must have broken every speed limit on the books while driving to Jessica's house, including running a red light. I just couldn't get there fast enough. I felt so high you'd have thought I just had one of Greg Barrow's injections. I mean I was in overdrive.

My excitement continued after I arrived. I must confess I tore Jessica's panties in my frantic haste to get her undressed, and I acted exactly like that mouse I had just witnessed performing amazing sexual feats. And then, like him, I collapsed, exhausted.

"Oh, daddy," Jess said, "what's *with* you today?

Why, you're as randy as a teenager. What a lover!"

"Get me a beer," I gasped, "and I'll tell you about it."

I sat up in bed, taking nourishment, and related what I had just seen on Greg's tapes.

She laughed delightedly. "You mean this stuff really works?"

"It sure as hell worked on mice. The chemist is going to try to dampen the aphrodisiac effect. We're trying to produce killers, not rapists. And, of course, we still don't know if it will have the same effect on humans."

"It sure had an effect on *you*," she said. "You better take it easy. Remember your ticker."

"Screw my ticker," I said. "If I hadn't known you were waiting for me, I'd have popped a gasket. Sorry I ripped your panties, Jess. I'll buy you more."

"You can strip me bare ass whenever you like. I love it. So you think this ZAP thing is going to be a success?"

"It looks like it. At the rate Greg Barrow is going, we may be able to test it on human volunteers within a few months."

"Volunteers? Who'll volunteer?"

"Barrow will be the first," I told her. "He insists on trying his new products on himself first. I admire him for it, but I think he's a fool. Enough about business, baby. Let's you and I have—"

"Oh," she interrupted me, "I forgot to tell you. I'm having more trouble with my car. It's really silly to keep paying out good money for repairs. I guess I need new wheels."

"Anything," I said. "Anything at all for my baby.

Buy a new car. Pick out something nice, and I'll pay the tab. It will be a little bonus."

"Oh, daddy," she said, sighing, "why are you so good to me."

"Because you're good to me," I said, reaching for her. "You always do whatever I want."

"I want what you want," she said. "Like this?"

"Yes," I said. "Oh my, yes!"

23

TANIA TODD

Well, I did what Uncle Chas said I should and told my mother he had phoned and invited me to have lunch with him on Saturday. It was going to be a private lunch, just him and me. She could drive me out there but she couldn't stay. Then she would pick me up later.

She laughed and said that was okay because she had some shopping to do on Saturday. She also said she would make some chocolate brownies that I could take to Uncle Chas because you should never go to visit someone without bringing them a gift.

I didn't say anything to Chet Barrow about this because I still wasn't sure my uncle was going to lend me the hundred dollars I asked for.

Anyway, Mother drove me out there, this was a little past noon, and came in with me to kiss and say hello to Uncle Chas, and then she left like she had promised.

I gave him the brownies, and he said that was great because he had bought some almond ice cream which we could put on top of the brownies for dessert. But first he had pizzas, two different kinds, and cream soda to drink, so I knew it was going to be a nice lunch, more like a party.

We started eating, and he got right down to business.

"Tania," he said, "I'm going to lend you the hundred dollars no matter what, but I'd really feel a lot better about it if you'd tell me why you need it."

"I knew you were going to ask me that," I said, "because a hundred dollars is an awful lot of money, and you just can't hand it over without wanting to know what it's for. I thought about it, and I decided that I would tell you if you promise not to tell my parents."

"I promise," he said.

"Cross your heart and hope to die?"

He nodded.

"You've got to say it," I told him.

"Cross my heart and hope to die," he said.

"Well," I said, "I need the money because I'm going to run away from home. With Chet Barrow."

He stopped eating his pizza, looked at me, then started eating again. "Who's Chet Barrow?" he asked.

"His real name is Chester Barrow. He's a boy who lives next door to us. He's a year older than I am, and he is very nice. Also, he is smart."

"Uh-huh," Uncle Chas said. "Is running away from home his idea or yours?"

"He thought of it first. He hasn't even said he'll take me with him. But I thought if I told him I had a hundred dollars, then he'd have to take me because I don't think he's got much money."

"Good thinking on your part," my uncle said. "Why does Chet want to leave home?"

"Because he is unhappy there. His father doesn't talk to him, and his mother watches TV all the time."

"I see. And why do you want to run away, honey?"

"Because I'm unhappy also. My father drinks alcohol all the time, and he doesn't come home for dinner. And then, when he does come home, he smells from perfume, and he and Mother have these terrible arguments, and once he slapped her and she cried. So I don't want to live there anymore."

He didn't say anything for a while, and we each had another slice of pizza. It had a very thick crust but it was good. Mostly I ate the topping off.

"Where will you go?" Uncle Chas asked finally. "Have you decided?"

"No, not yet. Chet is planning it."

He sighed very sorrowfully. "Tania, have you thought this over carefully? I mean, you won't have your own room anymore, or your own bed, or three meals a day. And where will you go to school?"

"School's out for vacation."

"Oh, yeah, I forgot. But won't you miss the other things?"

"I suppose," I said. "But I'll get used to it. And it will be better. Can we have dessert now? I'll fix it."

"Sure, honey. The ice cream is in the freezer. If it's too hard, heat the spoon under hot water."

"I know how to do it," I told him. "Uncle Chas, did it hurt when you lost your legs?"

"Sure it did. And for a while I thought they were still there. I mean I kept trying to wiggle my toes even though I knew I didn't have any toes. It was like having an itch you can't scratch."

"I feel sorry for you," I said.

"Thank you," he said.

I brought him his brownie with ice cream on top.

"That looks good," he said. "Why don't you bring the things over here. Then if we want more we can help ourselves."

"I'm not going to have more," I said. "I don't wish to get fat. Now I suppose you're going to tell me I shouldn't run away. Well, it won't do you any good because I've made up my mind."

"Hey," he said, "I wasn't going to try to persuade you not to. It's an important decision, and obviously you've given it a lot of thought."

"I have," I said. "And once I make up my mind, I do it."

"Sure," Uncle Chas said. "You're very determined; I can see that. But we may have a problem. Now look here. . . ."

He pulled out his wallet and spread five twenty-dollar bills on the desk.

"That's a hundred dollars, Tania," he said.

"I know," I told him. "I can add."

"Of course, you can. But the problem is, what are you going to do with it until you actually leave home? I suppose you could give it to Chet to keep, but then he might run away and not take you with him."

"He wouldn't do that."

"He *might*. It's possible, isn't it? Don't bite your fingernails, honey. And if you hide it in your room or someplace else around the house, your mother or father might find it and want to know where you got it and what it's for."

"I can hide it good."

"Maybe you can, but there's always the chance they may find it. Now, I'll put this hundred dollars aside for you. When you and Chet are ready to leave, you take a cab out here. Tell the driver to wait, and I'll pay him for the trip. Then I'll hand over the hundred dollars, and you and Chet can go wherever you like. How does that sound?"

I thought about it. "You promise to give us the money, Uncle Chas? When we leave home and come out here?"

"Of course. Here it is. I'll put it in a special envelope marked with your name. I won't touch it. It's yours when you come for it."

"Well, all right," I said. "I'll tell Chet about it, and then he'll have to let me go with him."

"Sure he will. If he's as smart as you say he is."

"He kissed me," I said suddenly.

"He did?" Uncle Chas said. "Did you get mad at him?"

"No," I said. "I liked it."

He laughed, wheeled his chair over, and hugged me.

"What's not to like?" he said.

Mother came for me like she promised and we went home. I went looking for Chet and finally found him at the swimming pool. This was a pool for all the people who live in our development. I don't go in very much because the stuff they put in the water turns my hair green. Chet was sitting by himself on the grass, and he was wearing clothes so I knew he hadn't been swimming with the other kids.

I sat down beside him. He was eating a Butterfinger and gave me a piece.

"Listen," I said, "I've got something to tell you." And I told him all about how my uncle promised to lend me a hundred dollars. It was put aside for me in a special envelope, and when we decided to leave home, we could take a cab to his place and he would pay the driver, and then he would give me my money.

"Wow," Chet said. "That's keen. We can go anywhere on a hundred dollars. I've been studying the map, and you know where I'd like to go?"

"Where?"

"Alaska. It's a nice place, and also it's so far away that our parents would never think of looking for us there."

"Aren't there bears in Alaska?" I asked him.

"I guess so," he said. "But they wouldn't bother us. There are alligators in Florida, but look how many people live here and never get bitten."

"And wolves," I said. "In Alaska."

"Okay, okay," he said angrily. "Where do *you* want to go?"

"Wherever you say," I told him. "Alaska is fine."

But I really wanted to go to Paris, France. That's where Sylvia Gottbaum was going with her mother and father.

24

DR. CHERRY NOBLE

He called me on Saturday right after his niece left, but I had just come from the beach and had to shower and dress. I stopped on the way to pick up a chilled bottle of Frascati and arrived at his studio about five o'clock.

We sipped the wine from his ridiculous jelly jars and nibbled on brownies that had apparently been baked by his sister-in-law. They were quite good. Chewy, with walnuts.

Chas told me about his lunch with Tania and how he had promised to hold the hundred dollars for her until she actually left home.

"Do you think that was wise?" I asked him.

"Can you suggest an alternative?" he said. "What I was really trying to do was stall for time. Look, Cherry, the kids might change their minds and forget all about running away. If they do go through with it and show up here someday asking for their money, then I'll just have to play it by ear."

"You know, Chas," I said, "aiding and abetting

134

runaway children may be against the law; I don't know. But even if it isn't, you're going to make enemies out of the children's parents and possibly leave yourself open to a civil suit."

"I know that," he said, "but I didn't have much choice, did I? Unless I want to snitch on the kids, which I don't."

"You said the boy's name is Chet?"

"It's actually Chester, but Tania calls him Chet. Chester Barrow."

I put down my wine and stared at him. "Barrow?" I said. "Is his mother Mabel Barrow?"

"I wouldn't know. They live next door to my brother's place. Herman has eyes for her. He calls her a dumpling so I guess she's plump. And one of the reasons Chet wants to leave home is that she watches TV all the time."

I drew a deep breath. "I shouldn't be telling you this, Chas, but I trust your discretion. Mabel Barrow is a patient of mine."

"Oh, lordy."

"And I can understand her son's desire to run away. It's obviously not a happy home."

He looked at me. "What do we do now, doc?"

"There's not a great deal we can do. Getting Mabel straightened around is going to take time—if I can do it. She's talking about divorce."

"Oh, shit," he said. "And, of course, the boy senses what's going on."

"Of course. Children are much more aware than their parents suspect."

"Poor kids," he said.

"Poor everyone," I said.

"What's that supposed to mean?"

I poured us more wine. "An occupational hazard," I told him. "I'm sure dermatologists get to thinking that everyone in the world has skin problems, and psychiatrists get to thinking that everyone in the world is screwed up."

He laughed. "Maybe we are," he said. "We're all nuts."

"Then what's the norm?" I asked him, but he didn't answer.

He hadn't turned on the lights, and the studio was filling with the mellow luster of the setting sun. It had a purplish tint, almost mauve. The air seemed perfumed with that glow. It had a soothing effect, warm and intimate.

"He kissed her," Chas said in a low voice.

"Who kissed whom?"

"Chet kissed Tania. She said she liked it. Is that the norm?"

"It's a good start," I said.

Again we sat in silence, both of us seemingly content. It was a rare moment, a good time to say what I had to say. And if I lost, my life would go on. Changed, but it would go on.

"I love you, Chas," I said quietly.

I thought he wasn't going to reply, but finally he did.

"I don't deserve it," he said.

That infuriated me. "Stop it!" I said angrily. "Now just stop it. Let me be the judge of whether or not you deserve it. I'm the one doing the loving."

His laugh was rueful. "Yes, doctor," he said.

I waited patiently, knowing that eventually he

would try to explain himself. He was an honest man, he really was.

"You know I want to," he said finally. "Not just the sex; that's only part of it. It's the giving, the surrendering, I find so hard. When I bought it in Nam, I was sure I was going to die. No pain yet, I was still in shock. But I looked down and saw my legs were gone. I just wanted to let go, let death take me. It seemed so easy—just to let go. But it wasn't easy. It was so tough that I couldn't do it."

"Chas, are you equating death with loving?"

"Of course not. I'm just saying that I thought letting go would be easy and I'd just drift away. It didn't happen. Almost against my will I fought back—or my body did."

"The instinct to survive."

"If you say so, doc. But it meant pain and the miseries. Now it seems so easy to keep on living the way I have been."

"And loving me means pain and misery?"

"Be honest," he said to me. "You know it does."

"It also means survival."

"Turn on the light," he cried. "My God, it's dark in here."

I switched on the lights, and he turned his head away from me. I wondered if he was weeping.

"I wish you had talked this way when you were under treatment," I told him. "I failed to draw it out of you."

"Don't put yourself down," he said. "Maybe the only reason I can talk this way now is because of the treatment. Your treatment."

"I know it's difficult for a man like you," I said.

"Yes, loving will mean surrendering, giving up a part of yourself."

"I don't have many parts left," he said wryly, looking down at his stumps.

"And you're right," I went on. "It will mean pain, for both of us. But the stakes are so high, it's worth the gamble."

He grinned at me. "No pain, no gain—right, doc?"

"Right," I said. "I'm supposed to be an expert on human behavior. But nothing I've read or studied or experienced in my practice can explain the way I feel about you, Chas. It's not analyzed in any of the textbooks. Perhaps because it's not abnormal."

"It is for me."

"Maybe. In your present mood. You see it as surrender. I see it as sharing. All I know is that I love you and want to make you happy. I think I can. But I have absolutely no desire to analyze the way I feel and understand *why* I'm acting the way I am. I just accept it. Besides, it's Saturday, and I don't work on Saturdays."

He laughed. "All right," he said, "since you won't analyze yourself, let me do it. You feel sorry for me."

"Bullshit."

"You're attracted to me the way a lot of people are attracted to freaks."

"Total bullshit."

"Or I represent a professional challenge; you don't feel my therapy is complete. Your love is strictly professional, all in the line of duty."

"You've got it all wrong, Chas. I love you because I love you. Can't you accept that?"

"It's too simple."

"Love *is* simple. It's a plain, elemental human emotion. Yes, as you said, the results may be pain and misery. But the feeling itself is clean and uncluttered. Nothing complicated about it. It just exists. And if you deny it, you risk more pain and misery than love can ever cause."

"Now you're preaching," he said.

"Yes, I'm preaching."

"Fighting for my soul, are you?"

"If you want to call it that. I don't want to see you wasting your life, Chas, that's for sure. But more important, I don't want to waste mine. If that sounds selfish, so be it. You're not going to ask me to stay for dinner, are you?"

"No."

"Just as well," I said. "It would be anticlimactic. Is there anything I can fetch you before I leave?"

"Yeah," he said. "I do believe that right now I need something a little stronger than white wine. Mix me a whiskey and soda, will you?"

"Which whiskey?"

"Whatever."

I made him a brandy and soda with a lot of ice and brought it to him.

"Thank you, Dr. Noble," he said.

"You're quite welcome, Mr. Todd," I said.

"Bend down," he said, motioning.

I leaned over his wheelchair. He crooked an arm about my neck, pulled me close, kissed me on the lips. A long, lingering kiss. Then he released me.

"I liked it," he said. "Is that the norm?"

"It's a good start," I said.

25

WILLIAM K. BREVOORT

Listen, I've been around the block twice, and the way Big Bobby Gurk was acting was making me antsy.

First of all, he phoned me at least four times wanting to know if I had a sample of the ZAP pill yet. I told him I was working on it, but I didn't like those checkup calls. When guys you've got a deal with get that eager you begin to think (1) it's bigger than you figured, and/or (2) they're conniving a way to cut you out.

Then suddenly Bobby wanted me to meet this twitch. Now when guys do that, it usually means they want to dump the broad and hope you'll take over, or she's such a gem and you're such close pals that he wants you to share the goodies. I didn't figure Gurk had either of those reasons.

But I went along with him because I was curious about what was on his mind, and also I didn't want to get him sore at me because I needed him if I was going to score big with bets on the fights and football games using the ZAP pill.

Bobby's woman turned out to be a big, friendly judy who was no slouch in the brains department. After we got to know each other, I asked her how come she had teamed up with a pig like Gurk, who sucked up his spaghetti like a vacuum cleaner and probably had the first buck he ever stole framed on the wall of his office. Also, he didn't smell so great. So how come she picked him?

"Beggars can't be choosers," Laura said. That was her name, Laura Gunther. "I've always had lousy luck with men."

Then I told her about The Luck and how I always had it. She said that was wonderful, and she wanted to keep seeing me in hopes some of it would rub off on her.

I got married years ago, but I don't know where she is now. Since then I've had a few women, but to tell you the truth, it wasn't all that important to me. But Laura and I hit it off right from the start, and I began seeing her two or three nights a week. I'd take her to ritzy restaurants and nightclubs where she could show off her rags and play the lady.

"You're the last of the big-time spenders, Willie," she told me. "I like that."

"Easy come, easy go," I said.

"Where does it come from?" she asked. "You got a business?"

"The information business," I said. "I buy from people who know and sell to people who want to know."

"Hey," she said, "that beats flipping hamburgers for sure."

After a while we found out we had both been in the

skin trade, which gave us something in common. And finally I told her about my hobby of cross-dressing. It didn't spook her.

"Look," she said, "you like to do drag and I like to smoke cigars. So what's the big deal? Live and let live is my motto."

The beauty part was that I could wear most of her dresses and lingerie because we were about the same size. I bought a lot of stuff from the boutique where she worked, and sometimes we'd go to a fancy shop and pick out gowns we both liked. She'd try them on before I bought them. It saved me a lot of bucks for alterations, and I liked wearing things she had worn. We kept all the new clothes at her place.

Also, she showed me some tricks with eye shadow I hadn't known about.

As far as sex goes, we never did connect, if you know what I mean. But we'd smoke a joint together or maybe do a line of coke and just play around. It was fun and no one got hurt. I helped her out a few times when she had the shorts, but she never really leaned on me for money.

The one thing I didn't like was that she was always asking questions about my business: who did I buy from and who did I sell to. You'd think a been-around twist would know better than to pry. After all, a man's business is private and she should have respected that.

I never told her word one, but she kept pestering me. So one night I took her out to a French place, and over the brandy and espresso I put it to her straight.

"Laura," I said, "I like you, and we've had a lot of laughs together. But if you keep digging into my private business I'm going to dump you. I'm sorry, but that's the way it is. I've worked hard to build up my career, and I'm not telling you or anyone else how I manage it. Okay?"

She took out one of those long, thin cigars she smoked, and I held a light for her. I noticed her hands were shaking.

"Willie," she said, "you've always treated me square, and I don't want you to dump me. It's true I've been trying to nose into your business, and now I'm going to tell you why."

And she told me that Big Bobby Gurk had put her on the pad to find out who my contact was at McWhortle Laboratory. She didn't know what the deal was between me and Gurk; all she knew was that he wanted to cut me out.

"Uh-huh," I said. "I figured it might be something like that. I admire your coming clean with me. I owe you a big one."

"Jesus, Willie," she said, "you won't tell Gurk, will you? He's got some muscle in his organization, and they'll feed me to the sharks if he finds out I snitched."

"Of course I won't tell him, Laura. What kind of a rat do you think I am? You just keep stalling him until I figure out how to handle this. It's got to be something cute because Gurk can be a mean bastard when he's crossed."

I gave it some heavy thought for the next few days, but I couldn't finagle a way to dump Gurk. If I expected to score by betting on fighters and football teams that had been doped with ZAP, I needed Bobby because he knew bookies all over the country and could cobble up a giant swindle.

Then I got a call from Jessica Fiddler, and I went over to her pad in the early evening. She told me she had balled McWhortle that afternoon.

"The old man came on like a young stud," she said. "And when I asked him how come he had so much juice, he told me he just watched a TV tape of some mice who had been injected with that testosterone stuff."

According to McWhortle's story, the injected male mouse had kept porking female mice until he fell over in a dead faint. Then, after he rested awhile, he started all over again.

"That's interesting," I said. "You mean the ZAP injection gave the mouse a rat-sized hard-on?"

"That's what McWhortle said. He also told me the chemist working on it is trying to cut down on the Spanish fly effect because they want the pill to produce killers, not rapists."

"It must be powerful stuff. Did he say when it would be ready in pill form?"

"No, but he said it might be tested on human volunteers in a couple of months."

"Did he happen to mention the name of the chemist working on it?"

"No," she said, "he didn't."

"Try to find out, will you, Jess. It's very important."

"How much important?" she asked.

This doll was developing a galloping case of the gimmes, but there was nothing I could do about it. She was a key player, and I needed to keep her happy.

"An extra grand for the chemist's name," I told her.

"Come on, Willie," she said. "You can do better than that."

"Get the chemist's name first," I said, "and then we'll talk business. Okay?"

She nodded, and we left it at that.

I drove back to Laura's place to dress for a big affair at my private club. It was called Waltz Night in Old Vienna, and I had bought a lovely bouffant ballgown in peach-colored taffeta. Laura had promised to set my strawberry blond wig in a Veronica Lake style.

I was excited about Waltz Night, of course, but I was even more excited by what Jessica Fiddler had told me. If the ZAP pill produced a sexual rush, there was more money to be made from that than from feeding it to some palooka heavyweight or second-rate football team.

What I had in mind was getting hold of a sample pill, having it copied, and bootlegging it all over the country as the first space-age aphrodisiac. You know how much men would pay to get it up whenever they wanted and keep it up as long as they liked? Millions!

The best thing was that I didn't need Big Bobby Gurk to pull off that caper; I could do it myself. Why, I could even peddle the stuff mail order as a vitamin or diet supplement before the Feds shut me down or thieves moved in, swiped the formula, and began hawking cut-rate imitations. I figured to make a mint before either of those things happened.

"Hey, Willie," Laura said, as she helped me with my mascara, "you're really high tonight. Good news?"

"It's The Luck," I said. "It hasn't deserted me yet."

26

MARLEEN TODD

I must confess I was horrified by my reaction to direct inhalation of oxytocin in its aerosolized form. When I plugged that soaked inhaler into my nostrils, I had no idea what the results might be. But all ethical researchers must test new products on themselves before recruiting other human volunteers.

My behavior after inhaling the hormone was extremely embarrassing. The odd thing was that I was fully aware of my ridiculous conduct at the time but unable to control it. I knew I was being overly affectionate toward Greg Barrow, my daughter, and my husband, but I could not resist the urge to exhibit my love.

Fortunately my excessive elation proved to be temporary. It ended when I suddenly became so sleepy I feared I might collapse if I didn't get to bed immediately. When I awoke the next day, I could discern no aftereffects other than a slight dryness of the nasal passages.

It was obvious to me that aerosolized oxytocin was much too powerful to be used in a perfume in an unadulterated form. But its ability to modify mood and behavior convinced me that in the proper strength it would be a unique and valuable base for the new fragrance I was creating. It could truly make Cuddle the warm, intimate, *caring* scent it was intended to be.

And so I set to work on the long trial-and-error process of combining a diluted measure of the hormone with more conventional essences. I recall that during this period of experimentation I didn't doubt for a minute that I would achieve my goal of producing a perfect Cuddle. I never stopped to consider the consequences, and that eventually proved to be a nearly fatal error.

But meanwhile I was faced with a worsening crisis at home. My husband's drinking and philandering had become so outrageous that I was driven to an open and possibly final confrontation.

It began with the clichéd cause of so many marital discords: Herman forgot our wedding anniversary, the tenth. I had prepared a fine dinner: a roast beef, twice-baked potatoes, and *haricots verts* with almonds, to be served with a very expensive bordeaux bottled the year we were married. Herman didn't come home for the anniversary dinner, of course, and poor Tania and I were forced to make the best of it and pretend it was a special party.

Herm finally arrived around ten-thirty, after Tania had gone to bed—thank God! He wasn't completely inebriated, but it was obvious he had been drinking heavily. I was seated in the kitchen when he came in. He headed directly for the refrigerator—for a cold beer, I presumed—but then noticed the unopened bottle of wine on the countertop.

"Hey," he said, picking it up to examine the label, "what the hell is this? Expensive stuff."

"Note the vintage?" I asked.

"Sure. It's ten years old. So?"

I looked at him, and his face froze in a goofy grin.

"Oh, shit," he said. "The year we got married. Is today our anniversary, hon?"

I didn't answer.

"Well, what the hell," he said. "I'll make it up to you. Maybe we'll go out tomorrow night for a nice dinner."

"I prepared a nice dinner," I told him. "A roast beef. But you didn't come home."

"Well, jeez," he said, almost aggrievedly, "you should have said something about it. How was I to know?"

It was at that moment that I made up my mind. Certainly I had suffered more serious slights and disappointments, but at that instant I decided I could no longer endure his boorish behavior.

"Herman," I said, "I want a divorce."

He blinked a few times. "Come on, hon," he said in a thick voice, "you don't really mean that."

"I really do. I suggest you sleep in the spare bedroom tonight. I'll see a lawyer tomorrow, and then we'll talk about permanent arrangements. I don't wish to continue living with you."

"Why the hell are you so pissed?" he demanded. "So I came home late for dinner. I forgot our anniversary. What's the big deal. It happens all the time."

"It's not just tonight," I said. "It's all the nights

you haven't come home. Your drinking. Your playing around. I've had it, Herm. I want out."

"I don't know what you're bitching about," he blustered. "Haven't I provided a good home? You got your own car. Who paid for that roast beef? A lot of women would like to have what you've got."

"What have I got?" I said furiously. "A drunken husband who makes no effort to conceal his infidelities. A lousy father who never spends time with his only child. A miserable lover who's lost all interest in his wife. You think other women would like to have that? Think again, buster."

"Look," he said earnestly, "I admit I haven't been perfect—but what man is? I'm under a lot of stress at the office, a lot of pressure to produce. I have to unwind or I'll go nuts. Maybe I haven't thought enough about how it bothers you and Tania, but it's not because I don't love you. I do, I really do. Listen, if I didn't have a home to come back to, I'd be lost. Divorce isn't the answer, Marleen, you know that. You still love me, don't you?"

"Yes," I said, "God help me, I still love you. But love isn't enough anymore. Not for me and not for Tania. We both need love in return. We need a man of the house who listens to our problems and helps solve them. We need a husband and father who *cares*. And you just don't care, Herman."

"Well, screw you!" he said wrathfully, glowering down at me. "If you don't like the way I act, then get your goddamned divorce. Who needs you? You're more interested in that stupid job of yours than you are in me. And when it comes to the job you're supposed to do in bed—forget it! You're a total washout."

"How the hell would you know?" I screamed at him. "How long has it been since you've even tried? And if you did, you'd be too soused to do anything. So don't talk to me about sex. Go fuck one of your chippies. God knows what you've picked up from them. I always make sure I wash a glass you've used. I don't want to catch anything."

"What the fuck are you talking about?" he yelled. "You think I don't use—" Then he caught himself and didn't finish what he was going to say. He took a deep breath. "Listen," he said hoarsely, "we're both upset. I admit I forgot our anniversary, and I apologize. But let's both sleep on this divorce thing. I don't want to lose you, Marleen, really I don't. I'll sleep in the spare bedroom, and maybe tomorrow we'll both see things more clearly and can talk it over like mature adults. Okay?"

"I'm going to bed," I said. "There's cold beef in the fridge. Just like you, lover boy—cold beef."

He uttered one awful curse, and with a sweeping motion of his arm knocked the bottle of anniversary wine to the floor. It shattered into a million slivers, and the red bordeaux spread everywhere. We both stared at what he had done, shocked.

Then I looked at him. "What are you trying to prove?" I asked. I really wasn't sure what I meant.

I went upstairs and listened at Tania's door. I couldn't hear her crying or stirring about, so I hoped she had slept through the argument. I went into my own bedroom and locked the door. I didn't even have the energy to wash up, just pulled on a nightgown and got into bed.

I thought of what he had said and what I had said,

and what I should have said. The whole situation was just so sad that I wanted to weep, and I did, for a short while.

It suddenly struck me that the day had been utterly bizarre. I had spent eight hours trying to create a fragrance that would make people more loving, more caring, and I had ended the day screaming at an uncaring mate whose love seemed reserved for himself.

I think it may have been then, in the hour or so that it took me to fall asleep, that I began to wonder if the solution to my personal problems might not lie in the solution to my professional problems.

It was possible.

27

MABEL BARROW

The reason I was putting on weight was that I was so unhappy. I told that to Dr. Noble, and all she said was, "Mmm." But I really believed it. I know I wore a size 6 when I got married and now I wore a 12. That tells you something, doesn't it? When you're unhappy, you're snacking all the time, like Pepperidge Farm cookies and M&Ms.

I wasn't a fatso, not yet I wasn't, but I was more zaftig than I wanted to be. I know my boobs were bigger and also my fanny. That was okay; I could live with that. But I was beginning to get flab under my upper arms, and my thighs were getting loose. That revolted me.

I mean I used to have a fantastic figure; everyone said so. I wore the world's teeny-weeniest bikinis. But I guess those days are gone forever. Now I wear a swimsuit with a built-in bra and a skirt, for God's sake. I knew I looked exactly like what I was: a plump housewife with a freezer full of frozen packages of macaroni and cheese.

That's why it gave my ego a boost when Herman Todd came on to me. I knew he played around a lot, but it was good for my morale to know there was at least one guy who had the hots for me. I sure as hell wasn't getting any heavy breathing from my husband.

One morning, after Marleen and Greg had left for work and the kids were out playing, Herm came over for a cup of coffee. I made instant for both of us and sat down at the kitchen table with him. I put out a plate of jelly doughnuts.

"What's with you?" I asked him. "You look down."

"I guess," he said, sighing. "Marleen and I had a big go-around last night."

"Yeah? About what?"

"I forgot it was our anniversary. She made a special dinner and bought a bottle of wine. I came home late, and she got sore."

"She'll get over it," I told him.

"I don't think so," he said. "She wants a divorce."

"Oh, shit," I said.

"My sentiments exactly. We talked about it again this morning before she left for work, and she's bound and determined. She's going to see a lawyer."

"I'm sorry, Herm."

"Yeah. I am, too. Listen, Mabel, I hope you won't tell anyone about this. Not even Greg."

"Of course not. What happens now?"

"I don't really know. I guess I'll move out and take a motel room somewhere. Maybe if I'm not around for a while, she'll calm down and change her mind."

"Maybe," I said.

We finished our coffee and doughnuts. I stood up

and started putting the dishes in the sink. I was wearing an old ratty robe and my hair was up in curlers, but it didn't seem to bother him. He got up and moved me around so I was facing him. He loosened the belt on my robe and opened it. I was wearing white cotton panties, but that's all. He gave me a once-over.

"You're some woman, Mabel," he said. "We could make each other happy." He leaned down to kiss my bazooms, then looked up at me. "If I get a place at a motel, will you come visit me?"

I didn't answer, and he bent down to kiss me again. He sure had a wicked tongue.

"Will you?" he repeated.

"All right," I said.

I said it without hardly thinking of what I was saying. I just said, "All right," like it was something I had thought about for a long time and finally decided to do. But it wasn't like that at all. It was more a spur-of-the-moment thing. I think it was his tongue.

But after he left, I thought about it and I got scared. I mean if Marleen wanted a divorce, maybe she already had a private detective following him. To get evidence, you know. And if I shacked up with him, maybe we'd get caught and I'd be named in court as the Other Woman, and that would just kill me, let alone what it would do to Greg and Chester.

I thought about it all day and ate a whole can of honey-roasted peanuts. I didn't feel much like cooking that night, so I made a big platter of spaghetti and meatballs, using three frozen packages. And I cut up some iceberg lettuce and doused it with Paul Newman's salad dressing. He's such a great actor.

After dinner, Chester went outside, to play I guess, and Greg went into his den to work, as usual. I watched a two-hour television travelogue on Tibet. How about those yaks?

Chester came home and went to bed. I cleaned up the kitchen and then went upstairs to take my shower like I do every night. While I was drying off, I looked at myself in the full-length mirror and wondered if I should have things done. You know, like a tummy tuck, an ass lift, and stuff like that. Also, they can vacuum fat out of your thighs. I saw it on a TV special.

I was doing my nails in the bedroom when Greg came in.

"Did you lock up?" I asked him.

"Doors and windows," he said. "All secure."

We said exactly the same goddamned thing every goddamned night.

What I had done was put on that black see-through lace teddy I had bought from Laura at Hashbeam's Bo-teek. I wasn't going to sleep in it, of course, but I thought it might tickle Greg's fancy, if you know what I mean.

I waited for him to notice, but he didn't even glance at me. He went into the bedroom for his shower, and when he came out, he was wearing his pajamas. I don't know why but when my husband wears pajama jacket and pants, it looks like a business suit.

I stood up and posed like a model. "How do you like it?" I asked him.

He looked at the lace teddy. "Very nice," he said, and went to the bed to turn down the covers.

"It's supposed to be sexy," I reminded him.

He looked again. "Very attractive," he said, which was an improvement—but not much. He got into bed and pulled the top sheet up to his chin.

I went over and sat on the edge of the bed at his side. "I feel horny," I told him. "Please don't tell me you've got a headache."

That made him smile. I turned off the lights, took off my teddy, and slipped into bed next to him, naked as a skinned rabbit. I took his hand and cupped it around one of my lungs.

"Look how big I'm getting," I said.

"I've noticed," he said.

"That's okay with you, isn't it?" I said. "I mean you don't have any objections, do you?"

It was the first I had heard him laugh in a long time. It wasn't much of a laugh, just a little chuckle, but it was *something*.

"You're very hot," he said in a low voice.

"Hotter than you think," I said. "Do you remember what to do next?"

He laughed again, a little louder this time. "It's like riding a bike," he said. "You never forget how."

"Why don't you take off your suit," I suggested. "And start pedaling."

He got out of bed to do it, stumbling around in the darkness. Then he got back into bed. Greg is nicely put together.

I ran my hands over his body. "Hey," I said, "what have we here? Hello, there! Long time no see."

He kissed me a few times. Adequate, but nothing to write home about. I pulled the sheet off us and kicked it aside. I inched up in bed and moved his head down to my bosom, wanting him to do a Herman.

"Try it," I said. "It's better than spaghetti and meatballs."

Then I stopped coaching him. He did what men are supposed to do. I mean he knew all the moves, even though he was never going to be a mad, impetuous lover. He was so methodical, like he was working his way through a sex manual. Something published around 1810.

Sure I got aroused; I'm not wood, you know, and right then it was thank God for little favors, though I wished he wasn't so polite.

"Am I too heavy on you?" he inquired.

You know, I really felt sorry for him. I mean he was *trying*. But when it came to making a woman happy, he had the words but he just didn't have the music.

28

HERMAN TODD

I wasn't going to take my problem to my brother; Chas has his own troubles. And if I told him Marleen was talking divorce, he wouldn't say, "I told you so," but he'd give me a look that would mean the same thing.

It was a funny feeling, not funny ha-ha but funny strange. I mean I was a sociable guy, "Herm" to half the population, always ready for party time. But now, with my life falling apart, I couldn't think of a shoulder I could cry on.

I should tell you that I hate solitude. If I had to live like Chas, I'd go nuts. I like to be part of a crowd, everyone knocking back the drinks and laughing up a storm. Suddenly I felt alone, deserted, with no one but myself to talk to. I couldn't handle it, I admit it, and I was afraid of just giving up and crawling into a bottle of Absolut to end my days.

I was really down, dragging ass, when I got this great brainstorm. There was someone I could talk to, a professional who would listen to my tale of woe and maybe tell me how to get out of the mess I was in. I phoned Dr. Cherry Noble.

"Is this about Chas?" she asked me.

"No," I told her, "it's about me. I need help."

"That's a good start," she said.

So we set up an appointment. I didn't even ask her what it was going to cost. At that point in time her fee was the least of my worries.

I was afraid she might want me to lie on a couch, which would have been ridiculous, but she didn't even have one in her office. She sat behind a desk for which I was thankful because I think I told you she's got the greatest legs in the world, and if she sat where I could see them, I'd probably end up making a pass and that would queer the whole deal. I sat in an uncomfortable armchair facing her across the desk.

I told her I was in deep shit with Marleen, that she had said she wanted a divorce and sounded serious about it. I also told her about the anniversary dinner I had missed.

"Surely she doesn't want a divorce because you forgot an anniversary," Dr. Noble said.

"Nah," I said. "That was just the final straw. I admit I've been a bad boy. Too much drinking. Too much partying. Too many beds, if you know what I mean."

"You were aware your behavior offended her?"

"I guess I knew it," I admitted, "but either I didn't care or I didn't think it would rile her all that much."

"And what is it you want from me, Herman—absolution?"

"Look, doc, the big problem is this: I can crawl on my knees to my wife, swear I'm going to straighten up and fly right. And maybe she'll give me another chance. Maybe. But I know that I won't be able to do it for long. Sooner or later I'll go back to my old ways because, let's face it, I enjoy living like that. So what I want from you is to be told why I act the way I do, why I'm hooked on drinking and whoring around. Maybe if I can understand *why* I do it, I can figure out how to stop permanently."

"Mmm," she said. "You don't want to lose Marleen?"

"Hell, no!" I said. "I love that woman, and my little girl, Tania. I guess I haven't proved it to them, but I do love them. I'm a self-centered sonofabitch, I know that, but I don't seem capable of changing."

"Do you honestly want to change?"

"Honestly I don't. I told you I like the way I've been living. But if changing is the only way I can hang onto Marleen and Tania, then I'll do it. What I want you to do is tell me how."

"What you're asking is that I help you learn why you drink so much and why you're a womanizer?"

"That's about it, doc."

"Mmm. Have you told Marleen that you were going to consult me?"

"No."

"If I take you on, do you intend to tell her?"

I thought about that for a moment. "Probably," I said finally. "It may be the only way to keep her from going ahead with a divorce. If she hears I'm getting help, maybe she'll be patient until she sees if I'm really serious about mending my ways."

"And are you serious?"

"Would I be here if I wasn't?"

She was silent awhile, and I stared at her. She was a handsome woman. Great cheekbones. If a woman has high cheekbones and long legs, she's got it all—right? Marleen had high cheekbones and long legs.

"I wouldn't care to be used, Herman," Dr. Noble said softly. "I don't like the idea of your thinking of therapy as a ploy to keep Marleen from seeking a divorce. If I took you on, your treatment could conceivably take a long time. Perhaps months. Perhaps years. Meanwhile, do you intend to keep living the way you have been?"

"I see what you're getting at, doc," I said slowly. "I can't ask Marleen to put up with my bullshit just because I'm going to a shrink. Is that what you mean?"

"Something like that."

"That doesn't leave me much hope, does it?"

"There may be a way of working it out," she said evenly. "Let me think about it. Phone me early next week. I think you've done a good job of analyzing your problem, but whether or not I can help you is a question. I hope you realize that the success of therapy will depend on you. Not on me, on *you*."

"Sure, I know that. Okay, I'll call you next week." I got up to leave. "Have you seen Chas lately?" I asked her.

"Yes," she said. "I stopped by his place last Saturday."

"How's he doing?"

"Better," she said. "Are you going to tell him about your problem?"

"No. He's got his own worries."

She nodded, rose, and opened her office door for me.

She was wearing a pantsuit so I never did get a good look at her legs.

It was then about three in the afternoon, and I didn't feel like going back to work. I could have gone out to the club and hoisted a few, but that didn't appeal to me right then. So, believe it or not, I went home. I guess I wanted time to think about what Cherry had said. She hadn't agreed to take me on, I noted, but she hadn't said no either. I figured my chances were fifty-fifty.

When I got home, I pulled into the driveway and didn't even get out of the car. I just sat there with the engine running and the air conditioner on. I saw Tania and Chester Barrow. They were both in their bathing suits, and they were having a hose fight across our two lawns.

They were having a helluva time, running around and screaming and dousing each other with water. I envied them. They ate, slept, enjoyed life, and that was about it. You had to grow up to have troubles.

I watched Chet Barrow, a good-looking boy, and thought about his mother. She was primed, and I knew if I had to move into a motel room, she'd be my first guest. I was glad I hadn't mentioned that project to Dr. Noble. She'd have thrown my ass out of her office for sure.

Tania came running over to the Lincoln, and I lowered the window.

"Why are you home so early, Daddy?" she asked.

"Just stopped by for a minute," I said. "Having a good time, honey?"

"It's okay," she said. "Better than going in that smelly pool."

Then Chet came close and sloshed her with water from his hose. She shrieked and ran away. He followed. I put up the window and watched the two of them scampering about, not a worry in the world.

I decided I wanted some of that. I backed out of the driveway and headed for the club. By the time I got there the Happy Hour would be starting.

29

GREGORY BARROW

That was a curious summer. I had six weeks of accumulated vacation time, and Mabel and Chester were continually asking when we were going away, and where. I told them how busy I was at the lab and mumbled something about taking time off in October. I didn't tell them that even a fall vacation was iffy.

The truth was I had no desire to go anywhere. I was totally engrossed by the ZAP Project, possibly the most interesting research I had ever done, and I even resented taking Sundays off. I wanted to be in the lab every day with my mice and video cameras.

The problem was to develop a testosterone formulation that increased aggressiveness without inflaming sexual desire at the same time. After several failed experiments, I began to wonder if the two might not be inextricably linked.

My first small success resulted from the addition of potassium nitrate and sodium nitrate to the solution of synthetic testosterone. I had clear evidence (on

TV tape) that male mice injected with the altered testosterone showed a small but discernible lessening of their desire to copulate.

To achieve even this minor reduction required countless experiments. And as I began a search for other chemicals that might further decrease the sexual consequences of the hormone injection, my notebooks filled with the record of seemingly endless trials, all of which ended in failure. One cause of that, naturally, was that I had no prior research by others to guide me. I felt like Edison who reportedly tested hundreds of materials before finding a filament that worked in his incandescent lamp.

While I was so deeply involved in the ZAP Project, I must confess that I was completely unaware of the worsening crisis in my relations with my wife and son. I thought we had arrived at a plateau of unhappiness, unpleasant but endurable. I suppose I was content because things didn't seem to be getting worse.

I expressed these sentiments to Marleen Todd, and she was scornful.

"Greg," she said, "you simply can't let matters drift. That's like neglecting to seek a cure for an illness because you've become used to the pain."

I admit I was somewhat miffed. She wasn't treating me like the village idiot, exactly, but she made no effort to hide her exasperation with my predilection for letting things slide. She may have had a point; I do hate to make waves.

"And what do you suggest I do, Marleen?"

"Either have a long, intimate talk with Mabel and get things straightened out between you two, or take some other action to end your estrangement."

"I wouldn't call it an estrangement," I said lamely.

"No? Then what would you call it?"

"I don't know," I said helplessly. "A coolness, I suppose. We inhabit the same house, but we seem to be living in different worlds. It's a very unsettling situation, Marleen, and I suspect most of the fault is mine. I know I'm not the husband Mabel wants me to be. She thinks I'm a failure as a man."

"Not all women think that, Greg," she said quietly.

Then an event occurred that was to affect profoundly all our lives.

On the morning of July 27, I heard the sounds of people running in the corridor outside my private laboratory and shouts I could not comprehend. I feared a fire might have broken out—a terrible danger since we had so many inflammables on the premises—but the alarm didn't go off.

A moment later my lab phone rang. It was Marleen, excited and breathless.

"Did you hear?" she gasped. "It's Mr. McWhortle. He collapsed on his putting green. They're giving him CPR."

I went out there as quickly as I could. The company doctor was in attendance, now using a portable oxygen tank. He and a nurse worked frantically for several minutes, while a crowd of employees that had assembled stood a respectful distance away.

"It's his heart," I heard someone say. "The doctor gave him a shot, but he hasn't moved since I've been here."

Then we all waited in silence. A fire rescue truck arrived followed by an ambulance. They had additional equipment, and the paramedics joined the doctor in ministering to the fallen man.

It was almost a half hour before the medical personnel gave up, turned away, and began to pack their gear. The ambulance crew wheeled a stretcher across the putting green. The company doctor came over to the assembled employees.

"He's gone," he reported.

The sudden death of Marvin McWhortle shook all of us. He really was a generous, beneficent employer, and after mourning his demise, we all began worrying about the future of McWhortle Laboratory. I think my greatest anxiety concerned the continued funding of the ZAP Project.

The laboratory was closed for three days, but those of us conducting animal research were allowed entrance to feed and care for our subjects. The laboratory reopened the day after the funeral. All employees were summoned to a meeting in the cafeteria where Mrs. Gertrude McWhortle, Marvin's widow, spoke to us.

She was a large, imposing woman, and no one could doubt her sincerity and determination. She said she was now the sole owner of McWhortle Laboratory, had every intention of keeping the business going, and saw no reason not to follow her late husband's plans for expansion.

She also told us she would act as chief executive officer until she could hire a more experienced CEO with the aid of a management consulting firm. All of us were to continue working at our assigned projects;

all contracts with clients would be fulfilled. The company was in excellent financial condition, she added, with ample cash reserves.

Good news indeed!

And so, with only a brief interruption, I returned to my assignment with renewed enthusiasm, as I think other employees did as well. I even heard several, including Marleen Todd, express satisfaction that a woman was now in charge of our company.

"I suppose it's selfish of me," Marleen said, "but I'm hoping Gertie will increase the budget of the perfumery. We've been trying to get our library of essences inventoried and computerized for ages. Greg, now is the time for you to put in a requisition for that electron microscope you've always wanted."

"It would be nice to have, Marleen," I said, "but it's really not essential."

"What an old stick-in-the-mud you are," she said, laughing.

I tried to laugh too, but couldn't. Her remark rankled, as did her previous comments about my tendency to let things drift. She seemed so vehement about what she considered my wishy-washiness that I had a feeling of being pressured, of being manipulated to fit a scenario she had designed. It was a disquieting notion.

But I had other, more important matters to consider. A week after Mr. McWhortle's death I succeeded in adding a chemical to the solution of synthesized testosterone that had a very definite, easily observed effect of diminishing, if not totally eliminating, the sexual aggression of injected male mice. I cannot identify the chemical for proprietary reasons, but I can state it was an inexpensive ingredient found in many common household soaps and detergents.

Repeated experiments with the new formulation yielded the same gratifying results, and I pondered my next move. Logically, I should have repeated my final experiments on larger mammals: guinea pigs, dogs, and chimps. But I was so excited by my recent success that I decided to progress immediately to trials on human volunteers—myself first, of course.

Analyzing my own conduct in this regard, I see now that I had an ulterior motive for wishing to try the hormone formulation on myself. I had no desire to become more physically aggressive; that is simply contrary to my nature.

But I did hope to become more assertive, to express myself and act more forcibly. I believe I had some vague notion of proving to Mabel and Marleen that I was a real man. Macho posturing had nothing to do with it. It was simply a matter of masculine pride.

30

JESSICA FIDDLER

On July 27 I was lying on a chaise out by my swimming pool, naked as a jaybird. I had my portable radio tuned to an oldies station. The local news came on, and I heard the announcer say Marvin McWhortle, a well-known businessman, had dropped dead that morning on his private putting green.

I immediately dashed into the house, phoned the Pontiac dealership and canceled my order for a white Bonneville. Thank God I hadn't signed a contract yet. Then I poured myself a vodka on the rocks, took a gulp, and started crying.

Part of my boohooing was because I had lost my sugar daddy; I admit it. But part was because I really felt sorry the old man had shuffled off. I mean he was always straight with me, never beat me, and he wasn't all that kinky. I knew I'd never find another john like him.

I finished my drink, dried my tears, and tried to figure out where I stood. The house was in my name, I owned my old heap, and I had about ten thousand in cash, most of it from Willie the Weasel. I knew that wouldn't last long, and I also knew that as soon as new management took over at McWhortle Laboratory, my no-show job as a consultant would be gone with the wind.

I had to discuss my predicament with someone in the same fix, so I phoned Laura Gunther at Hashbeam's and asked her if she'd like to share a plate of lasagna that night. She said she had a dinner date and couldn't make it.

"Anything wrong, Jess?" she asked. "You sound down."

"Yeah," I said, "I just had some superbad news."

"Look," she said, "suppose I stop by for a drink after work. I can stay an hour or so."

"I'd appreciate that," I said gratefully. "I can use some sympathy."

By the time Laura showed up, I had my act together and was thinking, what the hell, I wasn't so bad off. I had a roof over my head, a car, and money in the bank. I was surviving, and if I had to go back on the street again, I could do that; the body was used, but it was still a bargain.

I poured Laura a Chivas, which she dearly loves, and put out a bowl of Doritos. Then I flopped down on the couch next to her and took a deep breath.

"Okay, kiddo," she said, "what's the bad news you want to unload on me?"

"A man named Marvin McWhortle dropped dead today," I told her. "I guess it was a heart attack."

She was startled. "Don't tell me he was the guy who owned McWhortle Laboratory?"

"That's the one."

"Shit," she said. "That'll screw things up." She looked at me. "But what's it got to do with you?"

"Laura," I said, "McWhortle kept me. He was my one and only trick. He bought this house for me and put me on his company payroll."

"Son of a bitch," she said. "I knew you were balling an old geezer, but I had no idea it was McWhortle. Tough luck, Jess. You think he left you anything in his will?"

"I doubt it," I said. "But he was going to buy me a new Bonneville. That's out the window now, of course. But that's not the worst of it. Listen to this . . ."

I told Laura how McWhortle was always bringing me samples of new products his laboratory had developed, and how he liked to gab about new clients he had landed and projects the lab was working on. Then I'd sell the samples and stuff he had told me for a nice buck to a guy who was in the information business.

"It was a sweet racket," I mourned, "but with McWhortle dead, that cash cow just dried up, and I've got to think about hustling again."

Laura drained her Chivas and held out the empty glass. "Another," she said hoarsely. "Please."

I brought her the bottle and told her to help herself. She poured a double, at least, and took a hefty belt.

"Jess," she said, "this guy who bought information from you—his name wouldn't be Willie, would it? Tall, thin, dresses like a fashion plate?"

It was my turn to be startled. "Sure it is," I said. "William K. Brevoort. I call him Willie the Weasel because he's got a long, pointy face. You know him?"

"Oh, Jesus, do I know him!" she said. "This is the damnedest thing. Now you listen to this, Jess . . ."

Then she told me how Big Bobby Gurk and Brevoort had a deal cooking that involved a ZAP pill being developed by McWhortle Laboratory, and how Gurk wanted to cut Willie out and had hired Laura to find the name of the chemist feeding Willie the information.

"So I cozied up to Brevoort," Laura went on, "and he's twice the guy Big Bobby is. Also he smells better. So I told him Gurk was planning to dump him as soon as he found out the name of the chemist."

I laughed like a maniac. "Willie doesn't know the chemist at the lab. He knows me; I was the one selling him what McWhortle told me."

"Well," Laura said, taking another slug of her scotch, "I guess that's that. With McWhortle gone, the whole caper comes to a screeching halt."

I stared at her. "Not necessarily," I said slowly. "I know the name of the chemist."

"Oh my God!" Laura cried. "McWhortle may be dead, but we're still alive."

We talked it over, excited, with dreams of a big score. At first we figured that the two of us, working together, could somehow get a sample of the ZAP pill from the chemist. But then we realized that even if we could, we wouldn't know what to do with it. We just didn't have the contacts and the know-how to sell it for heavy bucks.

"We'll have to bring Willie in on the deal," Laura said finally. "I wish the two of us could manage it ourselves, but that's a pipe dream. Willie has the experience; he'll know how to finagle it."

"You trust him?" I asked her.

"Absolutely," she said, grinning. "Because I know something about him that'll keep him honest."

"Okay," I said. "I'll give him a call and tell him to get over here right away."

"Don't bother," Laura said. "He's waiting for me at my place. Let's go."

We took Laura's wheels, a Ford Taurus, figuring there was no point in driving two cars. We were at her condo in twenty minutes, and when we walked in together I thought William K. Brevoort was going to faint.

"What's going on here?" he said in a cracked voice.

We made him sit down, and Laura fixed drinks, which we all badly needed. Willie had heard of McWhortle's death and figured his hopes of making a mint on the ZAP pill were just as dead. He said he naturally thought he'd have to dump me as a source of information—and what else did he have?

"I'll tell you what we've got," Laura said. "Jess knows the name of the chemist working on that cockamamy pill."

Brevoort looked at me. "Is that straight?" he said.

I nodded.

"What's his name?" he asked eagerly.

I let him sweat a minute, pretending I was thinking it over. "Even thirds on the profits?" I said finally. "You, Laura, and me?"

"My word on it," he said. "And I don't cross ladies; it's not my style. What's his name, Jess?"

"Barrow. McWhortle called him Greg, so I guess it's Gregory Barrow."

Laura jerked and slopped her drink. "Barrow?" she said. "Has he got a wife named Mabel? Mabel Barrow is a good customer of mine at the store. I've got her address and phone number."

"I'll check it out," Willie the Weasel said. "If Mabel is his wife, it could give us an opening to Greg."

"And then?" I asked him.

He thought a moment, and I could almost see his grifter's gears turning. "Jess, maybe you can arrange to meet him accidently on purpose when his wife isn't around. Come on to him hot and heavy, and hook him. You know how."

"What if he doesn't go for me?"

"He will," Brevoort said confidently. "He's a man, isn't he?"

31

CHESTER BARROW

I never told this to anyone, but I don't think my parents are my *real* parents. I think I was adopted. I mean I'm so different from them that it makes sense, that they're not my real mother and father. And they don't treat me like the other kids I know get treated by their parents. They don't beat me up or anything like that, but they don't treat me like I was really their own kid.

I think my real mother and father were killed in a plane crash when I was little. Like we were all flying someplace neat like Disney World, and this plane got engine trouble and crashed. And while it was going down my real mother and father held me in their arms and protected me so I wouldn't get hurt when we hit, and I wasn't but they were both killed.

So then the police advertised if anyone wanted to adopt a little kid whose real parents were killed in a plane crash, and that's how I came to live with my mother and father, because they didn't have any kids of their own. But they've never told me I was adopted and that my real father was an astronaut and my real mother was a movie star who gave up her job so she could be my mother. I think that's what happened.

If they were my real mother and father and loved me, I wouldn't want to run away, would I? So that proves it.

When Tania told me her uncle was going to give her a hundred dollars so we could run away, that was keen. He said we should take a cab out to where he lived, and he would pay the driver, and then he would give us the money and we could go anywhere we liked.

Tania and I talked about it a lot, and we decided we would go to Alaska, like I wanted, but first we would go to Disney World, which was closer and which we had never seen. All the kids we knew had been, and they were always bragging on it.

"When should we go?" Tania asked me. "I think we should set a time because Mother wants me to start taking piano lessons."

"I think we should go before school starts," I told her. "Like if we go during vacation, we could leave in the morning, and then they probably won't know we're gone till that night. But if we go after school starts, then they'll call our parents right away when they take attendance and we're not there."

"That's very true," Tania said. "We should have a head start before they notice we've gone and maybe call the police. Chet, what do you think I should wear?"

I didn't know what she meant and shrugged. "What you always wear, I guess," I said. "Like shorts and a T."

"No," she said, "I can't wear that for traveling. Maybe I'll wear jeans and my nylon jacket because the nights might get chilly. And I'll put my dress-up things in my suitcase."

"Suitcase?" I said. "What do you need a suitcase for? It'll just get in the way."

"I'll need more clothes than what I'm wearing, and so will you. Have you got a suitcase?"

"I got like a bag," I said. "It's cloth but it holds a lot."

"Then you should pack it, Chet," she said. "And don't forget all your favorite things."

"Like what?"

"Well, maybe your little radio. And what about your stamp collection?"

"I forgot about that," I said. "It's in big books. I guess I'll have to leave them. I can always start a new collection when we get to Alaska."

"How long do you think it'll take us to get there?"

I thought awhile. "It depends," I said.

That night I looked around my bedroom and Tania was right; I did have a lot of favorite things. Like I had a rock I had found that looked like it had gold in it, and some swell shells I had picked up on the beach, and a plastic skull I had bought at a flea market with my allowance. I knew I'd never be able to take all that stuff with me, and I felt like crying but I didn't.

Then something started that I couldn't figure out. It was the beginning of August, and Tania and I were talking almost every day about running away and making plans. Right then it seemed to me that my mother and father got a lot more friendlier.

Like Mom was bubbly almost all the time and would make jokes and kid around with me. And my father would ask me what I had done that day, and he even bought me a really cool fishing cap with this long bill that shaded your eyes. They both seemed a lot nicer, and one night we all went to Bobby Rubino's for ribs.

I didn't know why they were acting like that. I told Tania about it, and she said they were probably just going through a phase.

"What's a phase?" I asked her.

"It's like a thing that doesn't last long," she said. "And then they go back the way they were."

I didn't understand, but I didn't tell Tania that because I didn't want her to think I was stupid.

Then something really unreal happened.

We had a nice ficus tree on our front lawn, and one morning Mother asked me to give it a good soaking with the hose because the leaves were beginning to look dried out and the tips were yellow. So after she left to go shopping, that's what I was doing when this great silver Infiniti pulled up in front of our house. The guy driving it lowered his window and motioned to me. I went over but not too close because I didn't want to be kidnapped and held for ransom.

But the man didn't look like a kidnapper. I mean he was well-dressed and all, and he didn't try to drag me into the car or anything like that. And he was smiling.

"Hiya, sonny," he said. "Hot work on a hot day—right?"

"Yes, sir," I said.

"Say," he said, "am I at the right place? Is this Mabel Barrow's home?"

I nodded.

"Glad to hear I'm not lost," he said, still smiling. "Do you know if Mabel is home?"

"No, she's gone into town."

"You sure?" he said.

"Sure, I'm sure," I said. "She's my mother so I should know."

"No kidding?" he said. "You're Mabel's son? Well, I'll be darned. What's your name?"

"Chet. It's really Chester, but I like Chet better."

"So do I, Chet," the man said. "And your father is Gregory Barrow—right?"

I nodded again.

"And I suppose he's at his job out at McWhortle Laboratory. Am I batting four hundred?"

"Uh-huh," I said. "He won't be back until tonight."

"Sorry I missed him," the man said. "I'm an old friend of your father's. We went to chemistry school together. Well, I'll just have to come back another time."

"What's your name?" I asked him. "So I can tell my folks you came by while they were out."

"Listen, Chet," he said, "you like surprises, don't you?"

"Some."

"Well, what I want to do is surprise your mother and father. You know, just walk in on them some night unexpectedly. I haven't seem them in years. Will they ever be amazed! So what I'd like you to do is not tell them I stopped by this morning. Because that would spoil my surprise. Okay?"

"Sure," I said. "I won't tell them."

"Attaboy," he said, still smiling. He dug in his pocket and took out some money. He held a five-dollar bill out to me. "Here," he said, "this is for being so helpful."

"Nah," I said, "that's all right."

"Take it," he insisted. "Buy your girlfriend some ice cream. You've got a girlfriend, haven't you?"

"Sort of," I said.

"Sure you do," he said. "A good-looking dude like you. Take the money, Chet. You deserve it because you've been so polite and you're not going to tell your mother and father I was here and ruin the surprise."

"Okay," I said.

So I took the five dollars, and he waved and drove away. I looked at the bill. It had Abraham Lincoln's picture on it. I knew who he was.

I put the money in my pocket and decided I wouldn't buy ice cream with it until Tania and I got to Disney World.

32

DR. CHERRY NOBLE

I made no decision, I planned nothing, and yet I suddenly became aware that I was spending more and more time with Chas Todd. I'd drive out to his studio two or three evenings a week, and sometimes visited on Saturday or Sunday afternoon.

He never invited me, exactly, but always seemed pleased when I arrived and regretful when I left. I felt much the same way for I enjoyed his company, his interest in my opinions, and the give-and-take of our frequent disagreements. Our arguments might have been spirited but they never became embittered. We differed on everything from the best wine for linguine and clam sauce to the influence of feminism on the fashion industry.

I was conscious of a growing intimacy, and I think Chas was, too. I don't mean physical, for our contacts never went beyond a light kiss. But we became increasingly comfortable in each other's presence, silences didn't embarrass us, and we both developed a heightened sensitivity to the other's moods.

The subject of his impotence was never mentioned,

and gradually it became "no big deal" to both of us. I must confess that during that summer I decided to make his studio more habitable and attractive. I have never been domestic, but I was offended by the primitive conditions in which he seemed content to live and work.

I insisted he buy new glassware, china, and cutlery. I had cheerful curtains and drapes made for his windows. I suggested he make his bed each morning and use a patterned satin coverlet since the bed was in plain view of visitors. I also persuaded him to purchase a few comfortable chairs for guests and a table he could use for dining rather than his cluttered desk.

"When are you going to put chintz ruffles on my wheelchair?" he asked.

He affected to treat the improvements with amused scorn, but I think he secretly was delighted, not only with the refurbishment of his home but with the wifely interest I was taking in his well-being. He might have joked about my efforts at interior decoration, but I noticed he was shaving every day, keeping his hair trimmed (via a barber's house calls), and his fingernails were reasonably clean. He also made arrangements with a florist to have a fresh gladiolus delivered every week.

"My brother says the place is beginning to look like a New Orleans cathouse," he remarked.

This conversation occurred the day after Herman Todd consulted me. It was an opening I welcomed and had no compunction using.

"Herman should know," I said lightly. "I imagine he's spent a lot of time in bordellos."

"There you're wrong, doc," Chas said. "My goofy brother is the kind of guy who'd never pay for sex. He thinks if you have to pay for it, it's a sign of failure. He prefers making a conquest. After all, he *is* a salesman."

"You make him sound like a predator."

"Maybe he is, in a way."

"Chas, I have a theory about men like that. Listen and tell me what you think. It's not really sexual pleasure they're seeking; it's the chase and the eventual surrender that excite them. That's why they're inveterate womanizers."

"An interesting idea," he said slowly. "You're saying they get their jollies from the hunt?"

"Something like that. And they go from prey to prey."

"If you're right, Cherry, then a man like that should never marry. A long, stable relationship with one woman would bore him to tears. Or else he'd become a compulsive cheater."

"Do you think that describes your brother?"

"Too close for comfort. How about mixing us a nice, dry gin martini, sharp and cold. Use the new glasses."

I mixed our drinks, brought Chas his usual double, and curled up in a new armchair facing him.

"Why do you think Herman is like that?" I asked.

He thought a moment. "Hard to say. It started when he was in high school. Even then he was chasing skirts. His nickname was Hotrocks. I think he was proud of it."

"But *why*, Chas?"

"You're the psychiatrist, not me, Dr. Noble. You tell me why."

"I don't know enough about Herman. All I can do is generalize. But you're his sibling; you grew up with him. You must have a clue."

"It's a crazy notion," he said, "but what it *might* be is that Herm was an absolute klutz when it came to sports and games. His eye-hand coordination is lousy. My God, the guy can't even catch a ball. I was the jock of the family, and all my energy went into physical activity, especially running. I ran around a track, my brother ran after girls. Does that make any sense at all?"

"Mmm," I said. "Do you think Herman was jealous of you? Jealous of your prowess as an athlete?"

Chas frowned. "That never occurred to me," he said, "but it's possible. I won some medals and cups. An article about me was in the sports pages of our local newspaper. Sure, it would be normal for Herm to be jealous, wouldn't it? Or envious?"

"Or both," I said. "And unconsciously decided to excel at another activity—seducing women. He wouldn't win any medals or cups, but he'd have the satisfaction of succeeding and earning a reputation as Hotrocks."

"It makes a nutty kind of sense," Chas said.

"It's a very neat explanation of why he does what he does," I said, "but I don't think it's the whole story. Ready for a refill?"

"Always," he said.

We spoke no more about the behavior of Herman Todd. I had some additional thoughts on the subject, but I was afraid they might offend Chas and felt it best to talk of other things.

But when I returned home later that night, I sat at

my desk and scribbled notes on what might evolve into a case history. What Chas had told me about his brother was not conclusive, of course, but it did suggest several approaches to Herman's problems.

I thought it justifiable to reckon that the subject had been jealous of his brother's athletic success and had determined to prove his own prowess in a quite different arena. He could have selected chess, for example, or music or any of the other arts to test his talent and skill. But Herman chose seduction. I thought more than sibling rivalry was involved.

If not wholly sibling rivalry, then what? I saw Herman's behavior as possibly an attempt to establish his bona fides as a "real" man. Inept at sports and games, he had to assert his masculinity by aggressive conduct toward women. He became an obsessive lothario, and each conquest added to his self-esteem.

All this could be bullshit, of course. The subject wasn't in therapy yet; I had hardly spoken to him. But I had learned to trust my instincts, and in this case I was convinced I was on the right track: Herman was continually seeking to conquer because his mistrust of his own masculinity needed constant assuaging.

This preliminary analysis troubled me because it was one short step from determined seduction to a more overt and brutal form of physical aggression toward women, culminating in rape. I wondered if Herman had ever struck his wife or any other woman.

Complicating Herman's dysfunction might well be his brother's war record. Chas had volunteered, fought bravely, and had been grievously wounded. Herman might express scorn for his brother's decision to go to war, but I was certain his admiration and envy of Chas existed, no matter how deeply they were hidden. Chas had proved himself a man. Herman constantly doubted his own maleness, and those doubts were driving him to a form of aggression that was threatening his marriage and might ultimately destroy his life.

All this was speculation on my part. But I had learned that no one who works in the field of human behavior really *knows*. We can only make educated guesses—and hope we are right. So when Herman Todd phoned early the next week, I told him I thought I might be able to help him and suggested he come to my office to begin a series of therapeutic sessions.

He thanked me for my interest but said he had been giving his situation a great deal of thought and had decided he could solve his personal problems by himself, without professional assistance.

I wished him good luck and assured him I stood ready to help if he found he needed it. I confess it was a disappointment, and I hung up with a premonition of a tragedy waiting to happen.

33

BOBBY GURK

Nobody messes with Big Bobby Gurk—nobody! I didn't get where I am today by being Mr. Nice Guy. You mess with me, and I mess with you. Only I mess *first*! You snooze, you lose.

Laura Gunther is getting nowhere with Willie Brevoort, and I tell her I don't like it.

"What are you going to do," she says, "feed me to the alligators?"

"Don't talk like that," I says. "It ain't nice."

"Nice-schmice," she says. "I'm balling the guy, but he just won't spill. What am I supposed to do—beat his kidneys with a rubber hose? You'll have to give me more time, Bobby."

"Okay," I says, staring at her. "You keep trying."

But I still don't like it. Listen, I know the odds. I learnt them all my life. And I know if your best friend *can* screw you, he *will* screw you.

Well, Gunther isn't my best friend, and neither is Brevoort. But I suspicion the two of them might have got *too* close and are figuring on giving Big Bobby

Gurk the shaft. It's possible. Look, there's a bundle involved here, and money can make people act like rat finks.

Right then, while I'm wondering if I'm being screwed, blewed, and tattooed, I get a phone call from Willie Brevoort.

"Bobby," he says, "I got bad news for you."

"Yeah?" I says. "What's that?"

"The old guy who owned McWhortle Laboratory dropped dead—you can look it up—and now the whole business is closed down. Settling the estate, you know. So they're not doing any work, which means the ZAP pill is on hold. I don't know when they'll start working on it again, if ever, but right now the deal is cold. Sorry about that."

"That's okay, Willie," I says. "It didn't cost me a dime, so no harm done."

I hang up and think: In a pig's ass! So I looked up the number in the phone book and call. A chirpy bird answers, "McWhortle Laboratory."

"Hey," I says, "you still in business?"

"Of course we're still in business," she says.

"I thought with your boss croaking and all, maybe you closed down."

"Mrs. Gertrude McWhortle is now our chief executive officer," she says. "The laboratory is functioning normally, and all contracts will be fulfilled."

"Thanks, babe," I says.

Oh Willie, Willie, Willie, I think. And you're the guy who kissed my ass for starting you on a new career. I owe you one, you said. Rat fink!

So I call Tomasino down in Miami and ask if I can borrow Teddy O. for a special job. I will pay Teddy a sweet per diem and also pay Tomasino a grand for the borrow. He says sure, he'll send Teddy up as soon as he gets back from Tampa where he's gone to persuade a deadbeat he should do the honorable thing and pay Tomasino what he owes him so the deadbeat's wife won't get an acid facial.

This Teddy O. is an enforcer and one of the best in the business. Look at him and you'd think he sells shoes for a living. But how many guys who sell shoes carry a sharpened ice pick in a leather sheath strapped to their shin? He is a little bitty guy and talks polite. And he is true-blue, absolutely dependable. He just likes to hurt people, that's all—but what the hey, no one's perfect—right?

He shows up, and I tell him all about Willie Brevoort and the ZAP stuff that's supposed to put lead in a guy's pencil. I also tell him what I want: the name of the chemist at McWhortle Laboratory who is leaking information to Brevoort.

"I get it, Mr. Gurk," Teddy O. says. "You want I should lean on this guy."

"No, no," I says. (Usually Teddy leans a little too hard.) "I figured first you could tail Willie awhile and see where he goes and who he meets. If we can't do it that way, then we'll do it your way."

"Okay," he says. "Is there a good barber in town? I need a trim and a manicure."

It takes maybe a week, no more, when Teddy shows up with a notebook full of stuff he's written down. He's got the names of all the guys Willie Brevoort had a meet with during the week and where they work. Don't ask me how Teddy does it. I told you he was good, didn't I? But anyway, none of the men

Willie met work at McWhortle Laboratory, so we got zip there.

"But here's something cute, Mr. Gurk," Teddy says. "This Willie putz likes to do drag. He belongs to a private club where the guys all wear women's clothes."

"No shit?" I says. "You know, I always thought he might be a flit. He dresses too good."

"I'm not sure he's a flit," Teddy says. "He's got two broads on the string."

"*Two!*" I says. "I know one of them. Laura Gunther. I paid her to pump Willie, but so far she's come up with zilch. Who's the other twist?"

Teddy puts on wire-rimmed cheaters and looks in his notebook. "Her name's Jessica Fiddler. A real pretty blonde. Looks like a high-class hooker. That's all I got on her."

"Teddy," I says, "we're getting nowhere fast. Well, let's give it some more time. Keep on Brevoort's ass; there's still a chance he might meet with the McWhortle chemist. And while you're at it, see what you can dig up on the blond hooker."

He comes back to me two days later.

"This Jessica Fiddler . . ." he says. "Just for kicks I called Hymie Rourke in Miami Beach. He's been in the skin game all his life and knows every pro in South Florida. He made this Fiddler dame right away. She used to dance in a nudie club in Miami and then quit to free-lance at the convention hotels. Rourke says he hasn't seen her around for at least a couple of years."

"That's inarresting," I says. "I wonder if she's hustling up here."

"If she is," Teddy says, "she's making out like gangbusters because she owns her own home."

"That don't sound kosher," I says. "You can't buy a house from turning tricks in this burg."

"I went out there," Teddy says. "Good neighborhood. I talked to an old lady who lives across the street and likes to watch her neighbors more than she likes to watch television. I told her I was a private dick working for a married woman who thought her husband was cheating with Jessica Fiddler and wanted to get evidence for a divorce.

"Well, the old bitch wouldn't talk until I slipped her fifty bucks for an outfit she belongs to. It's called SOS, for Save Our Salmon. Then she tells me Fiddler has two guys who visit her maybe two or three times a week. They both drive big cars, one silver, one white. I figure the silver is Willie Brevoort. He owns a silver Infiniti. I don't know who drives the white."

"So what do we do now, Teddy?"

"I want to get inside Fiddler's house to look around. I'll use a con that's worked for me before. I got a fake ID with my picture on it. It says I'm from the property tax appraiser's office, and I tell her I want to come inside for a little while just to count the rooms."

"Slick," I says.

"It's always worked," Teddy says. "But if she wants to check me out, I'm going to give her your phone number. Will you be here at noon tomorrow?"

"Sure," I says. "What do I do?"

"Just tell her it's the property tax appraiser's office, and yes, John R. Thompson is a legit appraiser. That's the name on my fake ID."

"Got it," I says.

The next day my phone rings about five minutes after twelve. I pick it up and says, "Property tax appraiser's office."

A woman asks, "Have you got a John R. Thompson working for you?"

"Oh, yes, ma'am," I says. "One of our best appraisers. He's been with us seventeen years now."

"Thank you very much," she says, and hangs up.

Teddy O. comes strolling into my office about an hour later.

"It went like silk," he reports. "That's a nice place she's got there. Two bedrooms and a swimming pool. And the furniture didn't come from the Salvation Army."

"Find out anything?"

"Yeah. She's got like a jillion jars and bottles in her bedroom and bathroom. They look like perfumes and lotions and makeup stuff. Most of them have plain white labels on them that just say McWhortle Laboratory with a code number."

"Son of a bitch!"

"So I says to the Fiddler broad, 'You must like perfume.' And she says, 'Free samples. From my boyfriend.' "

I look at him. "How do you figure it, Teddy?"

"I'm guessing the boyfriend is the guy in the white car. He's the chemist at McWhortle Laboratory you been looking for. Willie Brevoort isn't getting his information from the chemist; he's getting it from Jessica Fiddler."

I think about that awhile. "Yeah," I says, "that makes sense. She pumps the chemist and sells Willie everything the guy tells her."

"That's how I see it."

"So all we gotta do is find out who's driving the white car. Once we do that, we can offer him a piece of change for the ZAP pill. And if that don't work, you can lean on him."

"What if I can't find out who's driving the white car?"

"Then you can lean on Jessica Fiddler."

"I'd like that," Teddy O. says.

34

MARLEEN TODD

T he development of Cuddle was taking more time and effort than I had anticipated. As a professional perfumer, I have always believed that scents have the ability to alter moods. But now I was working on a fragrance that would, if successful, alter behavior. And I found that prospect somewhat disturbing.

I was familiar with pheromones, of course: those chemical substances secreted by animals that have the power to alter behavior of other animals of the same species. It seemed to me that in developing Cuddle I was attempting to create a human pheromone, and I wasn't certain of what the final effect might be.

During our drive to the laboratory one morning in August, I asked Gregory Barrow if he had ever worked with psychoactive drugs that affected behavior and personality. I think the question startled him.

"I've had limited experience," he said. "Why do you ask?"

"I was wondering if you had any strong feelings about them, for or against."

"I think they can be a benefit," he said carefully, "when properly used."

"But you see nothing ethically wrong in psycho-chemicals per se?"

"No," he said. "If drugs can be used to alleviate physical pain and treat human disease, I see no reason why they shouldn't be used to ease mental pain and psychic disorders. If a drug was developed to cure or control schizophrenia, for instance, how could one possibly object to it."

"I suppose you're right," I said doubtfully. "But drugs that alter behavior and personality make me a little uneasy. It's like playing God, isn't it?"

"So is prescribing aspirin," he said.

"I'm not doing a very good job of explaining what I mean," I said. "What about things like marijuana, LSD, heroin, and cocaine. They affect mood, behavior, personality. Would you defend them?"

"Of course not. They can be psychologically or physiologically addictive and do a great deal of harm. But psychochemicals that benefit the subject, that enable him or her to function as a normal human being, are certainly defensible."

I looked at him. "What is a normal human being?" I asked. "Please define."

He gave me a half-smile, but he didn't answer.

It was not a smartass question on my part because, to be perfectly frank, I was beginning to doubt my own normality. I had been acting very strangely.

Usually when I make up my mind to do something, I do it. I had chided Greg for being indecisive, and now I found myself behaving just as irresolutely. I told Herman I intended to consult an attorney about a divorce. At the time I said it, I meant it. But I was postponing that final act, finding all kinds of reasons to put it off.

I tried to analyze myself, to understand why I was dithering. The answer, which came as more of a shock to me than perhaps it does to you, was that I loved the man.

He was everything I've said he was: a boor, a drunk, a philanderer. But love, I sadly concluded, is not a rational emotion. Even recognizing Herman's faults and excesses could not kill what I felt for him. I was at once astonished and ashamed of myself, and even wondered if my intense caring for him was not an aftereffect of my inhalation of aerosolized oxytocin.

I went back to my laboratory with renewed determination to succeed. What had been a vague idea now became a definite plan that might, just *might*, provide a solution to my personal problems.

If I could develop a hormone-based fragrance that increased tender affection, it seemed possible that I could alter Herman's behavior in a way that would benefit our family. At that point in my research I couldn't even guess if the effects of such a psychoactive perfume would be temporary or lasting. That was a question that could only be answered after the scent was created.

But I was so excited by the prospect that I simply rejected all those qualms that had made me ask Greg Barrow about the ethicality of behavior-altering drugs. It seemed to me that Cuddle, if perfected, could have no ill effects on the user or on persons who smelled the fragrance.

I had now developed a few ounces of a perfume that contained a minuscule amount of the aerosolized oxytocin. I then used an alcohol solution as a diluter and put the mixture into a spray bottle that resembled an atomizer. I applied the scent to the inside of my left wrist and sniffed cautiously.

All I could recognize were the floral essences that served as a carrier for the hormone. There was no aroma of mauve, and I was aware of no changes in my mood or behavior. So I strengthened the formulation in stages, gradually increasing the proportion of the oxytocin and decreasing the volume of the alcohol diluter.

It was while these time-consuming experiments were proceeding that I had another conversation with Greg Barrow about psychochemicals. We were heading home one evening (I was doing the driving that week) when he suddenly said, "You may be right."

I was startled. "About what, Greg?"

"About psychoactive drugs. You said that anything designed to alter behavior and personality made you uneasy. You said it was like playing God."

"Well, I've changed my mind about that," I told him. "If psychochemicals can be a benefit and don't have any bad side effects, I see no reason why they shouldn't be developed and prescribed."

"You seem to have overcome your doubts," he said, "but you have stirred up mine. Let me give you a hypothetical case. What would you think of a psychoactive drug designed to make the user behave in a manner that is generally considered to be antisocial?"

"I would be against that," I said. "Definitely."

"Even if it was intended for limited and strictly controlled use? Even if the end result could be shown to have, say, a patriotic benefit?"

"Greg, you're not working on a poison gas, are you?"

"Of course not."

"Well, your hypothetical case sounds like it. If a psychoactive drug results in the user flaunting the norms of society, then it's wrong. It's unethical and immoral to develop it and prescribe it. Patriotism is no excuse. Humanity comes first."

He sighed. "I wish it was as simple as you make it out to be, but it isn't. There is no absolute 'good' and no absolute 'bad.' There are infinite gradations. For instance, suppose a psychoactive drug was developed that would cause the user to renounce all personal ambition and desire for worldly gain. One pill or injection would induce him to become a Jesus-like personality, give all his wealth to the poor, and spend his days in meditation and seeking spiritual salvation. Would such a drug be a benefit or a curse? To the individual using it and to humanity?"

I considered that a long time. "It's a tough one," I said finally. "Probably a benefit to humanity and a curse to the subject. But I really don't know. It's a philosophical question, isn't it?"

"Ethical," he said. "It's an ethical problem to the research chemist developing the drug. But it illustrates what I said about the difficulty of choice. We just can't be *sure*, can we? What troubles me most is using a drug to make the subject into a person he or she is not by nature. In other words, changing personality to conform to one's own standards, or one's employer's standards, or one's nation's standards—which may or may not be to the subject's benefit."

I knew what Greg meant, but his scruples didn't deter me. I was resolved to alter the personality of my husband. I might succeed in making him into a person he was not by nature. But it was the man he ought to be.

35

GREGORY BARROW

The death and funeral of Marvin McWhortle caused a slippage of three days in my detailed schedule for the ZAP Project, and early in August an additional day's work was lost when I received an unexpected visit from Colonel Henry Knacker. He demanded a progress report in the development of what he insisted on referring to as a "diet enrichment."

He sat in my private laboratory and viewed all the videotapes I had made. The colonel was favorably impressed with the results.

"Looks good to me, boy," he said when the final tape ended. "You figure you've got a handle on the sex angle—correct?"

"Yes, sir," I said. "The most recent formulation resulted in increased physical aggression with normal or lessened sexual drive."

"Lessened?" he said sharply. "Not totally, I hope. We don't want to make eunuchs out of our fighting men, do we, son?"

"No, sir," I said. "I don't believe there is any danger of that. The last two tapes you viewed, taken at twenty-four hours and forty-eight hours after the initial injection, show quite clearly that the increased aggression and decreased sexuality are temporary phenomena."

"Any side effects?"

"I've observed none so far," I told him. "Of course, it's always possible a delayed reaction to the hormone may turn up later, but I have no evidence of that."

"Good-oh," he said, rubbing his palms together with satisfaction. "Now what's next on your program?"

"I have two objectives, sir," I said, "and failure to achieve them might possibly threaten the success of the entire project."

He frowned at me. "I don't like the sound of that. What's the problem, boy?"

I resented being addressed as "boy" or "son," particularly since the colonel appeared to be only a few years older than I. But I made no objection. After all, he *was* the client—or represented the client—and I had no desire to endanger the funding of my research.

"The first objective," I said, "is the conversion of the liquid formulation to a solid. In other words, a pill or powder. Such a conversion is usually a relatively simple process. But I should warn you that sometimes a new drug proves not to be orally active. It has no effect when ingested but must be administered by injection to achieve the desired result."

"That's ridiculous," he snapped, as if it were my fault. "We can't spend time giving shots to a regiment of grunts about to go into combat. The logistics would be impossible."

"I realize that, sir," I said as patiently as I could. "But if a ZAP pill does prove ineffective, there is another method that should be considered. It might be possible to structure the testosterone formulation for transdermal delivery. The drug would be carried in small patches applied directly to the skin."

"Now you're talking!" Knacker cried enthusiastically. "The bugle blows, our boys stick on their patches, and pick up their rifles. Correct?"

"Yes, sir," I said. "And I suspect a skin patch might have a longer-lasting effect than injection or pill."

"Sounds good to me," the colonel said. "Now what's the other problem?"

"The conversion of the ZAP formulation for use by humans. There are actually two questions involved here. First of all, sir, you should be aware that sometimes drugs have effects on laboratory animals that cannot be duplicated in humans. The physiologies, of course, are quite different. The testosterone works on mice, as you have seen. Whether or not it will work on humans remains to be proved.

"The second part of the same question is what quantity of the formulation should be recommended for human use. Usually this is a technical problem in which the body weights of mouse and man are compared to calculate the proper volume of the human dose. Conversion is an inexact science, and too much testosterone may be given in the human dose or too little. Really, the most effective conversions result from trial and error."

The officer looked at me with a pitying smile. "That's no problem, son," he said. "You get your pill made in the strength you think best and give me a shout. I can provide all the human guinea pigs you need. Listen, we have plenty of fuck-ups in the stockade right now who'll be happy to volunteer to gulp down a ZAP pill if they'll get time knocked off their sentence. You follow, boy?"

"Yes, sir," I said. "Then you wish to go directly from rodent to human tests without trials on larger laboratory animals?"

"You've got it, son, and the sooner the better. You give me the ZAP pill, and within a few days, a week at the most, I'll be able to tell you if you've got a winner or a washout. Okeydokey?"

"Yes, sir," I said.

I locked the door after he departed. I thought he was a dreadful man, but at least I had won his approval to go directly from mouse testing to man testing.

Of course I had no intention of providing Colonel Knacker with a supply of pills, assuming I was successful in developing an oral form of the sex hormone. I had absolutely no wish to use imprisoned soldiers as "human guinea pigs." That would be such an immoral thing to do that I had rejected it even as he had proposed it.

My only ethical course of action, obviously, was to test the ZAP pill on myself. I doubted if it presented any mortal danger, but that had to be proved. And self-administration would give me much more precise observation of the results than if the drug was tried on other volunteers.

I must confess that I was eager to try the ZAP pill. I assure you again that I had no desire to become more aggressive. At the same time I recognized that it would do no harm if I became, even temporarily, bolder and more assertive.

Both my wife and Marleen Todd had, on occasion, remarked on my indecision and a lack of determination that amounted to what they apparently saw as insipidity. Their comments disturbed me. I was curious (and hopeful, I must admit) as to what effects the sex hormone would have on my behavior and personality.

That evening, before dinner, Mabel said to me, "Guess what? We've been invited to a cocktail party."

"Oh?" I said. "Who's giving it?"

"Laura Gunther. She takes care of me at Hashbeam's Bo-teek. I've known her for years. Well, she's having a cocktail party at her condo for all her best customers and their husbands or boyfriends. It sounds like fun."

"When is it to be?"

"Saturday afternoon at two o'clock."

"I'm afraid I won't be able to make it," I said at once. "I have to work on Saturday. But why don't you go. I'm sure you'll have a good time."

"I don't want to go alone," she protested. "Laura specifically asked that I bring you. She wants to meet you. I don't see why you can't forget your job for one Saturday afternoon."

"You don't understand," I said. "I'm behind schedule on a very important project, and I've just got to get caught up."

"You never want to go anywhere with me," she said angrily. "Sometimes I think you're ashamed of me."

"That's not true, Mabel," I said.

"Well, I'm not going to the party by myself. I'll just spend another lonely Saturday afternoon at home. Laura will be so disappointed when we don't show up."

I sighed. "I'll tell you what, Mabel; suppose I take an hour or so off from work and meet you at the party. I'll have a drink or two and then go back to the lab. Will that be satisfactory?"

"I guess it'll have to be," she said. "What an old fogy you are."

36

CHAS TODD

My life was changing. I was aware of it, but the odd thing was that I didn't seem responsible for the changes. I mean I wasn't *consciously* doing things differently. It was more like I was an observer, sitting back and noting my own metamorphosis.

I knew a lot of it was due to Cherry Noble. After she spruced up my studio, almost immediately I spruced up myself. It just seemed wrong to live like an unshaved bum when she had gone to all that trouble to make my home attractive.

But those were just the physical changes in my life. As a matter of fact, I duplicated the situation in my new book, *The Romance of Tommy Termite*. Lucy, his girlfriend, cleans up Tommy's nest, and before he knows it, he's bathing in rainwater every day and wearing a tie.

My more important transformations were things you couldn't see because they were happening inside me. The only way I can describe them is to liken them to a thaw. Something that had been frozen was warming. It was the damnedest thing. I knew it was

207

happening, but I didn't know why or what it portended.

For instance, on the days Cherry didn't visit, I'd phone her at home. We'd have long, inconsequential talks, but I'd always hang up smiling. And when she did show up at my place, I'd usually read to her what I had written about Tommy Termite's romance, and we'd discuss it and sometimes we'd argue. Cherry had some great ideas.

I don't think there was any exact date when it popped into my mind that I was in love with this woman. There was no sudden revelation, just a slow, gradual realization of how much she meant to me and how arid my life would be without her. It scared me.

My brother came over for our usual Thursday lunch, and I was tempted to tell him how I felt. But I realized that was hopeless because I really didn't know *how* I felt. And besides, all he wanted to talk about were his own problems.

He mixed us heavy bourbon highballs in my new glasses, and we sat at the new dining table wolfing down the roast beef sandwiches and potato salad he had brought.

"I wasn't going to tell you this, Chas," he said, not looking at me. "What the hell, you've got your own troubles. But Marleen wants a divorce."

"Shit," I said. Then I groaned.

"Yeah," he said, "that was my reaction. But if that's what she wants, I'm not going to stand in her way."

I stopped eating to stare at him. He didn't look so good. His face was puffy, eyes bloodshot, and he had put on so much lard that everything he wore looked a size too small. He was beginning to get a few red lines in his nose, and his cheeks were mottled. Pop began to look like that about five years before his liver gave out.

"Herm, you're an asshole," I told him. "Marleen is a fine woman. If you had half a brain you'd do whatever you could to hang on to her. And there's Tania to think about."

"I know," he said miserably. "But what's the use? I'm never going to change."

"You can change. If you want to. You just don't want to."

"Oh, I want to," he said, "but I can't. I just don't have the gumption."

"Balls!" I said furiously. "You can go to AA or get dried out at some drunk farm. And you can stop chasing chippies. That doesn't take gumption. A little common sense will do it. You're just too goddamned selfish."

"You're right, brother. As usual."

He gave me a twisted grin, but I could see he was hurting. All the anger went out of me and I couldn't yell at him anymore. I felt sorry for him, and I worried about him. After all, he was my brother, and that counted.

"Herm, do me a favor, will you?"

"What's that?"

"Go see Dr. Cherry Noble. She helped me; she can help you."

He continued working on his lunch and didn't look up. "I already have," he said. "One interview. We talked and she said she'd let me know if she'd take me on. But then I thought about it and decided what's the point; I'm never going to change."

"Man, you're sick," I said.

"I guess," he said. "But it's my choice, isn't it? If I want to go down the tube, down I'll go."

I felt like weeping.

He glanced at his watch. "Hey," he said, "I've got to get back to the office. I may be a lush, but I'm a functioning alcoholic. You take care, y'hear."

He poured himself a tot of sour mash, knocked it back, and started for the door. Then he turned to face me.

"Still brothers?" he asked.

"Sure," I said huskily. "Always."

I just sat there, not moving, after he left. I found myself thinking about a guy in my squad in Nam. He was shooting smack and couldn't stop. He told me he knew he'd OD someday, and he did. Of course he had plenty of reasons. I could understand where he was coming from.

But I couldn't understand my brother. He had a nice home in South Florida, a good job, a loving wife, a great daughter. But he was destroying himself as surely as my buddy did in Nam. What is this thing with people that drives us to screw up our lives?

I knew I had to do something about Herman. I'd probably fail, but I had to try. I figured my best bet would be to ask Cherry for advice. If Herm had talked to her, maybe he had dropped some clues as to why he behaved as he did.

When my phone rang, I wheeled over to the desk hoping it was her and she'd tell me she was coming to visit that evening. But it was Tania, and I perked up.

"Hiya, honey," I said. "Enjoying your summer vacation?"

"Yes, I am," she said in that serious manner she had that always made me smile. "Uncle Chas, do you still have my hundred dollars?"

"Of course I do," I said. "It's in a special envelope marked with your name, just like I promised. Tania, have you and your boyfriend changed your minds about running away?"

She giggled. "Well, he's not *really* my boyfriend. And we haven't changed our minds. First we're going to Disney World, and then we're going to Alaska. That's why we need the money."

"Uh-huh," I said. "Honey, you know your parents are going to feel terrible when you leave home. I'll bet they'll cry."

"Maybe my mother will but not Daddy."

"Why not him?"

"Because he doesn't love me."

I caught my breath. "Tania, I don't think that's true. I believe your father loves you."

"No, he doesn't," she insisted. "Or he wouldn't do the awful things he does. Uncle Chas, I've got to go. I'm going to help Chet decide what to pack. He's not very good at it."

"Pack?" I said. "Then you're leaving soon?"

"Real soon," she said. "Before school starts. Bye now!"

I hung up slowly, confused and saddened. I had a wild idea of telling Herman that his daughter planned to run away. It might shock him into changing his ways. But I decided I couldn't risk it. It would betray Tania's trust and probably convince her that neither father nor uncle loved her.

I phoned Cherry at her office, something I rarely

did. The receptionist said Dr. Noble was busy at the moment, but she'd give her my message. I stared at the blank screen of my word processor and waited patiently. It was almost twenty minutes before Cherry returned my call.

"Can you come over tonight?" I asked her.

"Chas," she said, "is something wrong?"

"I need you," I said.

37

MABEL BARROW

I hadn't been to a party in ages, and I got real excited about going to Laura Gunther's shindig. Of course I had nothing decent to wear so I went down to Hashbeam's Bo-teek.

"Laura," I said, "I bet the only reason you're having this bash is so that all your customers come in for new outfits."

"You got it," she said, grinning. "Believe me, you're not the first. Listen, Mabel, I hope your husband will be there."

"Well, he's working on Saturday but he promised to show up for an hour or two."

"Good enough," she said. "I'm eager to meet him. Now let's pick out something for you that'll knock everyone dead."

She had some great sequined sheaths that were to die for, but I had to admit I was a bit too tubby to get into them. We finally settled for an embroidered chemise-type number, tight across the fanny and with a neckline low enough to show cleavage.

"No bra," Laura warned. "Let it all hang out."

"Suits me," I said, and I imagined what Herman Todd's reaction would be if he saw me in that dress. Maybe it could be arranged.

I left Hashbeam's in time for my appointment with Dr. Cherry Noble. I told her about the party on Saturday, and how happy I was to get out of the house for a change.

"Is your husband going?" she asked.

"At first he didn't want to. He's working on Saturday, and that stupid job of his comes first. But finally he agreed to stop by for a drink."

"Mmm," she said. "No argument?"

"Not really. Sometimes I think he's trying. We even made love the other night. Whoopee. On a scale of one to ten, about a five. I wish there was a pill I could slip into his macaroni and cheese that would give him a little more oomph."

Dr. Noble smiled. "I'm afraid there's no pill like that, Mabel."

The rest of the session was all about my self-esteem and why I needed to have men wanting me—the only way I could feel important. I figured all women felt that way, but the doc said not so, that self-worth had to come from within, how I felt about myself, and not from the approval of others.

I thought that was a squirrelly idea but I didn't tell her that. And I didn't tell her about the new cocktail dress I had just bought that made my knockers look like a baby's ass.

By the time Saturday rolled around I was in a state. But it was a nice feeling, a real high I hadn't felt for a long time. I had my hair done that morning and even splurged on a manicure. I rushed home a little before noon to shower and dress before driving to the party, fashionably late. I certainly didn't want to be the first one there.

Chet was in his bedroom with Tania Todd. A lot of his junk was spread out on the floor, and the kids were sorting the stuff into piles.

"What's going on?" I asked.

They looked up at me. "It's for school, Mrs. Barrow," Tania said. "When we go back, we'll have to give talks on how we spent our summer vacations. I'm helping Chet pick out some things for his show-and-tell."

"That's nice," I said. "Chet, I'm going out for a while around two o'clock, but I'll be back in time to get supper on the table. Maybe we'll have hot dogs and beans. If you kids get hungry this afternoon, there are jelly doughnuts in the fridge. Have a good time."

I spent the next two hours getting dolled up. It made me feel ten years younger, and the finished product looked sharp, if I say so myself. I had that glow I used to get when I was going out on a date before I was married. Those were the days! And I was such a dope I thought they'd last forever.

I had to be careful sliding onto the driver's seat of the Roadmaster because that embroidered chemise was snugger than I thought, and the last thing in the world I wanted right then was a split seam. I checked my makeup in the rearview mirror and wiped a fleck of lipstick off a front tooth.

There were at least a dozen people already there when I sashayed into Laura's condo. There was a bar set up with a hired bartender, a yummy boy with a great tan. There was also a table with plates and bowls of nibbles like macadamia nuts and miniature pretzels. No one was sitting down, everyone was standing and mingling, carrying their drinks and talking up a storm. I knew it was going to be a good party.

Laura grabbed me the moment I walked in and gave me a quick once-over.

"Mabel," she said, "you look fantastic. That dress is *you*. Where's your husband?"

"He'll be along," I said. "Can I have a drink?"

"I'll get it for you, hon," she said. "Then I want you to meet some of these wonderful friends of mine."

I must have been introduced to a dozen guests in the next fifteen minutes. I didn't remember their names, of course, but they were all dressed to the nines, and none of them looked like they had to worry where their next buck was coming from. But there was nothing stuck-up about them, and I got a lot of compliments on my dress. I could see where the men were staring.

Laura left to greet some new arrivals, and I got me a second rum and Coke from the dreamy kid behind the bar. One of the couples I hadn't met came up and we all introduced ourselves. His name was William Brevoort ("Just call me Willie!") and she was Jessica Fiddler, a real model type, tall and blond, but kind of hard-looking if you know what I mean. They seemed to be close friends, but I didn't get the feeling they were making it together.

They were really good company, just as friendly as they could be. Jessica was wearing one of those sequined sheaths from Hashbeam's that I loved but couldn't get into, and Willie had on a plaid silk sport jacket with lime green slacks. We talked clothes—just to break the ice, you know—and then Brevoort asked, "What does your husband do, Mabel?"

"He's a research chemist," I said. "He invents new drugs and things like that."

"No kidding?" he said. "What a coincidence. I'm in the pharmaceutical line myself. I'd like to talk to him. Is he here?"

"Should be along soon," I said. "I'll make sure you meet. Jessica, who does your hair? It's beautiful."

"Thank you," she said, "but the fall isn't mine." She added, "Willie lent it to me," and we all laughed.

I saw Greg come through the door, and I went over and grabbed his arm. He was wearing his old three-piece navy blue suit like he had just been confirmed. In that flashy crowd my poor hubby looked like a sorry-assed refugee from Lower Slobbovia.

I got him a drink and brought him over to meet Jessica and Willie. We chatted of this and that for a while, and then Jessica drew me away to the food table where Laura had just put out a big platter of boiled shrimp with a fancy plastic toothpick stuck in each one. When I looked back, Willie was talking a mile a minute to Greg, and I guessed they were talking business, which men like to do at parties.

After a while Greg came over to where I was standing with Jessica and took one shrimp.

"Enjoying the party, Mr. Barrow?" Jessica asked.

"Very nice," he said. "I wish I could stay, but I'm afraid I've got to get back to work."

"You just got here," I protested. "Stay a little while longer. Jessica, you hang onto him while I get him another drink."

A lot more people had arrived, and the bar was mobbed. It must have been five minutes before I could get back to Greg. He was still talking to Jessica and had a funny look on his face. I thought maybe she had told him a dirty joke. My husband doesn't like dirty jokes.

Jessica smiled and moved away when I came back. "Hope we meet again, Greg," she said. "Don't work too hard."

I handed him his drink. "Isn't she pretty?" I said.

"Yes," he said. "Very. Listen, Mabel, I'm going to finish this and then I've really got to go. You stay as long as you like. Don't worry about making dinner. Maybe we'll go out tonight. You're all dressed up, so we'll go someplace nice."

"You like my new dress?" I asked, twirling so he could see it back and front.

"I do," he said, smiling. "I really do. Just don't take a deep breath."

I was sort of stuck with him, which I suppose is a mean thing to say, but you don't go to a party to associate with your husband. Secretly I was glad when he finished his drink and said he had to get back to the lab.

He kissed my cheek. "Have a good time, Mabel," he said.

And after he left, I did.

38

WILLIAM K. BREVOORT

This was serious business. Jessica and Laura and I agreed on that. I mean we had all pulled small cons, penny-ante scams, the badger game, maybe rolling a drunk now and then. And we had all been in the skin trade. Been busted, did time. But that was two-bit stuff compared to ripping off the ZAP pill. Big money was involved here, and we all knew it.

"We got two problems," I told the ladies. "How to glom on to that pill, and how to keep Big Bobby Gurk away from our throats."

I said I had told Gurk that Marvin McWhortle had croaked and the deal was dead. But I wasn't sure Big Bobby bought it, and we had to figure he was still interested. If he ever found out we had the pill and had double-X'd him, he'd come looking for us.

"Yeah," Laura said. "The guy's a slob, but he's a *heavy* slob—dangerous. He's still porking me every now and then. My heart really isn't in it, but I'm afraid to dump him; he might get physical. Also, by letting him jump my bones, I can keep an eye on him and maybe find out if he's got something nasty on his mind."

"Okay," I said, "you keep tabs on Gurk. That leaves the job of getting the pill. I checked out the address of Mabel Barrow and scammed her kid, a boy named Chet. He told me his pop is named Gregory, and he's a chemist who works at McWhortle Laboratory. So that confirms what the old man told you, Jess. Now we got to finagle a way to meet this Gregory and see how we can turn him."

We discussed a dozen different scenarios, but nothing clicked until I hit on the scheme of Laura throwing a cocktail party at her condo. She'd invite her best customers, including Mabel Barrow, and tell them all to bring their husband or boyfriend. Jess and I would be there and make a move on Gregory.

"I like it," Jessica said. "Maybe he'll get sloshed, which will make him easy meat for a come-on."

"Before you do anything," I said, "let me have a crack at him. He might be suffering from the shorts and ready to peddle the pill for cash. If I strike out, then you take over."

Laura said, "The only thing that bothers me about this party idea is what do we do if Bobby Gurk shows up unexpectedly. He might meet Gregory Barrow, and that could queer the whole deal."

"You could invite him," Jess suggested, "and then keep him so busy he doesn't have a chance to meet anyone."

"Invite him?" Laura said indignantly. "I wouldn't invite that bum to a funeral—unless it was his own."

But she finally agreed to go along with the party after I said I'd pick up the tab for the booze and food. Listen, it takes money to make money; everyone knows that.

We went over our plan again and again until we had it choreographed down to the smallest detail, like what Jessica would wear and how Laura would tip off the hired bartender to slug Gregory Barrow's drinks.

It was a good plot and it should have worked. But it didn't, and I began to wonder if The Luck had deserted me.

First of all, the chemist showed up late, stayed about an hour, and then took off. I don't think he had more than two drinks, and they didn't help us a bit. Jess and I met him all right—for all the good it did us. He wasn't a bad-looking guy, but he dressed like a zombie and wore brown shoes with a navy blue suit. Beautiful. I think maybe he smiled twice.

The party lasted until about six o'clock. Finally, everyone was gone, including the bartender, and we were left with the mess to clean up. But before we did that, we slumped in chairs, shared a joint, and tried to figure out what had gone wrong.

"The guy's a straight-arrow," I complained. "I think he bought my story of being in the drug biz, but he wasn't giving anything away. I as much as told him he was in a position to make big bucks if he'd be willing to share some of McWhortle's trade secrets. He looked at me like he was ready to phone the FBI. Listen, I've been clipping gulls all my life, and mostly you get to them through their greed. But this Barrow acted like he couldn't care less about gelt. And as for screwing dear old McWhortle Laboratory, forget it. I tell you the man's a fucking Boy Scout. He's not going to hand over that testosterone pill for love or money. Leastwise not for money. Jess, how did you make out in the love department?"

The folding bar was still in place, and a lot of the booze I had bought was still there. Jessica went over and poured a Chivas for Laura, a Sterling for herself, and a glass of club soda for me.

"You called him a straight-arrow," she said. "He's also a frost. I don't know what's with him. Either I didn't turn him on or he's so in love with that Betty Boop wife of his that he doesn't want to stray. Anyway, I gave him the full treatment, trying to convince him that I thought he was God's gift to women. But I just couldn't touch him. I think if I came right out and said, 'Wanna get naked?' he'd have said, 'I beg your pardon, ma'am.' Like I had my address and phone number written on a piece of paper and slipped it to him. The poor mooch didn't know what to do with it and finally stuffed it in his pocket. Maybe he'll call me, but don't bet on it. Let's face it: The guy's a natural-born wimp."

Laura took a big gulp of her drink. "No hits, no runs, just one big error," she said. "So where do we go from here, Willie?"

The two ladies looked at me, expecting a brainstorm. They were both good kids but limited, if you know what I mean.

"I'll come up with something," I promised. "I always have. Meanwhile, what say we go have some dinner. My treat."

They were more than willing. We closed the door on the full ashtrays and lipsticked glasses and went to a high-class seafood joint on the Waterway, where we all had lobster, pasta, and a salad. We didn't talk about the ZAP pill while we ate, just traded crazy war stories and had a few laughs.

There was a young couple sitting at the next table with a little boy who was working on a shrimp cocktail. He looked to be a few years younger than Chester Barrow, but maybe seeing him was what gave me the idea of how we could convince the chemist to hand over the pill.

I drove the ladies back to Laura's place, and then I returned to my own pad. My club was having an affair that night, a costume party called *Fête Parisienne*. I had rented the outfit of a cancan dancer, complete with black net pantyhose and ruffled skirt. I even had a mouche to stick on my cheek.

It was a good party with plenty of champagne, but there were two other cancan dancers, which spoiled the evening for me. The winner of the first prize was a policeman who dressed like Edith Piaf and sang "*La vie en rose.*"

I got home around two A.M., but I was too charged to sleep. I thought a long time about my new scheme for getting the ZAP pill from Gregory Barrow. I was sure it was doable, but I'd need the help of Jessica and Laura. It would be heavier than anything I had done before, and if it got screwed up I knew what the result would be: five-to-ten in the slammer with all those swell people.

I finally got to sleep, and it was almost noon on Sunday when I woke up. The first thing I did was phone Laura and ask if she could get Jessica over to her place at, say, three o'clock. She called me back about ten minutes later and said Jess was hungover and didn't want to go out in the sunlight, but we could meet at her place.

So that's what we did. Both the ladies looked like they had hit the sauce pretty hard after I left them the night before. I mean their faces were puffy, and they held their coffee cups in both hands: a sure tip-off that they had the shakes. But they listened attentively enough while I explained how we could get Gregory Barrow to cooperate.

I finished, and they stared at me. Then they turned and looked at each other.

"I don't know, Willie," Laura said slowly. "It could be a disaster."

"That's right," I agreed. "I wouldn't lie to you. But it could also go off without a hitch. Jessica?"

"It's a tough call," she said. "I've never done hard time and don't want to start now. Isn't there any other way, Willie?"

"I'm open to suggestions," I said.

They were silent.

"Look," I said, not wanting to push them, "I don't expect an answer this minute. But think about it—okay? If we pull it off, we'll be set for the rest of our lives."

"And if it flops," Laura said, "we'll be set for the rest of our lives making license plates."

"You've got it," I said. "The choice is yours."

"Tell me something, Willie," Jess said. "If Laura and I include ourselves out, will you recruit someone else and go ahead with it anyway?"

"Sure I will," I said. "I think it's too good to pass up."

That was a lie. If they said no, I was dead.

39

HERMAN TODD

Here's something I want to throw at you. If there was a way—let's imagine this—a guaranteed way that a married man or woman could cheat and be absolutely sure of never getting caught, how many faithful husbands and wives would there be in the world? Makes you think, doesn't it?

Well, I was thinking about it. What happened was that I was still living on Hibiscus Drive in Rustling Palms Estates, even if I was sleeping in the guest bedroom. And every time I asked Marleen if she had seen a lawyer, she'd say, "Not yet."

So naturally I figured the crisis was just melting away, and I had overreacted by going to Dr. Cherry Noble. I called that off and started giving serious thought to how I could hump Mabel Barrow without getting caught. Usually I had my fun and games in the woman's home, but I could hardly do that with Mabel, could I? And my Lincoln Towncar, roomy as it was, reminded me too much of my high-school high jinks on the lumpy backseat of a spastic Studebaker.

That got me to trying to devise a foolproof way of cheating with absolutely no possibility of discovery. I finally came to the sad conclusion there was none. But there were ways to minimize the risk, and after a lot of scouting I found a motel down near Fort Lauderdale. It wasn't the most elegant hot-pillow joint in South Florida, but it wasn't cheesy either. Best of all, it was out in the boonies, and the chances of running into someone who knew me or Mabel were practically nil.

I checked the place out. It was summer, customers were few, and the owner was perfectly willing to rent by the day. And he impressed me as the kind of guy who wouldn't give a damn who I had as a visitor. Also, there was an ice-vending machine in the lobby, and for an extra five bucks you could get a vibrating bed. All the room lacked were mirrors on the ceiling.

It was fun to plan all this. It was like I had come to a final realization that I was a bastard, always had been, always would be. If I was the way I was, why not relax and enjoy it? Soul-searching was a waste of time. If my wife was willing to put up with my shenanigans, who was being hurt?

Right about then Marleen decided we should have the Barrow family over for dinner.

"Can't we skip it?" I asked her. "Or postpone it?"

"No," she said in that bossy way she had. "We owe them."

So I didn't make waves. Thinking about it later, I decided it might not be such a bad idea after all. It would give me a chance to diddle Mabel and, by contrast with her dweebish husband, convince her that life offered pleasures she hadn't sampled yet, and Herman Todd was ready, willing, and able to share them with her.

My wife was a gourmet cook, and she went all out on that dinner: gazpacho, pasta with black olives and scallions, lamb chops with an herb crust and fresh mint sauce, caramelized onions and shoe-string candied sweet potatoes, mile-high apple pie. I provided the wine, including a duplicate of the anniversary bottle I had smashed. I hoped it would make amends, but Marleen didn't even notice.

It was a fantastic meal, but the pièce de résistance as far as I was concerned was Mabel Barrow, a piece I couldn't resist. She wore a tight embroidered dress with a neckline that just wasn't there, and I kept waiting (and hoping) for one of her boobs to plop into the soup.

There were six of us at the table, including the kids. Both Tania and Chet were finicky eaters, but they admitted it was a super dinner and cleaned their plates. After dessert the kids disappeared somewhere, and the four of us sat around awhile and chatted as we finished the wine.

Then Gregory and Marleen started talking shop, and Mabel and I wandered out to the backyard where I could smoke a cigar. Marleen didn't let me do it in the house.

It was a gorgeous summer night, just cool enough to be comfortable. It wasn't a full moon, but there was enough of it so I could see the gleam of Mabel's semi-exposed balloons.

"That's a great dress you're almost wearing," I told her.

"You like it?" she said, pleased.

"Love it," I assured her. "I'd buy Marleen something like it but it would be a waste of money; she'd never fill it the way you do."

"I'm glad you approve," Mabel said. "I wore it to a cocktail party last Saturday, and I got a lot of compliments."

"And passes from the guys," I guessed.

By that time we had strolled to the end of the backyard and were standing near a little herb garden Marleen had planted.

"Have you been thinking about it?" I asked her in a low voice.

"Thinking about what?"

"Don't play games, Mabel. You and me."

"You said you were going to move out and get a motel room," she reminded me. "But you're still here."

"That doesn't change how I feel about you. I found a motel. How about it?"

"Where is it?"

"The motel? Down near Lauderdale. Way off in the boondocks. Nothing elegant, but it's clean and away from everything. No one would ever spot us. We could meet there."

She didn't say anything.

"Look," I said, "I guess you know you drive me nuts. I don't think of anything but you. Even in my dreams. When you walked in tonight, I thought my knees were going to buckle. That's how you affect me. Do you ever think about me that way?"

"Yes," she said. "Frequently. But I'm scared."

"Nothing to be scared about," I told her. "No one's

going to find out. Nothing's going to change—except us. It'll be great for both of us, I just know."

Again she didn't reply. But I've been a salesman all my life, and I know the first rule of successful huckstering: Keep talking.

"Is Greg such a great lover?" I asked her.

"No," she said, "he isn't."

"Well, I am," I said. "And that's not bragging; it's the truth. I know how to pleasure a woman. Things I'll bet you've never even thought of."

"You're getting to me, Herm," she said with a throaty laugh. "If I decide it's a go—and notice I say *if*—how do we manage it?"

"Easiest thing in the world. We pick a time that's right for both of us. I'll give you the address and directions how to get there. You drive out in your own car. I'll get there first and be waiting for you. Believe me, you'll have no hassle at the desk. You're just visiting a guest at the motel—me. I'll be using my own name. That's how sure I am that we'll have no problems."

"I'm still scared," she said. "I've shacked up at motels, but that was when I was single. I've never cheated on Greg before."

"What he doesn't know won't hurt him."

"Yeah," she said, "I guess you're right."

"Life is short, Mabel," I urged her. "Let's grab a little fun while we can."

"I'm all for that," she said. "But now I think we better get back inside, or they'll be thinking we're grabbing a little out here."

We went back inside, and the Barrows finally left about eleven o'clock. Tania had already gone to bed, and I helped Marleen clean up the kitchen. I told her what a great dinner it was.

"Thank you," she said, and went upstairs to the master bedroom.

I stayed downstairs, kicked off my shoes, and mixed myself a big brandy and soda. I flopped into an easy chair and reviewed my sales pitch to Mabel Barrow. I figured it was right on target and a done deal.

I expected to feel the usual excitement and sense of triumph I get when I know I've scored, but for some reason I didn't feel those things that night. To tell you the truth, I was a little depressed. Maybe if Mabel had made more objections, I would have enjoyed my victory more. I always liked selling an insurance policy to a prospect who starts out by saying no and ends up a client saying yes.

But Mabel never said no. With her it was "maybe" from the start, and it doesn't take a dynamite salesman to convert maybe to yes. I'm not saying she was a pushover, but there was no challenge. I think I had caught her at a time in her life when she was more than ready.

Perhaps that was what depressed me. The thought occurred that if it wasn't me, it would have been some other man. You understand? It wasn't Herm Todd she had the hots for; I just happened to be the nearest guy available. If I hadn't made a move on her, she'd have found someone else; I was sure of it.

Once I realized that, I began to wonder about all the other women I had shagged, thinking I had succeeded in selling them a bill of goods, talking them into something they didn't want to do. Maybe I had the whole thing ass backwards; they were making the conquest, not me, and all their protests were playacting, either to make themselves feel virtuous or to tickle my macho ego.

Those were not pleasant thoughts, I can tell you that. Because if my fears were true then I had been used by women all these years, played for a fool, treated like a sex object, for God's sake!

I mixed myself another drink.

40

JESSICA FIDDLER

Listen, I admit no one would ever mistake me for Mary Poppins. I mean I've done a lot of scurvy things in my life—not because I wanted to but because I *had* to if I wanted to survive.

Sure, a lot of things I did were illegal, and even when I wasn't breaking any laws, a lot of people would say I was acting in an immoral way. Screw them! I couldn't afford to have morals. And I happen to know what the Bible says about casting the first stone.

At the same time I was living a sleazy life, there were some things I just wouldn't do, even though they would have made me a nice buck. For instance I never peddled dope. I've never done a woman, although I had plenty of chances, believe me. And the same goes for orgies. As Willie the Weasel would say, it's just not my style.

So I did have standards, even if you probably think them a laugh. To tell you the truth, all my life I wanted to go straight, but I could never manage it.

My thing with Marvin McWhortle was about as close as I ever came, but now that had ended and I was back to the sleaze again. It hurt.

You may not believe this, but *Town & Country* was my favorite magazine of all time. I liked to read about people riding to the hounds, going to formal parties, and all that stuff, and I liked to look at the photos of the women who just got hitched. You could tell they were marrying money, which is okay, but some of them weren't as pretty as me and didn't have the bod. But what the hell, life is unfair; everyone knows that.

I'm telling you all this to help explain why I decided to go in on Willie Brevoort's caper. It was the heaviest thing I had ever done, and I knew that if we got busted, we'd all do hard time. But it was a chance, you see—maybe the only chance I'd ever have to get out of the rat race and go straight. Because if it went down like Willie said, we'd all be on easy street.

I talked it over with Laura Gunther and told her how I felt.

"Yeah, kid," she said, "I know where you're coming from. It could be the answer to your dreams, and it could also be the end of the road. You know that, don't you?"

"Sure I do," I said. "And if I had a better choice, I'd take it. But the only other choice I have is hitting the clubs again or going back to hustling conventions. So I think I'll gamble on Willie. How about you?"

She sighed. "I guess I might as well," she said finally. "Right now I've got nothing in my future but

standing on my feet all day in that shitty shop and
boffing Big Bobby Gurk at night, that asshole. Yeah,
I guess I'll play along."

So we gave Willie a call, and he came over to my
place and we started planning.

This wasn't going to be a simple job like when you
smash a jewelry store window, grab a Rolex, and run.
This was a real scenario with a lot of details and
tricky timing, and everything had to go just right or
we'd all get racked up. So we spent plenty of time
discussing possibilities and how we'd handle things
that might go wrong.

We didn't get it all figured out at one meeting, of
course. We got together almost every evening, and
gradually it all came out smart and tight. The one
objection I had was using my place as headquarters.

"It's got to be, Jess," Willie argued. "My condo is
too small, and so is Laura's. We need a safe house,
and you've got two bedrooms. We can't rent a hotel
suite, can we?"

"I don't know," I said doubtfully. "I don't think I
can handle it by myself."

"Not to worry," Willie said. "I'll be right here with
you until it's over. Okay?"

So I agreed. Talk about your Fatal Errors!

Everything was going along fine, and we were getting to the point where we were ready to set a definite date for the Crime of the Century when Willie
showed up at one of our meetings looking worried.

"Something's happening," he said, "and I don't like
it. I didn't want to mention it to you ladies because
I thought I might be imagining it. But now I know
it's for real. About a week ago I thought I was being

tailed. I kept seeing this black Toyota Camry everywhere I went. Always driven by the same man, a little guy who wears wire-rimmed specs. Finally I decided I better check it out, so I jotted down his plate number. One of the members of my private club is a cop, and I slipped him five yards to have it traced. The Camry is registered to a shtarker I've heard about who's got a name so long that no one can pronounce it. So he's called Teddy O., and he works as an enforcer for Tomasino, a Miami shylock. From what I hear, Teddy O. is not a nice man."

"Why would he be following you?" I asked.

It was the first time I ever saw Willie lose his cool, and it scared me.

"Why?" he shouted. "Why? Use your goddamn head! I don't owe Tomasino, so Teddy O. must have come up from Miami on a special job for someone else. And who could that be but Big Bobby Gurk? All these South Florida heavyweights are buddy-buddy."

"You think Gurk is keeping an eye on you?" Laura said.

"What else?" Willie said. "He thinks the ZAP Project is still alive, and there's a buck to be made. So he puts this Teddy O. on my tail, hoping I'll lead him to the McWhortle chemist. Then Gurk moves in and takes over. I know how that fat slob works."

"So what do we do now, Willie?" I asked worriedly. "Call the whole thing off?"

He looked at me. "Not a chance. I'm just telling you ladies that it's suddenly become a lot hairier, and if you want to cut out, you're entitled. But I'm going to stick with the plan. Gurk may have the muscle but I've got the brain. If I can't out-finagle that stupe

I might as well go back to pimping. No, I'm not giving up just because a hatchet man is on the scene. If push comes to shove, I'll figure a way to handle Gurk and Teddy O. Now what about you two?"

Laura and I exchanged a glance. I was impressed by Willie's confidence, and I admired his sass. I think Laura did, too.

"I'll stick," she said. "What the hell, in for a penny, in for a pound."

I nodded. "I'm still in, Willie," I said.

He smiled at us. "You ladies are the real thing," he said. "I love you. We'll come out of this smelling like roses, you'll see. Now, Jessica, I want you to find the Barrow home and learn the neighborhood. Not only the main drags but the back roads. Make a couple of trips from the Barrow place to here at legal speeds, and time how long it takes. This whole caper is going to depend on timing."

So I did what he said. The Barrows lived in a nice clean development, a real family place where everyone seemed to have little kids and big lawns. There was nothing *Town & Country* about it, but it looked solid and respectable, and you just knew that no one who lived there had problems.

I drove around and learned how to get in and out of the development and the fastest route back to my home. I kept track of the times and how long it would take even if traffic was heavy or I got stopped by red lights. I also found another route that took a little longer: a two-lane road with no traffic lights.

On the second day I did this, I drove back to my home in the late afternoon and as I turned into my street, a black Toyota Camry passed me, going the other way. It had just gone by my house. I was spooked when I saw that car, the same model that Teddy O., the hit man, was using to shadow Willie Brevoort.

But that wasn't what set me shaking. I got a good look at the guy driving it, and like Willie had said, he was a small gink wearing wire-rimmed cheaters. I had seen him before. He was John R. Thompson, the property tax appraiser who had talked his way into my house to count the rooms—he said. I started cursing—and believe me, I know how to do it.

The moment I got home I looked up the property tax appraiser's office in the telephone directory. The number was different from the one Thompson had given me to call. Just to make absolutely certain I had been diddled, I phoned the legit number. They said they had no appraiser named John R. Thompson.

I hung up, so furious at myself I could scream. I had let that little prick con me, and it made me feel like a moron. I thought I was street-smart, and I fell for a crude scam like that.

Then I started thinking. If Teddy O. knew where I lived and had cased my home, he and Big Bobby Gurk would know I was connected with Willie Brevoort and the chemist at McWhortle Laboratory.

I thought about my choices a long time. I knew I'd have to tell Willie and Laura that our "safe house" wasn't so safe anymore.

But before I did that, I decided, I better call a real estate agent and get my beautiful home listed. I had a feeling I wouldn't be living in it much longer.

41

DR. CHERRY NOBLE

You would think, wouldn't you, that being a practicing psychiatrist with all my working hours filled with the problems of my patients, I would welcome a placid and trouble-free private life. But that wasn't the case at all. Sometimes I wondered if problems are necessary to feel truly alive. And if they don't come to us, we create them.

All I know is that my existence would have been unutterably empty and sterile if it hadn't been for my relationship with Chas Todd. My work was satisfying on a professional level, but it didn't totally engage me; I wanted something more. I suspected it might be a need for personal drama.

Chas asked for my advice on how he might assist his brother and how best to handle the intention of his niece, Tania, to run away from home. What was most significant to me was his confidence in my judgment and his willingness to seek my help. It was an added bond between us, another signal of our growing intimacy.

238

"Chas," I told him, "I find your brother's problems as troubling as you do, and I wish I could suggest a simple and guaranteed solution, but I can't. Some problems are insoluble, you know that."

"I don't want to believe it," he said. "It means I can't do a damned thing but wait for a disaster to happen. Herman told me he went to see you."

"He told you that?" I said, mildly surprised. "Yes, we had a single introductory session. Then he called and said he had decided not to continue."

"My brother is an asshole," Chas said gloomily. "Even he knows it, but he's unwilling to make an effort to change. And as for Tania, she says she and Chester Barrow plan to leave home before school starts after Labor Day. Cherry, do you think I should tell their parents?"

"Yes," I said, "I think you should. I know you feel it will be a betrayal of Tania's trust, but the physical safety of the children comes first."

"Yeah," he said, "I guess you're right. And maybe if I tell, it'll convince the parents that they better start paying more attention to their kids. I'll think about it. Will you fix us a drink?"

"I thought you'd never ask," I said. "It's a good night for it."

I was referring to a heavy rain that had started early in the evening and was continuing with no sign of a letup. I had driven to Chas's studio after dinner, through flooded streets and over palm fronds blown down by a blustery wind. The rain was still rattling against the roof of his barn and streaming down the windows, but we were snug and dry.

I poured us glasses of a tawny Spanish port we were

both developing a taste for. The only illumination in the big room came from the desk lamp. It made a cone of light, holding back the shadowed corners. Chas wheeled his chair in reverse until his face was in semidarkness.

"Hey," I protested, "I can't see you."

"That's the way I want it," he said. "Because I have a confession to make to you, Cherry."

I waited.

"Remember when I was under treatment, I told you about a woman named Lucy I was engaged to?"

"I remember," I said. "She was killed in a car crash."

"It was all bullshit. There never was any woman named Lucy. I made the whole thing up."

"Why did you do that, Chas?"

"I don't know. Maybe I wanted your sympathy. I really don't know why the hell I told you that lie. It just seemed a good idea at the time."

"And why are you telling me now that it was a lie?"

He took a deep breath. "Because," he said, "I don't want any more lies between us. Nothing fake, nothing make-believe. No more bullshit."

"Perhaps you told me about Lucy to persuade me that you had been attractive to women before you were injured."

"That's possible," he acknowledged. "At that stage in my therapy I wasn't thinking too clearly."

"Chas," I said, "Lucy is the name of Tommy Termite's girlfriend in your new book, isn't it?"

He wheeled his chair back into the lighted area and stared at me. I had no doubt whatsoever that he was startled.

"My God," he said, "that's right. And I never made the connection. What does it mean, doc?"

"It means you're Tommy Termite," I said, laughing. "Searching for romance."

He looked at me thoughtfully. "You know," he said, "you may be on target. I'm writing a fucking autobiography."

"Only it's not about your life," I reminded him. "It's about the way you want to live—a projected autobiography."

I was still taking it lightly, but Chas wasn't. I could see he was shaken.

"I was going to have them marry," he said slowly. "Tommy Termite and Lucy. If the book was a success, I planned sequels. They'd have kid termites, raise a family. It could go on forever. Was I dreaming of me?"

"Only you can answer that, Chas."

He laughed suddenly. "I could have picked a more impressive insect than a termite to serve as my alter ego."

"Oh, I don't know," I said. "Termites have some admirable qualities. They're determined, they work hard, and they survive despite exterminators. They also happen to have a soldier caste."

"Crazy," he said, shaking his head. "Chas the termite."

"May I be Lucy?" I asked him.

He wheeled his chair over to where I was sitting and took my hand.

"Do you think that's possible?" he said, looking sternly at me. "No bullshit now. All I'm asking is, do you think it's *possible*?"

"Yes," I said, "I think it's possible."

He set his glass on the floor and reached for me. I put my glass aside and leaned to him. It was a twisted, strained embrace, fumbled and awkward, but we managed. We kissed.

"Tommy," I said, stroking his cheek.

"Lucy," he said, and we both giggled.

I don't know what they call it now; necking, petting, smooching—it all sounds so old-fashioned. But that is what we did: kids in a secret place, exploring while the rain surrounded us and blanked out the world. It was sweet, so sweet.

We stopped, breathless, and stared at each other.

"Give me time," he said in a voice that was almost a croak. "I need time. Please."

I nodded and smoothed his hair back from his brow. We picked up our glasses and finished our wine without saying another word. After a while I rose, gathered up my things, and gave him a farewell peck. I left him slumped in his wheelchair, head bowed.

I drove home slowly through a downpour that seemed to be worsening. I tried to sort out my feelings, but they were too chaotic for easy classification. It was only after I was safely home, showered, and in bed that I was able to put my thoughts in order and determine what I wanted to do.

I must have this man; I decided that. With marriage, without marriage, with sex, without sex—none of that seemed important. I just needed him in my life, and I thought he needed me. He had lost his legs and would never regrow them. I had lost—or was in danger of losing—part of myself as well. The loving part. I didn't want that gone. I wanted it to thrive.

I felt I knew Chas. I recognized his weaknesses and deficiencies as clearly as I did my own. But what of that? Love, if not blind, is uncaring. I mean there are really no requirements or standards, are there?

These meandering musings before I fell asleep had a curious conclusion. They made me question if I had been correct in my analysis of Mabel Barrow and Herman Todd. I had labeled them insubstantial personalities intent only on sexual gratification. Now I wondered if I truly understood them.

Perhaps, like me, they were simply hopeful searchers, aching to give, eager to have their tender passion requited. Just to love and be loved in return— it sounds so simple, doesn't it? So easy. So *right*.

Then why is it so rare?

42

TANIA TODD

I told my mother that I didn't think Chester Barrow was a very practical boy, and she laughed and asked me why I thought so.

"Because," I said, "his father bought him a fishing cap with a long bill that shades your eyes. But Chet wears it backwards so the bill shades his neck and the sun is always in his eyes."

"Well," she said, "maybe that's a fad with boys these days. I see a lot of them wearing their caps backwards."

"I think it's silly," I said.

I didn't tell her the other ways that Chet wasn't practical, because it was about our running away. For instance, I had to tell him what to take and help him pack. And I was the one who looked up the telephone number of the cab company so we'd have it when we were ready to leave home and go out to my Uncle Chas to get the hundred dollars.

"Now here's what I think," I told Chet. "Labor Day is on September seventh. Then school starts on

Tuesday, the eighth. So I think we should leave on September second, which is a Wednesday."

"Why on that day?" he asked me.

I sighed. Sometimes I have to explain things to Chet twice or maybe three times. I know he's smart, but he just doesn't pay attention.

"We decided we would leave before school started," I said. "And September second is just as good a day as any. Also, it's in the middle of the week, so it will be easier getting a cab than if we leave on a Saturday or Sunday. And besides, your mother and father might be home on the weekend, and mine, too. So Wednesday is when we'll leave."

"I guess," he said.

"Now you must be all packed on Tuesday night," I said. "And I'll be ready so we can just take off on Wednesday anytime we want. I think we should go around noon, which will give us time to pick up the money from Uncle Chas and start out before it gets dark."

"Boy," he said, "you sure are bossy."

"Well, my goodness," I said, "somebody's got to think of these things. And I wish you'd wear your cap the right way. You look silly."

"Do not," he said.

"Do so," I said. "But if you want to look silly, I really don't care."

"Listen," he said, "my folks haven't been so bad lately. Maybe we should talk about this some more."

"You mean you don't want to go? Chet, it was your idea."

"I know it was," he said like he was mad at me.

"I'm just saying maybe we should give them like another chance."

"Chester Barrow," I said, "if you back out now after all my work, I'll never speak to you again as long as I live."

"I'm not backing out," he said, getting that look he gets sometimes when he clenches his teeth. "I just mean my mother and father have been nicer to me lately, like I told you. Are your parents still fighting?"

"Yes, they are," I said, "and if you don't want to leave home, then I'll go by myself."

"Oh, no," he said, "you can't do that. I'll go, I'll go just like we planned."

"Promise?"

"Sure," he said, "I promise."

I felt sort of guilty because to tell you the truth my parents hadn't been fighting lately like they usually did. My father was still missing dinner and coming home late smelling from alcohol, but it didn't seem to bother my mother anymore, because she didn't yell at him, and she smiled a lot and was always humming.

Just because I'm a girl going on nine doesn't mean I don't notice things, and I wondered why she was acting so happy.

We were eating in the kitchen one night late in August, and I said, "I wish Daddy would come home to have dinner with us every night."

And Mom said, "Oh, I think he will. I think he'll change his ways real soon."

I wasn't so sure. "Can people change the way they are?" I asked her.

"Of course they can," she said. "People change all the time."

I thought about that awhile. "I think Chet Barrow is changing," I told her.

"Is he, dear? How is he changing?"

"I don't know," I said. "But sometimes he says things, and then he goes back on them. I don't like that."

Suddenly she looked sad. "Men are like that, Tania," she said. "As you get older, you'll learn that they frequently say things, promise things, they don't really mean."

"Well, that's just lying."

"Not exactly. Sometimes they'll say things because they want something, or to keep you happy, or because they don't want an argument."

"And all the time they don't really mean it? I think that's awful."

"Yes, it is," she agreed with me. "But you'll just have to learn to put up with it."

Well, she could put up with it if she wanted to, but I wasn't going to. So the next time I was alone with Chet I spoke right out.

"Now listen here, Chester Barrow," I said, "I don't like the way you've been acting."

He looked at me. "What are you talking about?" he said.

"Well, sometimes you say things because you want something, or to keep me happy, or because you don't want an argument. And all the time you don't really mean what you're saying."

"You're nuts," he said. "When did I ever do things like that?"

"All the time," I said. "Like I can tell that now you don't really want to run away. You're just pretending."

"Oh my gosh," he said. "I told you I'd leave with you, didn't I? I promised, didn't I?"

"But you don't really mean it," I said. "I can tell."

"I do so mean it."

"No, you don't. At the last minute you'll make some excuse not to go."

"You know," he said, "you can be a real pita."

"Pita?" I said. "That's like a bread."

"Yeah, I know," he said. "It also stands for 'pain in the ass.' And that's what you can be."

I started crying. "That's the worst thing anyone ever called me in my whole life," I told him, "and I hate you."

"Well, you called me a liar."

"Did not. I just said that sometimes you say things you don't really mean. Like running away."

"But I do mean it," he insisted. "Will you stop crying, for gosh sakes. Just because I said maybe we should think about it some more, that don't mean—"

"Doesn't."

"That doesn't mean I'm not going to keep my word. When did I ever go back on my word, tell me that."

"Cross your heart and hope to die that you'll absolutely, positively, run away with me on Wednesday, September second."

"All right," he said. "Cross my heart and hope to die."

"Well, that's better," I said, sniffing.

"You believe me now?"

"Yes, I believe you."

"We've got some frozen Milky Ways in our fridge," he said. "You want one?"

"Okay," I said. Making up after an argument is the best part.

"Hey," Chet said, "what you said about hating me— you don't really mean that, do you?"

"No," I told him. "I just said it because you called me a pita and I was mad, but I didn't really mean it."

"That's good," he said.

After we ate our frozen Milky Ways, we decided to put on our bathing suits and have a hose fight. So that's what we did. We were playing around, dousing each other, when suddenly Chet stopped and stared out at Hibiscus Drive. I looked and saw a big silver car driving slowly by.

"There's that guy again," Chet said.

"What guy?" I asked him.

"A man who knows my mom and dad. He says he's going to stop by when they're both home and surprise them. It's supposed to be a secret."

"What's his name?"

"He didn't say. But he gave me five bucks."

"That was nice of him," I said.

"Yeah," Chet said. "He's an okay guy."

43

BOBBY GURK

"Something's going down," Teddy O. says to me. "I can smell it."

"How do you figure that?" I ask him.

He squints at me through those crazy specs he wears. "The three of them, Brevoort and the two women, are thick as thieves. They get together almost every night. Usually at Fiddler's house, but sometimes at Gunther's condo."

"But never at Willie's place?"

"I've never spotted them there."

"Teddy, what do you think they're cooking?"

"You want me to guess?" he says. "That's all I can do—guess. I'd guess they haven't got the ZAP pill yet from the McWhortle chemist. Otherwise they'd be long gone. Am I right? But they know they're going to get it, maybe soon, and they're figuring how to handle it. If I was them, I'd grab the pill, get out of town, and set up business somewhere else."

I think about this a long time. "Yeah," I tell him finally, "I do believe you got it. And I can't stand the idea of getting the shaft on this deal. People are such rat finks—you know?"

"Maybe we should move on them right away," Teddy O. says. "Even before they get the pill. Make them tell us the name of the chemist." He takes his ice pick out of the sheath strapped to his shin and waves it at me. "I know how to do it," he says.

"Sure you do," I says. "And maybe we'll have to do it your way. But if we lean on them to get the chemist's name, then we need to pick up the chemist and lean on him to get the pill. So it gets messy—know what I mean? Maybe someone goes screaming to the cops—and then where are we? If it has to be done, then we'll do it. But first let me go see the Gunther dame again. Maybe she'll sing."

"I think she's in on the swindle," Teddy O. says.

"Maybe yes, maybe no," I says. "I'll sure as hell find out."

So I give Laura a call and tell her I'm stopping by that night. "That's nice," she says.

I shouldn't be telling you this because you might think I'm an airhead, but I had a thing for that crazy dame. Like what they call a soft spot in my heart. She's a tall, busty broad with a dirty mouth, but what I like about her is that she's always cracking wise and just don't give a damn. But, of course, my liking her has got nothing to do with business.

I barge into her place, and she's wearing these baby-doll pajamas that show a lot of skin and make her look as big as a house. I figure it's smart to knock off a piece before I brace her, because who knows what kind of a mood she'll be in after I lower the boom.

So after I get up off the floor, she pours us belts of Chivas, and we just sit around bare-ass naked and shoot the bull awhile. Finally I decide to lay it on her.

"Hey," I says, "I hear you and Willie and a blond twist have become palsy-walsy."

"Yeah?" she says. "Where did you hear that?"

"Oh, you know how word gets around. Who's the blonde?"

"A playmate of Willie's. Her name's Thelma something."

So right away I know she's lying, because the blonde is Jessica Fiddler, and if Laura is palling around with her she'd know her name.

"Uh-huh," I says, like I'm not really inarrested. "The three of you having a scene?"

"Now and then," she says. "You got any objections?"

"Not me," I says. "Live and let live. How about an invite to make it a foursome?"

"Not your style," she tells me. "Unless you do coke."

"Oh-ho," I says, not believing her for a minute. "Nose buddies, is that it?"

"That's it," she says. "Just to relax occasionally. Take our minds off our troubles."

"We all got 'em," I says. "Some more than others. What do you hear from Willie about the ZAP pill?"

"Not a word. Bobby, you might as well forget that deal. Since old man McWhortle croaked, all the work at his lab has come to a screeching halt."

"It don't make sense," I says. "There's a lot of loot to be made from that pill. Funny that they'd just drop it."

She shrugs and pours us a refill. She's really got all the goodies. Beefy but not fat, if you know what I mean. And good skin. Creamy. I'd hate to bat her around and spoil her complexion, but I could do it if I had to.

"What's Willie up to these days?" I ask her.

"How the fuck should I know?" she says. "He doesn't blab about his personal business. I guess he's doing what he did before: peddling information. Why don't you ask him?"

"I haven't seem him around lately. I thought maybe he's cooking up a big deal. I've done a lot for Willie. I hope he remembers who his friends are."

"You figure you're a friend of his?"

"Sure I am."

She laughs. "Come on, Bobby. You're the guy who was planning to shaft him."

"That was just business, but personally I like him. I hear he does drag."

She looks at me. "You hear a lot of things, don't you?"

"Does he or doesn't he?"

"As far as I know he wears pants."

"You've made it with him?"

"That's what you paid me for, isn't it?"

"Oh, I'm not complaining," I says. "I just won- dered if a guy like that can get it up."

"He's got no problems in that department," she tells me. "Trust me, I know."

"I'd like to trust you, babe," I says. "I really would. I'd hate to find out you've been diddling me. Then I'd have to come looking for you. You know?"

"How could I diddle you? I haven't clamped you for money, have I?"

"No," I admit, "you haven't. But there are all kinds of swindles. Like maybe you and Willie and the blond broad are figuring to glom on to that ZAP pill for yourselves and leave poor Bobby Gurk on the outside looking in."

She shakes her head. "If we had that fucking pill and were going to cross you, would we still be around? Use your head."

"Maybe you haven't got the pill yet," I says, "but you know how to get it. Then you'll split. I wouldn't do that if I was you, babe. You know what they say: You can run, but you can't hide."

"I don't know what you've been smoking late- ly," she says, "but you've sure got some crazy ideas. Hey, how about an encore on the floor?"

She wants to change the subject—right?

"No," I says to her. "You come over here and do me."

I want to get her down on her knees, because now I know for sure Teddy O. is right and the three of them, Willie and the two women, are fig- uring to dick me.

I had given Laura every chance in the world to come clean and let me in on what's going on. But, no, she wants to play it cute. So I got no choice but to do it Teddy's way.

I make a meet with him the next day, and we talk about how we'll do it.

"Listen, Teddy," I says to him, "I got a lot of guys in my organization, and a couple of them are heavies. So if you need some backup, just say the word."

"I don't think so," he says, "but thanks for the offer. We don't want a mob scene."

"Then you and me will manage it," I says. "What's the script?"

"I'm guessing the blonde, that Jessica Fiddler, is the key. She's the one banging the chemist—right? So we hit her when she's alone in her house. It shouldn't take long. All we want is the name of the chemist and where he lives."

"Piece of cake," I says. "I'd like it if we can scare the shit out of her without no rough stuff."

"Maybe she don't scare," Teddy says. "Then what?"

"Then you take over," I tell him.

He nods. "What I'll do is get to know her routine: when she's home, when she goes out. Then we'll pick a good time and pay her a visit."

"Whenever you're ready, just give me a call."

He looks at me. "You sure you don't want me to handle this by myself?"

"Nah," I says. "I'll come along. I want to get a look at this broad. Maybe after the chemist is out of the picture, she'll be cruising for a new boy-friend. Like me."

We both laugh. I'm bullshitting him, of course. I got no particular interest in the blonde. But I don't want Teddy O. leaning on her by himself.

Accessory to a homicide is a rap I don't need.

44

GREGORY BARROW

I know there are more inspired research chemists at work today, but I have frequently comforted myself with the belief (possibly mistaken) that few have my talent for self-discipline. This applies not only to my professional assignments but to my personal life as well. I think I can say without fear of serious contradictions that I am a singularly *regulated* man. I never act on whim or make capricious decisions.

So you can imagine my surprise and wonderment at what occurred during my brief attendance at a cocktail party given by the saleslady of a boutique patronized by my wife. In fact, I put in an appearance only to please Mabel. Ordinarily I try very hard to avoid social functions. I am just not very good at them, and I am certain my awkwardness and discomfort are obvious.

Two unusual things happened. First, I was engaged in conversation by an elegantly dressed man who claimed to be in the pharmaceutical business.

To my astonishment, he lost no time in making it very plain that he was prepared to pay me large sums of money if I would divulge to him trade secrets of McWhortle Laboratory. Naturally I rejected his offer immediately.

The second curious incident involved a shapely young woman, rather flashy but quite attractive. I can only report that she "came on" to me. She did not seem inebriated, and frankly I was bewildered by her behavior. I know very well that I am far from being the handsomest of men, and most people find me cold and aloof, not realizing that my reserve springs mainly from shyness.

In any event, I was nonplussed by her warm and intimate manner and then embarrassed when it became clear that she was suggesting a sexual liaison. Of course, I rebuffed her advances as politely as I could, but she insisted on giving me a slip of paper (obviously prepared in advance) with her name, Jessica Fiddler, and her address and phone number.

It was possible she was a prostitute and distributing her "business card" to all the men at the cocktail party, but I was inclined to doubt it. I had the feeling that she had singled me out, but for what purpose I could not have said.

But even more unaccountable was my reaction to that bizarre meeting. I have claimed to be the most self-disciplined of men, and I truly believe that. Yet in the days and weeks following the cocktail party I found I was thinking frequently of Jessica Fiddler, wondering about her motives, and fantasizing about what might have happened if I had accepted her generous invitation.

This invasion of my thoughts came at a particularly unwelcome time, for I was working very hard to bring the ZAP Project to a successful conclusion. I was being badgered frequently by Mrs. Gertrude McWhortle, who was in turn being constantly annoyed by Colonel Henry Knacker.

Actually, I was very close to completing the project. I had succeeded in developing a testosterone formulation I judged would be effective on humans, and I had converted the liquid into pills not much larger than a 325 mg aspirin. I produced a dozen pills and put them into a small plastic container. The only step remaining was testing on humans.

As I have stated before, I had every intention of trying the ZAP pill first. It was the moral and ethical thing to do. And yet now that the moment had arrived, I confess I felt a certain amount of, perhaps not fear, but trepidation. The chances of fatal poisoning were, I told myself, so slight that they could be ignored.

But I was entering the realm of behavior modification and, quite honestly, I was not certain of the ZAP pill's effects on humans. I thought ruefully that my situation was somewhat akin to that of Dr. Frankenstein, not knowing if I might produce a monster or a saint.

After a great deal of reflection, I decided it would be too risky to ingest a ZAP pill at the laboratory with so many people nearby. I thought it best to take the pills home, lock myself in the den, and swallow the pill in solitude. But before I did that,

I planned to leave a detailed document instructing my wife and the authorities what actions to take in case I died, lapsed into a coma, became unconscious, or began behaving in an antisocial manner.

It was then the last week of August. I took the container of ZAP pills home and carefully concealed it behind a stack of journals in the den. I did not inform Mrs. McWhortle or Colonel Knacker that the ZAP pill had been finalized. I hoped after my test I could assure them that it had no injurious consequences.

I could have conducted the trial immediately, of course, but I admit I dithered. It was not fear of death so much as fear of an irreversible personality change. After all, even if the pill had the desired effect of increasing aggression, I could not be absolutely sure it would not be permanent, even though the result had been temporary when the testosterone formulation had been injected into mice. And also there might be side effects I hadn't anticipated.

I wanted to become more assertive, but what if, after gulping one or more ZAP pills, I underwent a complete transmutation and became a totally different man? The danger that the testosterone might turn me into an insensate brute was very real to me. The possibility was there: I might lose the ability to feel anything but fury and hostility that demanded physical aggression for release.

This concern had an unexpected consequence: I realized how much I loved my wife and son. I confessed to myself that I had neglected my familial responsibilities. I had become an absent husband and an absent father.

It was during this period, when I was contemplating all the possibly dire results of swallowing the ZAP pill, that one night, while preparing for bed, I said to my wife in a low voice, "I love you, Mabel."

To say that she was astonished would be no exaggeration; she stared at me, eyes wide in disbelief.

"What brought that on?" she asked.

But having blurted out an intimate truth, I didn't have the courage to continue. It was all so new to me, you see. I was not in the habit of verbalizing my innermost thoughts and emotions. Somehow it seemed shameful. I know how ridiculous that must sound to you, but it was the way I was.

So I merely shook my head in answer to my wife's question and went to bed. I could see the disbelief in her face, and it saddened me.

I met the same doubts when I attempted to repair my relations with my son.

"Chet," I said to him one morning, "before school starts maybe I'll take time off from work, and you and I can spend a day together. How would you like that?"

He looked at me strangely. "Gee, I don't know," he said hesitantly. "I got a lot of things planned. I'm going to be awfully busy."

So I dropped it, discouraged by my failure to communicate with wife and son. I couldn't blame them; my behavior must have seemed suspect. They were so accustomed to my chilly reserve that my awkward attempts to demonstrate my love caused uneasiness. I began to wonder if I could ever convince them I was trying to change, to *improve*.

I admit I was confused, and ordinarily I might have confided in Marleen Todd, described my problem, and asked for advice. But she would surely inquire why I was suddenly intent in persuading my wife and son that they were important to me, that I loved them and wanted their love in return.

To answer that question truthfully, I would have to inform Marleen that I was about to test a pill that could conceivably turn me into a savage beast. And before that might happen, I wanted to establish myself as a warm and loving husband and father. I wanted to prove my *humanness*.

But, of course, I could tell Marleen nothing about the ZAP Project. First of all, I was sworn to secrecy. And second, if I did tell her, I knew what her reaction would be: She'd be horrified and outraged that I had developed a product designed to increase aggression in a world already awash in violence.

So I sat in my den, the door locked, and bounced those damnable white pills on my palm, reflecting they had the potential to utterly change my life. Whether for good or for evil I could not say.

But I knew I would soon find out.

45

MARLEEN TODD

I always had a very close relationship with my
daughter Tania. I was thankful, and proud, that
she treated me more as a peer than a mother.
She confided in me, asked my advice, and seemed
genuinely interested in my work.

But recently I had noticed a kind of secretive-
ness in her behavior. She wasn't as forthcoming
as usual, and she seemed to be spending an inor-
dinate amount of time with Chester Barrow.

"Tania," I said to her, "you have so many nice
friends, but you've hardly seen any of them this
summer."

"Mostly they've been away," she said. "Like, on
a trip with their parents. And Gloria Peretz went
to tennis camp, and Marsha Gilcrest had her tonsils
out. So not many of them have been around."

"I'll bet you'll be happy when school starts, and
then you'll see them all again."

She didn't reply to that, and I let the matter
drop. I wanted to mention that I thought she was

spending too much time with Chet Barrow, but if she was lonely during the day and he offered companionship, it seemed cruel to criticize.

Knowing what I know now, I realize I should have been more alert to her moods and resentments, no matter how fanciful. But to tell you the truth, I was so engrossed in my work at the lab that I neglected my duties as a mother. So part of what happened was undeniably my fault.

The development of Cuddle progressed faster than I had dared hope. Because of my personal situation with Herman, I had decided to reconstitute the aroma so that men might find it attractive as a cologne or after-shave. This was a relatively simple task of replacing the lavender and floral essences with sprightlier scents such as citrus, pine, and peppermint.

The most difficult problem was increasing what we called the "projection" of the fragrance. There are perfumes, for instance, that simply don't "carry"; only the user is aware of the aroma, and a person standing quite close might not even be able to sniff it. Other perfumes, of course, project so powerfully that the smallest amount can fill an elevator.

After trying several different top notes, I came to the conclusion that for chemical reasons I could not understand, the oxytocin had a deadening effect on other scents. When I tried it on my wrist, I was certainly conscious of the aroma. But when I asked the opinion of my coworkers in the perfume lab, they could hardly believe I was wearing a scent.

But as a mood and behavior modifier, Cuddle exceeded all my expectations. Repeated trials on myself proved that it had a fantastic ability to make the user feel relaxed, almost languid. More importantly, it increased sympathy for others, spurred a desire for loving togetherness, and heightened a sense of caring.

Darcy & Sons had asked McWhortle Laboratory to produce a new fragrance that would create a feeling of romance, intimacy, and warm understanding. I was certain Cuddle fulfilled those specifications and would be an enormous commercial success.

I was so proud of my triumph that I could not resist telling Greg Barrow what I had accomplished. We were driving home from the lab on the last day of August when I said: "Greg, I have something wonderful to tell you. But you must promise to keep it absolutely confidential."

"Of course," he said.

Then I related the whole story: the assignment to develop Cuddle, my serendipitous discovery of an aerosolized form of oxytocin, and how I had succeeded in using the sex hormone in a perfume that had amazing effects on mood and behavior.

"*Good* effects," I emphasized. "Cuddle just makes you love the world and everyone in it."

"Congratulations," Greg said. "It sounds like you've done an original and ingenious job."

I was driving and couldn't turn to stare at him. "I thought you'd be more excited," I said.

I heard him draw a deep breath. "Marleen, you deserve all the credit in the world. It was a creative idea. But I doubt very much if Cuddle can ever be marketed commercially."

I was stunned. "Why on earth not?" I demanded.

"The Food and Drug Administration," he said. "Can you really see them approving an over-the-counter product that contains a human sex hormone? I can't. The FDA would demand years of tests. And even if they eventually okayed it, I think there would be endless objections from consumer organizations. Look at the problems with getting the public to accept the growth hormone and genetic engineering. You had a remarkable concept and achieved what you set out to do. But I suspect the client will reject it out of hand. It's just not a salable product."

I knew at once that he was right, and I wondered how I could have been such a fool to think that Cuddle could ever be sold alongside Obsession, Passion, and Opium.

"Oh, God," I said, "what an idiot I've been! All those months of work wasted!"

"Not necessarily," Greg said in his serious way. "It's quite possible the aroma you have created might well find a use in psychotherapy. It would have to undergo rigorous testing, of course, but if it alters mood and behavior the way you describe, it could prove valuable in the treatment of, say, depression and suicidal tendencies. I certainly wouldn't junk it just because it'll never be a best-seller. It may turn out to be a very, very important discovery."

That made me feel a little better—but not much. I suppose that in some crazy way I had envisioned Cuddle being easily available to everyone and making for a kinder, gentler world. Greg had brought me down from cuckoo-land. But I found reality depressing.

That night, alone in my bed, I was still dejected, still wondering how I could have been such a simp to think for a moment that a fragrance containing a sex hormone could be sold at perfume counters in department stores. I had just been carried away by a rosy vision, never stopping to consider its practicality.

But, dammit, I told myself, it *was* a good idea, an original idea, and I really had nothing to be ashamed of. I had worked hard, and I had succeeded. And, as Greg had said, it was possible that my formulation might be a big help in the treatment of behavioral problems and psychic disorders. After testing, of course. And I knew of one behavioral problem on which I was determined to do the testing myself.

Herman didn't return home until after midnight. I heard him come stumbling up the stairs and slam his way into the guest bedroom, making no effort to avoid waking Tania or me. I listened to him preparing for bed, showering to remove the traces of his most recent infidelity, no doubt.

I had absolutely no qualms about what I intended to do.

The next morning, at the breakfast table, he looked like God's wrath. His face was puffy, eyes bloodshot, and he was barely able to get a cup of black coffee to his lips, his hands trembled so. But I made no comments on his appearance.

"Herm," I said as casually as I could, "I've been working on a new cologne for men at the lab, and I think I've finally got it right. I wish you'd try it and tell me what you think."

He looked up at me dully. I frequently gave him samples of new colognes and after-shaves, as I did to Greg Barrow and other male neighbors, to test their reactions and hear their suggestions.

"Sure, hon," Herman said. "Leave it on the bathroom sink in the guest bedroom, and I'll give it a go. It's not flowery, is it?"

"Oh no," I said. "It's a real he-man's scent: spicy, minty, and very refreshing. I think you'll like it. The client wanted something different and powerful."

"Sounds good," he said. "What are they going to call it?"

"*Stud,*" I told him.

"Hey," he said, perking up, "that's for me."

46

CHESTER BARROW

Girls can be bossy, you know that? Like running away from home was my idea, I thought it up. But then I told Tania Todd about it, and right away she was taking over. I mean she was going with me, told me what to pack, and even picked the day we were going to leave. Are all girls like that?

Of course, I admit she got her uncle to lend us a hundred dollars which we needed. And the other things she did weren't *wrong*; it's just that she acted like she was running things and I wouldn't be able to leave home without her. *That* was wrong. I probably would have done better without her tagging along. But I didn't tell her that because she'd start crying, and then I'd have to take it back.

So we were going to go on Wednesday, September 2, like she said. I had all my stuff packed in a bag I had shoved under my bed, because my mom never dusted under there. Also, I had decided to make some baloney sandwiches to take with us on the morning we left. Tania said that was a good idea but they should be ham and cheese. See what I mean?

The funny thing was that during that last week my father was trying to be real friendly and talking to me and all. He even wanted to take a day off from work and we would do things together. I couldn't figure out why he was acting so strange like that, and I wondered if maybe he knew I was going to run away and was trying to make up for how mean he had been to me so I wouldn't go.

I told Tania about it, and also how happy my mother suddenly was, laughing and joking with me all the time. Maybe she knew, too. But Tania kept saying it was just a faze (I think that's how you spell it) that they were going through and pretty soon they'd be right back to the way they were before and treating me miserable.

"I guess you're right," I said.

"I know I'm right," Tania said. "Sometimes my father is nice to me when he remembers to be, but then he's up to his old tricks again. I hope you're not thinking of backing out, are you, Chet?"

"Of course not."

"Because if you change your mind, I don't care. I'll just run away by myself."

"I'm not going to change my mind," I said. "How many times do I have to tell you?"

We were sitting in our garage where we went so no one could see us. We were talking about what would be the best way to get to Disney World after we left her uncle's place, like, should we hitch a ride or take the bus? And suddenly, right out of the blue, Tania said, "You don't care for me."

Boy, she really knew how to mix up a guy.

I said, "I do so care for you. I kissed you, didn't I?"

"Oh, that," she said. "That didn't mean anything to you."

"It did so, too."

"I bet you've kissed lots of girls."

"Well, I haven't."

"Never?"

"Well, maybe one or two," I said.

"Who were they? Do I know them?"

"Nah," I said, "you don't know them." That was a lie. "They were just girls."

"Why did you kiss them?"

"Holy moley!" I said. I was getting sore. "I don't remember why I kissed them. Okay?"

"You don't care for me," she said again, and we were right back where we started.

I began to think that if she was going to talk like that all the time, maybe it wasn't such a great idea to let her come along when I left home. I mean I couldn't figure out what she *wanted*.

"Look," I said to her, "I don't ask you how many boys you've kissed."

"Well, I haven't," she said. "You're the only one. So that proves how much I care for you. Because you're the only boy I've let kiss me."

"Tell me what you want," I begged her. "Just tell me what you want me to say, and I'll say it."

"That's no good," she said. "You've got to say it on your own."

Well, that was one talk we had in the garage, and I didn't know what she was getting at. I was all mixed up, and even though I thought about it a lot, I couldn't understand why she was, like, mad at me. I didn't do anything to her. I wished there was someone I could ask about it, but there wasn't.

I was hoping she'd forget about it, but she didn't. Almost every time we talked she'd ask if I cared for her. I mean she really picked on me.

"Now look here," I told her, "if we're going to be traveling, I'll take care of you. Don't worry about it."

"That's not what I mean, Chet," she said.

"Well, what *do* you mean?" I asked her.

"When I ask if you care for me, I mean do you like me?"

"Sure, I like you."

She was quiet a while, then she said, "Do you love me?"

Geez, she was something. First it was did I care for her, then it was did I like her, and now it was did I love her.

"Wait a minute," I said. "Kids are supposed to love their parents, and maybe their relatives and a sister or brother, if they've got one. But kids aren't supposed to love other kids."

"Who says so?" she said.

"Everyone knows that. When you get grown up, it's okay to love someone and then you get married. But kids can't get married, so what's the point of loving someone? It wouldn't do you any good."

"You can love someone and not get married," she argued. "Freddy Washburn told Velma Burkhardt he loved her, and they're just kids and can't get married."

"Who told you that?"

"Told me what?"

"That Freddy Washburn told Velma Burkhardt he loved her."

"Velma told me."

"Well, Freddy Washburn is a real nerd, everyone knows that, and he was probably lying."

"No, he wasn't," Tania said. "He gave Velma a friendship ring. It's got like this little blue stone in it. So that proves he loves her, Chet."

"He probably found it in a box of Cracker Jack."

"But he *gave* it to her. That's the point."

"Well, what do you want me to do—give you a friendship ring?"

"That would be nice," she said. "It would show you love me."

"I didn't say I did."

"Does that mean you don't?"

"I didn't say I did, I didn't say I don't. What's so important about it anyway?"

She sighed. "You just don't understand."

"I sure don't," I said. "Explain it to me."

"Well, if a boy says he loves a girl, then she is his girl and he can't love anyone else. And if a girl loves a boy, then she can't love anyone else either. It's just the two of them, forever and ever."

"That's stupid," I said. "What if one of them moves away?"

"Then they write each other or talk on the telephone."

"But what if one of them moves to like Russia and they never see each other again. What happens then?"

"It doesn't make any difference, Chet," she said. "They've got to keep on loving each other, because they said so."

"That's stupid," I said again. "It just don't make sense."

"Doesn't," she said. "And it's not stupid. It means the boy and girl belong to each other. And if one of them gets hurt or gets sick, the other one takes care of them."

I didn't say anything.

"If I get hurt or sick, Chet," she said. "I mean after we run away. Will you take care of me?"

"Sure," I said. "Of course I would. I wouldn't just leave you."

"Well, that proves you love me. And if you gave me a friendship ring, it would be like a sign."

"A sign of what?"

"That we belong to each other."

"Hey," I said, "it's awfully hot. Let's put our suits on and go to the pool."

"All right," she said.

I was glad she agreed. Talking about love and all that mush was making me nervous.

47

CHAS TODD

I sat in that stinking wheelchair every day, and every day I wondered if I had been a goddamned fool not to accept Uncle Samuel's offer of prostheses and elbow canes. I don't know why I opted for a chair. I think maybe I didn't want to display my infirmity in public. Or maybe I wanted to play the martyr. Who the hell knows. Do you always know why you do the things you do?

That's especially true of moral choices. They're a bitch, because no one gives you a guidebook when you're born. You're supposed to learn by education, training, and experience. But sometimes you're faced with conflicts that nothing has prepared you for. There are no precedents, and common sense can only take you so far.

What brought on that fit of introspection was the business of my niece, Tania, planning to run away from home. I figured that if I snitched on her, she'd never forgive me. But if I kept her plans secret, as I had promised, I could be endangering her safety. I didn't like to think of what kids like her and Chester Barrow might face on the road by themselves.

So I batted it back and forth, and I finally decided to inform their parents. I told Cherry Noble what I was going to do.

"I'm glad, Chas," she said. "Children are not just young adults, they're *children* and haven't yet learned to act in their own best interests."

"I guess," I said. "I keep wishing Tania may eventually forgive and forget I betrayed her. And maybe it'll make the parents pay a little more attention to their kids. It's a gamble."

"All our choices are gambles," Cherry said. "Aren't they? We try to calculate the odds and go with the decision that offers the best chance of success. But sometimes we go against the odds. That's called hope."

"Thank you, doctor," I said.

"How are you going to tell the parents?" she asked, ignoring my sarcasm. "Telephone them?"

"No, that's too cold. Herman comes here for lunch every Thursday. I'll tell him then."

"I think that's wise," she said. "Be sure to say or imply that you think it's the shortcomings of the parents that made Tania want to leave home. I wish you could talk to the mother, too."

"I will," I vowed. "I'll tell Herman to ask her to come out here so I can talk to her one-on-one. I'm going to be tough on them."

"Good," Cherry said. "Even if Tania is imagining her grievances, they should be aware of them."

So that was that: another crisis dealt with, a decision made. But I couldn't forget what Cherry had said about all our choices being gambles. The most important bet I had to make involved her.

What convinced me were things I had said and things she had said about my book-in-progress: *The Romance of Tommy Termite*. It didn't take a giant brain to realize I was writing about myself. All of Tommy's indecisions were mine, and all his hopes were mine. That included love, marriage, home, family—the whole megillah.

It wasn't that I was unhappy with the way things presently were between Cherry and me, but our relationship irked me because it seemed incomplete. There was something missing—and it wasn't just sex. It took me a while to figure out what was bugging me, but I finally identified it: There was no commitment.

I had reached the point in my narrative where Tommy the Termite decides to give up his bachelorhood and ask Lucy to marry him. (I could hardly wait to write the termite wedding scene; that was going to be fun.)

Anyway, Tommy goes through a lot of mental and emotional anguish before he decides to pop the question. He's afraid of giving up his independence. He's afraid of losing his freedom. He's afraid of taking on responsibilities he isn't sure he can handle.

I was afraid of those things, too, and in addition I had the fear of impotence to overcome. It was no use saying the decision was a gamble, take a chance, and what did I have to lose. I had a lot to lose—and so did Cherry Noble. Maybe it was because we had spent those years as analyst and analysand that I had little hesitation in talking to her about it.

"First of all," I said, "I want you to know that I realize this isn't wholly my decision to make. I have no idea what your reaction might be, but I know it's just as important or more important than mine. So you'll have your mind to make up after you help me make up mine. What I'm trying to say is that I'm not taking you for granted. I hope you understand that."

"I understand," she said quietly.

It might have been the first day of September but South Florida was still sweltering. I had finally sprung for a new air conditioner, a beast of a machine that could bring the inside temperature down to the point where you could hang fresh hams on the walls.

It wasn't quite that cold, but I kept it chilly enough so that Cherry always brought a light sweater along when she came to visit. We were sitting close to each other, working on a bottle of Frascati, when I started my confession.

I remember very well that the bathroom door was open and the light was on in there. It didn't provide much illumination for the big room, but it was a bright night, a full moon or close to it, and a pearly glow was coming through the windows. It was like being under water, looking up and seeing a wavery translucence, almost hypnotic.

Cherry was paled by that light. It made her eyes seem dark and enormous. I suppose I looked as masked to her, and I thought it odd, because that night I wanted no part of disguises.

"You must know I care for you," I started.

"Care?" she said with a small smile. "That's rather insipid, wouldn't you say, Chas?"

"How about I'm fond of you," I said. "Is that better?"

"Not much."

"You're a tough lady. All right, I like you. Will you buy that?"

"You can do even better," she said. "Try."

"First let me tell you what's bothering Tommy the Termite."

I told her about all his fears and the struggle he was going through trying to decide whether or not to propose to Lucy.

"Those are my fears, too," I told Cherry.

The bottle was in a bucket of ice at her feet. She leaned to refill our glasses. The wine looked as colorless as water in the moonlight.

"And what does Tommy decide?" she asked.

"That's fiction," I said. "This is us."

"And I thought you had made up your mind," she said mockingly. "After all, you did say you liked me."

"Oh, God!" I burst out. "Care for, fond of, like, have affection for—is there anything I've left out?"

She looked at me. Was she amused or hurt? "Whatever happened to love?" she said.

"Ah," I said, "the four-letter word. What is it? Tell me that."

I think she laughed. "Someone once asked Louis Armstrong what jazz was. He said, 'Man, if you gotta ask, you'll never know.' "

"At least tell me the symptoms."

"An ache, uncertainty, a hope, longing."

"That's it?"

"That's it."

"I may have it," I said.

All right, I was bewildered. You've got to picture me: a grizzled old fart planted in a wheel-chair. And there was that slim, elegant woman, brainy, with the greatest legs God ever created. And she wanted me to say I loved her. I knew she did. And I couldn't. You'd say I had been popping stupid pills, wouldn't you?

We stared at each other, and there were so many things unsaid, by me at least.

"This is worse than going into a firefight," I said.

"Is it so painful? I'm not pressuring you, you know. I wouldn't want you to think that."

"I don't think it. All the pressure is coming from me, and it's driving me nuts. Give me a clue, doc."

"Chas, you're thinking about it too much, trying to solve your problem by linear reasoning."

"Isn't that what I'm supposed to do?"

"Not in matters of faith. That is determined by emotions."

"Are you telling me love is a faith?"

"That's exactly what I'm telling you. You can analyze the bejesus out of any faith, tear it to tatters with logic and reason. But if it's strong enough, it will survive."

"That's heavy stuff," I said. "You want me to act on what I feel and not on what I think?"

She nodded. "Follow your heart and not your head. Is that banal enough for you?"

"Plenty," I told her. "It's what Tommy the Termite does. He decides to marry the girl, and they live happily ever after."

"Well?" she said.

48

LAURA GUNTHER

I don't scare easy, but I admit I was getting antsy. What happened was this: Willie and I had a meet with Jessica at her place, and she told us how she had spotted a black Camry driving past her house. But the guy behind the wheel, who Willie claimed was Teddy O., an enforcer from Miami, Jess made as John R. Thompson, who had conned his way into her home by posing as a property tax appraiser.

"A scam," she said angrily. "I checked with the county office, and they got no one by that name working for them. So the bastard diddled me. I should have my brain examined."

I was spooked by the story, but Willie didn't lose his cool.

"Let's not panic," he said. "I'm just guessing that Teddy O. is working for Big Bobby Gurk. But it's possible that he's cooking some caper of his own that's got nothing to do with the ZAP pill."

"That's crap," I said, and I told them about

Gurk's last visit when he told me he suspected the three of us were planning to dork him.

"Oh, he knows all right," I said bitterly. "And I'm betting he and his bloody playmate are plotting something nasty."

"Shit," Willie said, which surprised me, because usually he talked like a perfect gentleman.

"Hey," Jessica said, "I think right now we could all use a belt. Chivas for you, Laura, vodka for me, and club soda for you, Willie. Okay?"

She brought the drinks, and we sat there awhile without speaking. Jess and I were waiting to hear how Brevoort was going to handle these new developments. After all, the whole fucking deal was his idea, and he was supposed to be the ballsy honcho.

"I still think our original scenario is a good one," he said finally. "But now we'll have to make a few minor adjustments. First of all, let's move up the schedule and make our move before Bobby Gurk and Teddy O. can hit on us. Suppose we do it on Wednesday, September second, at noon. All right with you ladies?"

Jessica and I nodded.

"And since they may be tailing Jess's car and mine, let's switch to your Taurus, Laura. Okay?"

"Sure," I said. "Jess and I can trade cars for the day."

"We'll still use this for our safe house," Willie went on, "because I'm convinced it won't be for more than one day. Gregory Barrow will hand over the pill after the first phone call; I'm sure of it; he'll be at work in the lab. But now the problem is <u>how do we get Mabel</u>

Barrow out of the house on September second? If she's around, it might queer the whole operation."

"That's easy," I said. "I'll phone Mabel on Wednesday morning and tell her Hashbeam's Boteek got in some new lingerie that's just right for her. She'll come running; I can practically guarantee it."

"Good," Willie said. "Then I think that takes care of everything. Any questions?"

"You'll be with me in the Taurus?" Jessica asked him.

"Of course," he said. "That part of it will go just like we planned. We come back here, call the chemist at the lab, and that's it."

"Willie," I said, "are you sure this cockamamy thing is going to work?"

"I'm sure," he said. "It'll go like silk; you'll see."

He still had half his club soda left, but Jess treated me and herself to refills.

"Then what?" Jessica asked him. "Assuming we get the pill, what happens next? Go over it one more time."

"All right," he said patiently. "I take off as planned. I go to another city, probably another state. I get the ZAP pill copied and the business organized. It might take a month or so, but trust me. I'm not going to shaft you. It's not my style. And I figure that after a month or so Gurk will lose interest. After all, what can he do? He hasn't got the name of the chemist so he can't glom on to *another* pill."

"The asshole can come looking for us," I reminded

him. "Jess and I will still be here."

"That's right," he agreed, "but you both knew that when you signed on for this. If he shows up, just tell him that I suddenly disappeared, you don't know where I went, and to the best of your knowledge I never did get the ZAP pill. I honestly don't think he's going to lean on you."

We didn't say anything. Willie finished his drink and stood up.

"I don't think we should meet again," he said, "until this goes down. Let's stay in touch by phone. And by Wednesday or the day after this whole thing will be wrapped up, and we'll be on our way to easy street."

After he left, Jessica poured us another drink and we sat staring at each other.

"What do you think?" she asked me.

"I thought I could handle Big Bobby," I told her. "But after that last boff I'm not so sure. When Willie takes off, I think Gurk will come looking for us, and he might get physical. Him and that Miami killer."

"Let me tell you something," Jess said. "Something I haven't told Willie the Weasel, and I don't want you mentioning it to him. After I saw Teddy O. casing my home, and remembering what Brevoort said about him being a hatchet man, I decided to put the house up for sale. So I've got it listed with a real estate agent. After we get the ZAP pill, I'm leaving with Willie, and I'm never coming back. Wherever we go, I'll hire a lawyer to handle the sale of the house for me. But I'll be long gone with no forwarding address so Big Bobby Gurk and Teddy O. can't feed me to the sharks. Guys like that scare the hell out of me."

"My God, Jess," I said. "Then what happens to me? You and Willie will leave me to face the music. And like you said, those guys don't play nice when they think they've been dorked."

She thought a moment. "Laura, do you own that condo of yours?"

"No, it's leased."

"Then you can walk away from it. Take my advice and start packing. Do like I am: I'm taking two suitcases of stuff I really want and just leaving the rest of my shit. What the hell, if you can believe Willie, we'll have all the money in the world to buy new things."

I looked at her. "You know, Jess, I think you're right. I'll get ready to split as soon as we have the pill. The three of us will leave together."

"Also," she added with a twisty grin, "it won't do any harm to keep an eye on Willie the Weasel, in case he has any cute ideas of screwing us out of our shares."

"I like the way you think," I told her. "I'm beginning to have my doubts about that grifter. He's been running scared ever since he found out Teddy O. was on his tail. We'd be schmucks to let him take off by himself with the pill. We'd probably never hear from him again."

"That's the way I see it," Jess said, nodding. "So the two of us will stick to him like a second skin. Just to protect our investment, you know."

"Right on!" I said. "I'm going home now and

start packing. You have any idea where you'd like to go after we dump this burg?"

"I've been thinking about New Orleans," she said. "I've never been there, and I hear it's a wide-open town."

"Suits me," I said. "I'm ready for a change of scene. Anyplace where Big Bobby Gurk isn't part of the landscape."

I finished my drink, kissed Jessica good-night, and headed for home.

I turned into the parking lot of my condo just as a black Camry was coming out. I saw the driver in my headlights: a little guy wearing wire-rimmed specs. I could have sworn he smiled at me. I almost wet my pants.

I wasn't surprised that Gurk had told Teddy O. where I lived, but it was a shock to see him keeping tabs on me. I hurried inside, locked the door, drew the drapes. I pulled out two suitcases and started packing.

I had some nice things, and it was going to break my heart to leave most of them behind, but it had to be done. I finally selected *my* favorites, not the stuff William K. Brevoort was storing in my closets.

Wherever we were going, the sonofabitch could buy his own dresses.

49

HERMAN TODD

I got up Tuesday morning with the usual industrial-strength hangover. When I stared in the bathroom mirror, I could see what all the boozing and whoring was doing to me. I was beginning to look like an old lush, my face pasty and bloated. I wondered how long it would take my liver to collapse, just like my father's.

Marleen had left for work, and Tania was out somewhere, so after I showered and shaved, I wandered next door to cadge a black coffee. Mabel Barrow was sitting at her kitchen table flipping the pages of a tabloid magazine. She glanced up as I came in.

"Herm, you look shot," she said.

"I am shot," I admitted. "But nothing that your delicious coffee won't cure. How about it?"

She got up to make me a cup of instant and put out a plate of glazed doughnuts. She was wearing pink plastic curlers in her hair. That turns me off. But she was also wearing a T-shirt (no bra) and short shorts. That turns me *on*.

She sat across the table from me and nibbled on a doughnut. I know it will sound like I was around the bend, but the sight of her sharp white teeth biting into that doughnut was the sexiest thing I had ever seen, and I decided it was time to go for broke.

"Tomorrow's the day," I told her.

"For what?" she said, all innocence.

"What you and I talked about," I said. "The romance of the ages."

"I don't know," she said hesitatingly. "I'm not sure."

I reached across the table to take her hand. "Mabel," I said, looking directly into her eyes, "don't pass up this chance, or you'll regret it for the rest of your life—and so will I. You and I are meant for each other; I just know it. We think alike, and we feel alike. We both want the same thing—a little fun, a little happiness, before we get too old to enjoy it. Am I right?"

She nodded.

"Then let's *do* it," I urged her. "Tomorrow at noon. No one will know, no one will find out. Just you and me. It'll be our secret, and it'll be great."

She finished her doughnut and licked her fingers. "What should I wear, Herm?" she asked in a low voice.

I grinned at her. "Whatever you can get out of in a hurry. We're not going to be playing Chinese checkers, you know. Mabel, this is going to be the joy of a lifetime. I'm going to love you like you've never been loved before."

"I've got to get home in time to make dinner."

"That'll give us at least four hours together. Four hours of paradise."

"You'll get there before me?"

"Guaranteed."

"And there won't be any problems with the desk clerk?"

"Absolutely not. I'll grease his palm to make sure. There's an ice machine in the lobby. What do you want me to bring along to drink?"

"I like Galliano."

"You've got it. I'll even bring a lime. Now let me have a piece of paper, and I'll write down the address and how to get there."

Before I left the Barrow kitchen, we embraced and exchanged a soul kiss. My God, she was soft. And so ready! I could feel it.

"Wednesday noon," I whispered in her ear. "I'm going to take you to the stars."

"Don't forget the Galliano," she said.

I drove to my office as horny and excited as a teenager. The first thing I did was phone the motel and reserve a room for noon on Wednesday, September 2. I asked for a vibrating bed, figuring it might be good for a laugh.

I slaved all day, catching up on the paperwork I had been neglecting. I went out for lunch but didn't have a single drink. I was determined to stay sober and get to bed early. I wanted to be physically fit for the motel scene on Wednesday. I just knew it was going to be a memorable bang.

I was a Boy Scout for the remainder of the day: worked hard, treated my employees with respect (to their shock), and went directly home from the office. I did stop briefly to pick up fresh flowers and a key lime pie. Question: Why are married men who plan to cheat so attentive to their wives beforehand?

What a nice, peaceable, domestic evening that was! Marleen loved the flowers, and Tania loved the pie. But I think what they liked best was that, for the first time in a long time, I was acting like a "man of the house," a sober and solicitous husband and father. To tell you the truth, I didn't find it a trial. I think I enjoyed it.

I may have been wrong, but that night I had the feeling that with a little salesmanship I could have persuaded Marleen to let me into her bed. I didn't make the effort. All I could think about were sharp, white teeth biting into a glazed doughnut. I guess there are words for guys like me. Schmo is one of them.

"Oh, by the way, Herm," Marleen said, "that new cologne I told you about—I left a sample on your bathroom sink. I wish you'd try it and tell me what you think."

"Sure, hon," I said. "I'll use it tomorrow."

I awoke early on Wednesday morning. It was a strange feeling to get up unhungover. What a high that was! I heard Marleen and Tania moving about and talking downstairs, so I stayed in bed until the house quieted down and I knew Marleen had left for work. Then I started getting ready for the day's assignation—with emphasis on the first syllable.

I probably don't have to tell you, but in situations like this the man's preparations are as detailed and finicky as the woman's, if not more so. I mean I took extra care in brushing my teeth and shaving closely. I did a thorough job in the shower, too, and spent a lot of time in selecting my seduction costume: not too dull, not too flashy. It was, I thought, something like putting on a confirmation suit.

But before I dressed, I inspected the new cologne Marleen had left on the bathroom sink. It was in a spray dispenser and unlabeled. I spritzed a little onto one hand, rubbed my palms together, and sniffed the fragrance.

I liked it. As Marleen had said, it was spicy and minty and had a very refreshing after-scent. I sprayed my armpits and rubbed some on my chin, neck, and chest. It was cooling which, I supposed, came from the alcohol base. But even after that evaporated, I could smell the aroma. It wasn't overpowering, and I had the feeling Mabel Barrow would love it. That wonderful woman!

All perfumed and duded up, I went out into a perfect day: warm sun, cloudless sky, kissing breeze. What a great world it was! I saw Tania and Chet huddled in the Barrows' garage and waved to them. What marvelous kids! Both of them were winners, and I loved them, I really did.

The drive to the Fort Lauderdale motel was a delight. I just felt so good that I wanted it to go on forever! It was like being born again, seeing everything for the first time. Colors seemed so vivid, traffic sounds were music, and I even sang as I drove. I don't remember the tune but it was so bright and cheerful I had to laugh!

The people at the motel couldn't have been nicer; I had no problems at all. The room they gave me was spacious, sunlit, and spotlessly clean. It was only then that I realized I had forgotten to bring a bottle of Galliano. I went back to the lobby and from a vending machine I bought two cans of cold A&W diet root beer. I was happy with my choice. Mabel would be delighted!

She arrived about twenty minutes later, and she looked absolutely beautiful! She was wearing jeans and a pink cotton shirt, and her hair positively glistened. She was radiant, and I realized how fortunate I was that she loved me.

I took her in my arms and told her how I felt.

"Sweetheart," I said, "just being with you is all a man could want. These moments are so precious to me. You look so sweet I could eat you up."

"That, too," she said. "Where's the Galliano?"

"First," I said, "let's snuggle awhile."

She looked at me strangely. *"Snuggle?"* she said.

50

MABEL BARROW

Herm came over on Tuesday morning for a cup of java and gave me the motel pitch again. I figured what the hell, fish or cut bait, and I was tired of the should-I-shouldn't-I routine. So I made up my mind right then and told him okay, I'd shack up with him at noon on Wednesday. If he was even half the lover he claimed to be, it would be a hoot.

Finally deciding calmed me down. I mean I had been worrying the problem a long time, and now I felt better about things. I had a session with Dr. Cherry Noble on Tuesday afternoon and tried to explain.

"Look," I said, "I'm no great brain, and I know it. I happen to be a very physical woman, and I need my jollies. Is that so awful?"

"Quite normal," she said, smiling.

"So I've decided to kick over the traces," I went on. "One time, at least. I don't like the idea of cheating on my husband, but what he doesn't know won't hurt him—right?"

293

"Mmm," she said.

"I know I'm taking a chance," I said. "I mean if this guy turns out to be the world's greatest stud, I might get hooked. Know what I mean?"

"I know," she said.

"Then it would become a habit, and I'd turn into a bimbo. But I don't think that's going to happen. I may not be brainy, but I know what's best for me. Greg has a lot of good qualities. He's steady, a hard worker, and I guess he loves me in his own nutty way. And he brings home the paycheck. I'm not giving that up for a toss in the hay, even if the guy turns out to be Superman."

Cherry looked at me a moment. "I presume the man you're talking about is your next-door neighbor, the one you told me about."

"That's right. He's a boozer, which is another reason I can't see myself getting seriously involved. But he's fun, and that's something that's been missing from my life."

"By fun I presume you mean sexual pleasure."

"That's what I mean all right. Do you blame me?"

"No, Mabel, I don't blame you. I'm not going to tell you that you're doing the right thing or the wrong thing. It's your choice to make. Do you want to continue seeing me?"

That question surprised me because after I decided I'd give Herman Todd a hump, I also decided I didn't need Dr. Noble anymore. I mean I had found a cure for what ailed me, hadn't I? So why did I need a shrink? Besides, it cost plenty.

"I think I should stop," I admitted. "I really

appreciate your listening to all my complaints. It's been a big help talking to a smart woman like you. But maybe I'll try things on my own for a while. Okay?"

"Of course," she said. "I understand completely. I wish you the best of luck, and if you ever decide you'd like to talk to me again, I'll be here."

"You're a darling," I said. "You know that? Listen, doc, you got a guy?"

She flipped a hand back and forth. "Sort of," she said.

"Well, he's an idiot if he lets you get away," I told her.

She laughed. "Thank you, Mabel. I think so, too, but I'm not sure he does."

"What's the problem?" I asked her.

She looked at me in a strained kind of way. "Much the same as yours," she said finally. "With complications."

And that's all she'd say.

I spent all Wednesday morning getting ready. Chester was out in the garage with Tania Todd— I guess they were playing or something—so I had the house to myself.

I was going to get all gussied up because this was a big deal in my life. But then I figured what was the point because I'd be bare-ass naked all afternoon and didn't have to impress Herm with my duds. He'd probably rip them off anyway. So after I showered, I just pulled on jeans and a cotton shirt so if anyone saw me, they'd think I was heading for Sears or someplace like that.

While I was doing my hair, Laura Gunther phoned from Hashbeam's Bo-teek.

"Mabel," she said, all excited, "you've got to come down right away. We just got in a new shipment of lingerie, and you're going to love some of the things. I took one look and immediately thought of you."

"Aw, Laura," I said, "I can't make it today. I promised this friend to have lunch with her at Mizner Plaza. As a matter of fact, I was just leaving when you called."

"That's too bad," she said. "You'll be gone all day?"

"Probably," I told her. "But I'll try to stop by tomorrow."

"That's fine," she said. "See you then."

So I finished dressing. I didn't take a purse or handbag, just my wallet stuck in the hip pocket of my jeans. I didn't want to run the risk of leaving ID in the motel room.

"Chester, I'm going out now," I called into the garage. "Got some shopping to do. I'll be home for dinner."

"Okay, Ma," he yelled. "Take your time."

I got into the Roadmaster, took a deep breath, and started out for Fort Lauderdale. Herm's directions were easy to follow, and I don't think it took much over twenty minutes to find the motel. What can I tell you—it looked like a motel. It wasn't the Ritz-Carlton, but it seemed clean enough. The best part was that it was way off in the woods, and the chances of being spotted by someone I knew were practically nil.

Like Herman promised, I had no trouble at the desk. They gave me his room number right away with no questions asked. Up to that point, everything had gone without a hitch, and I was really beginning to get excited at what was going to happen now.

The room he had rented was nothing special, just your standard motel flop, but what the hell, we weren't going to *live* there. What was a shock was Herm's behavior. He greeted me with this sappy smile, and if I didn't know better, I'd have guessed he was stoned. Not drunk, but *stoned*.

After the door closed and locked, he grabbed me in his arms and held me tightly. He said he wanted to *snuggle* awhile. So we stood there clasped together like a couple of idiots for what seemed like five minutes.

"Oh, I just love to hug," he said. "Don't you just love to hug?"

"Well, yeah, sure," I said. "A hug is okay. Sort of like an appetizer—know what I mean?"

Finally he turned me loose and led me over to one of the beds. We sat close together. Now we'll get down to business, I thought. Then I noticed a thing on the bedside table that looked like a little vending machine. It had a long wire leading to the mattress.

"What's that?" I asked him.

"Oh, that's funny," he said. "You turn it on, and the bed starts to vibrate."

"No kidding?" I said. "I've never seen anything like that. Turn it on, Herm."

"We don't need it, sweetheart."

"I just want to see how it works. Switch it on."

So he did, and I turned the dial to High. Sure enough, the whole bed began to shake.

"Hey," I said as we started jiggling, "that's crazy. Now's a good time to have a swig of Galliano."

"Oh, I forgot to bring it," he said. "But I do have this cold A&W diet root beer. Isn't that great!"

I just looked at him, and he put an arm around my shoulders. "The important thing, Mabel," he said, "is caring. Don't you agree?"

"Oh sure," I said, wondering where the hell he was coming from.

"I care for you so much," he went on. "You have no idea. Do you care for me, dear?"

"Would I be here if I didn't?"

He held me tighter and nuzzled at my neck. "We must respect each other," he crooned, "and love each other. I want to tell you my innermost feelings, and I want you to tell me yours. I want us to be truly intimate, Mabel, to share all our secret thoughts and dreams."

Meanwhile that insane bed had warmed up, was going faster, and we were bouncing up and down like acrobats on a trampoline. Herm had trouble hanging onto me.

"Just to cuddle with you is so wonderful," he said, speaking louder because the bed was beginning to sound like a meat grinder. "I've wanted a romance like this all my life. I know now that if there can be warm understanding between a man and a woman, that's the most marvelous thing in the world."

"Herm," I said, "how do you turn this god-damned thing off?"

"You and I can create a whole new world of two," he babbled on, still with that sappy smile. "I want us to become so loving that nothing, not even death, can ever part us. Oh, Mabel, Mabel, Mabel, I love you so much."

"When?" I yelled. *"When?"*

He hugged me tighter to keep me from being bounced off. "Snuggling like this," he shouted in my ear, "is the answer to my dreams. I want to spend the rest of my life being the best, the truest, the most loving *friend* you've ever had. I want to—"

"Shit!" I screamed, and got off that galloping bed. I staggered a moment, caught my balance, and headed for the door.

As I ran down the corridor, I heard his echoing wail: "I love youuuuuu!"

51

EYEWITNESS TESTIMONY

I made a meet with Teddy O. on Wednesday morning, this is September 2, and I says to him, "Teddy, I'm sick and tired of futzing around. Let's do it today."

"Yeah," he says, "it's about time. I figure about one o'clock will be best. The Fiddler dame is usually home then."

"How do we do it?"

He shrugs. "Nothing fancy. We just bust in and ask her politely to give us the name of her boyfriend, the chemist with the ZAP pill."

"And if she clams up?"

"Then we unclam her," he says, grinning. "Believe me, she'll talk. Either the easy way or the hard way."

"Okay," I says. "Let's leave here at noon. Maybe we'll grab a burger and some fries first. We'll go in your car. Are you sure you won't need any backup?"

"I'm sure," he says.

*　*　*

I phoned Mabel Barrow on Wednesday morning, figuring to get her out of the house by tricking her into coming to the Bo-teek to look at a new shipment of lingerie. But she said she had a lunch date and couldn't make it.

So when Jessica and Willie showed up at Hashbeam's in Jess's car, I told them what had happened.

"But she said she'll be gone all day," I added. "So there's no need to change our plans."

"Good enough," Willie said. "As long as the kid is there by himself."

"Look," I said, "I don't want to sit here all day sucking my thumb. Give me a call after it goes down and let me know what's happening."

"I'll phone you," Jess promised. "Now give me the keys to your Taurus. You got enough gas?"

"Full tank," I assured her. "Listen, I wish you guys the best of luck."

"Piece of cake," Willie said, and I hoped he was. right.

I brought all my stuff over to the Barrows' garage on Wednesday morning after Mother left for work. Chet had already brought his things down, so we were all ready to go. But Mrs. Barrow was still in the house, and we talked about how we could run away while she was there.

"We didn't think of that," Chet said. "How are we going to call for a cab if my mom is here? She'll want to know what's going on."

Then we saw my father wave to us, and he left in his car.

"Now we can move all our stuff to my house," I said, "and call a cab from there."

"Gee, I don't know," Chet said, and I could see he was worried. "Mom could be looking out the window and see us leave."

We were still talking about what we should do when Mrs. Barrow shouted from inside the house and said she was going shopping and would be home in time for dinner. So we waited until she drove away, and then we went into the Barrows' kitchen to phone.

I drove Laura's car with Willie the Weasel in the passenger seat. He wasn't saying much, and I could tell he was going over our scenario in his mind, figuring how to react if something went wrong.

"No rough stuff, Willie," I warned him.

"Nah, Jessica," he said. "It's not my style. I've got a scam all worked out. The kid knows me, see, and thinks I'm a friend of his dad. So I'm going to tell him his old man was hurt in a lab accident and is asking for him."

"You think he'll fall for it?"

"Sure he will. Then once he's in the car, I can handle him."

"I hope you're right."

"Trust me. And as soon as we get to your place, I'll phone Barrow at McWhortle's."

"It's tricky, Willie."

"It's a sure thing," he said.

"The last time someone told me that, I got busted, had to pay a fine, and was lucky I didn't get tossed in the slammer."

"You worry too much," he said.

Tania and I waited in the garage until my mom drove away. Then we went into the kitchen and phoned the cab company. Tania wanted to do the talking, so I let her. She gave the man our address and told him to hurry. She was real bossy.

"He said it'll be about twenty minutes," she reported. "So now all we have to do is wait."

"Maybe we should move all our stuff out to the curb," I said.

"No," Tania said. "Someone might see us and ask where we're going. We'll have the cab pull in the driveway and we'll load up right here."

"Listen, Tania, do you think you should call your uncle and tell him we're coming? He might be out."

"He can't go out," she said. "He's in a wheel-chair and never goes anyplace. But maybe I'll phone anyway and tell him we're on our way."

So she did and talked to her uncle a few minutes. Then she hung up and said, "He's there, and everything's okay."

"Are you sure he'll give us the money?"

"I know he will," she said. "He promised, and I trust him."

We were standing outside in the driveway, watching for the cab, when a Ford Taurus pulled up in front of our house. A man and a woman got out and came walking toward us. I recognized the man. He was the guy in the silver Infiniti who said he was an old friend of my dad.

* * *

Tania phoned me a few minutes before noon on Wednesday and said she and Chester Barrow were all packed and ready to go, and she had already called for a cab. They would be out at my place within a half hour to pick up the hundred dollars.

That was the worst news I could have heard. I had planned to tell Herman about the kids' intention to run away when he came for lunch on Thursday. But now I only had thirty minutes to figure out what to do, and I admit I was totally flummoxed. So I called Cherry and explained the situation.

"How do I handle it?" I asked her. "Give them the money or try to talk them out of it or what? I need quick advice, doc."

She was silent a moment. Then: "I can cancel my afternoon appointments, Chas. I'll have my receptionist tell them I have a family emergency. It's a half-truth. I think I better come out to your place. Perhaps I can help you with the kids."

"God bless," I said. "I write books for children, but this is something beyond me."

"I'm on my way," she said.

I hung up thinking what a true-blue woman she was. I realized then how much I had come to depend on her. Not just for offering to help with Tania and Chet, but for doing her damnedest to make me a whole man again. It took this crazy emergency to make me see it.

I made up my mind right then. She might say no, but if I didn't at least try, I didn't want to imagine what my future would be like. They don't give you medals for regret.

Jessica and I got out of the car, and I saw Chester Barrow standing in the driveway outside his house. There was a little girl with him.

"There's the boy," I told Jess.

"Who's the girl, Willie?" she asked.

"Never saw her before," I said. "A complication, but I can finagle it. Let's go."

We walked up to the kids, and I took the boy by the arm.

"Hiya, Chet," I said. "How you doing?"

"Okay," he said, looking at me.

"Listen, I got some bad news. Your dad's been hurt in an accident at his laboratory. He's been taken to a hospital, and he's asking for your mother."

"She's not home," he said.

"Then you better come along with me," I said, tugging at his arm. "Your dad should have family with him."

"Don't go, Chet," the little girl said. "Phone the lab first and see if he's telling the truth."

I knew right then it was going to go sour if we didn't move fast.

"Jessica," I said, "hold the loudmouth until I get the kid in the car."

Jess got a good grip on the girl, and I started to drag the boy toward the Taurus.

"Is this a snatch?" he asked me.

I almost laughed out loud. That kid had been watching too many crime shows on TV. "Yeah, it's a snatch," I told him, talking tough. "And I got a big gun. I'll blow your head off if you give me any trouble."

I pushed him into the backseat and climbed in after him. Jessica released the girl and came running. She got behind the wheel, and we pulled away with a chirp of tires.

"How much ransom you going to ask for?" the kid wanted to know.

I was in my office on Wednesday morning, working on a reformulation of Cuddle. After what Greg had said about the objections of the FDA, I realized a perfume or cologne containing a sex hormone could never be marketed commercially. That did not mean, of course, that I could not produce a limited amount for my private use if the sample I had given Herman to try had the desired result of modifying his behavior.

I was preparing to go down to the employees' cafeteria for lunch when my phone rang. It was my daughter, so excited she was almost incoherent.

"Tania," I said patiently, "I can't understand a word you're saying. Now just slow down and tell me why you're calling."

"They just took Chet Barrow away!" she shouted.

"What? Who took him away?"

Then she told me a man and woman had pushed Chet into their car and driven away with him.

"They kidnapped him," she said, and I could tell she was trying not to cry. "And the woman held me, and I tried to kick her and bite her, but I couldn't. She really held me tight, and I bet I have bruises tomorrow."

"Tania, where are you now?"

"I'm in our house, in the kitchen."

"I want you to stay inside. Lock all the doors and windows. Don't go out and don't let any strangers in, no matter what they say. You understand?"

"Yes, Mother. Should I call 911 and tell them what happened to Chet?"

"I'll take care of it, dear. You just stay inside."

"Can I call Daddy's office and tell him?"

"Yes, you can do that. And I'll tell Mr. Barrow immediately. We'll be home as fast as we can get there."

I hung up and rushed down to Greg's private lab.

I worked all Wednesday morning on the final ZAP Project report. I left the Conclusions section blank until I had tested the testosterone pills hidden in my study at home. Those were the only tablets I had produced, and I didn't intend to make more until I had observed their effects on myself.

My phone rang shortly after twelve-thirty. I did not recognize the man's voice.

"Mr. Gregory Barrow?"

"Yes. Who is this calling, please?"

"It's not important. What is important is that we're holding your son, Chester."

"What are you talking about?"

"Your son has been kidnapped, Mr. Barrow."

"I don't believe it!"

"Would you care to talk to him? Just a minute."

I waited, frightened and trembling. Then: "Hi, Dad," Chester said cheerfully.

"Are you all right, Son?"

"Oh sure. They haven't hit me or anything. They just pushed me in a car outside our house and drove me here. It's a snatch, Dad."

"Chet, put the man on again."

After a moment he came back on the line and said, "Satisfied, Mr. Barrow?"

"You hurt him, and I'll kill you," I said.

"No need for threats," he said calmly. "We have no intention of harming the boy—if you agree to our terms."

"How much?" I asked hoarsely.

"Not money," he said. "Just a few of the ZAP pills."

I caught my breath. "How did you know about that?"

"What difference does it make?" he said. "That's the ransom, Mr. Barrow. You hand over a few testosterone pills to us, and the boy walks away unhurt. You refuse, and I can't guarantee his safety. Think it over. I'll call you in about an hour, either at the lab or at your home, and give you instructions for delivery. I suggest you refrain from informing the police. That wouldn't be smart, Mr. Barrow."

Then he disconnected, and I sat staring at the dead phone in my hand. There was a pounding on my lab door. I unlocked it, and Marleen Todd rushed in.

"Greg," she said in a stricken voice, "Tania

just called and said something dreadful happened
to Chester."

"I know," I said. "I've got to get home."

"I'm going with you," she said.

Willie sat in the backseat, hanging on to the boy
while I drove. I was afraid the kid might scream
or start crying but he was no trouble at all. He
just kept asking how much ransom we were going
to demand. To tell you the truth, I think he was
enjoying it, like it was a big adventure he could
brag about to his pals.

When we got to my place, we hustled him inside
and closed all the venetian blinds. Our original plan
was to tie him up in case he got any ideas of making
a break for it. But he was so well-behaved we didn't
have to use the clothesline I had bought. I brought
him a Coke and some Doritos and he thanked me
politely. Nice kid.

Willie called Gregory Barrow at the lab and let
him talk to his son a minute to prove we had
him. Then he told Barrow we wanted the ZAP
pill and would call again in an hour to tell him
how to make the drop.

"Let him sweat awhile," Willie said after he
hung up.

"My Dad don't sweat," the kid said.

Willie said, "Doesn't." I thought that was funny.

I got myself a vodka and a club soda for Brevoort.
Then I phoned Laura at Hashbeam's like I had promised and told her everything was copacetic. We were

all just sitting there waiting for the hour to pass when my front door bell rang.

"Don't answer it," Willie said in a whisper. "And everyone keep quiet."

Just to make sure, he got a grip on the Barrow boy and put a hand over his mouth.

The bell rang again, a good long ring, but we sat there without making a sound.

Then suddenly my front door burst open. It was locked and chained, but there was a splintering sound, and I thought it was coming off the hinges. It didn't, but it swung wide open, hung crazily, and the elephant who had put his beef to it came stumbling in. And right behind him was a little guy wearing wire-rimmed glasses.

I knew who those bums were.

Believe me, I've busted through heavier doors than that one. So Teddy O. and me go barreling in, and there's this classy-looking head, Willie Brevoort, and a little kid, a boy who was maybe ten years old, about that.

"Well, well, well," I says. "May we join the party?"

No one says a word.

"I bet you're Jessica Fiddler," I says to blondie. "Am I right?"

She doesn't answer.

"And what's your name?" I says to the kid.

"My name is Chester Barrow," he says, "and I have been kidnapped. I think you should call the police and these people should go to jail."

I look at Teddy O., and he looks at me.

"Kidnapped?" I says to the boy. "Why should they do that? Is your daddy rich?"

"They don't want money," he says. "This man phoned my father at the laboratory where he works and told Dad he wants some kind of pills, and when he gets them I can go home."

I grin at Teddy O., and he grins at me.

"Beautiful," I says. "Just lovely. And is your daddy going to hand over the pills?"

"I guess," the boy says. "This man told my father he'd call him again in a little while and tell him how to deliver the pills."

"Stoolie," Willie says.

"Hey," I says, "watch your language. He just wants to go home. Am I right, kid?"

"Yes," he says, "and they should go to jail."

"They certainly should," I says. "Willie, phone the boy's daddy and tell him to deliver the pills here."

He doesn't make a move.

"Teddy," I says, "persuade him."

That guy was some slick operator. With one fast swoop he's got the sharpened ice pick out of the ankle sheath and he's holding the point under Brevoort's chin.

"Make the call, Willie," I says gently. "Tell the chemist to bring the pills here."

"Very well," he says.

Teddy O. looks disappointed.

After I left Herman Todd at that funky motel, I drove home as fast as I could. I had never been so humiliated in my life. I mean, after the way he pitched me, I was primed for a world-class hump, but he turned out to be all talk and no do. All I got was an earful of caring, respect, warm understanding, and cuddling. What kind of bullshit is that?

When I got home, Greg, Marleen Todd, and Tania were standing in the driveway talking and all excited. They filled me in on what had happened, and I almost fainted. My first thought was that God was punishing me for going to the motel with Herm. I was glad we hadn't screwed, or maybe I'd never see Chester again.

"Greg," I said, "what are we going to *do*?"

"Wait for the phone call," he said grimly, "and then do whatever they want to let Chet go."

"Maybe we should call the police."

"No," he said, "definitely not."

Then Marleen saw a pile of bags and suitcases stacked just inside our garage door. "Tania," she said, "what is your overnight bag doing out here?"

The girl started crying. "Chet and I were going to run away," she sobbed.

"Oh my God," her mother said, flopped to her knees, hugged Tania, and started crying herself. Then I started crying. What a scene that was!

But then we heard the phone ring inside our house, and Greg dashed into the kitchen with me right behind him. He grabbed up the phone.

"Yes," he said. "Yes, this is Gregory Barrow. That's correct. Yes, I understand. Would you repeat the address, please. Thank you. I'll be there as soon as possible."

He hung up and rushed into the den with me on his heels.

"How much money do they want?" I asked him.

"They didn't say."

I watched him root around under a pile of magazines and dig out a little plastic container. He opened it and shook two white pills into the palm of one hand.

"What are you doing?" I said.

He shoved the pills into his mouth and gulped them down without water or anything. Then he shuddered, closed his eyes, and grabbed the edge of his desk. I think he was shaking.

"This is a hell of a time to be popping aspirin," I yelled at him.

His eyes opened slowly, and he stared at me. What a look that was!

"Shut your big, fat mouth," he said.

Well, when those two guys came busting through the door, there was a huge one and a little one with glasses, I thought everything was going to be okay. I mean I figured they would call the police, and I would tell them how I got kidnapped. Then those crooks would go to jail, and the cops would take me home.

But it didn't work out like that. It looked like they all knew each other. The guy who claimed he was a friend of my dad, his name was Willie, and I think he was lying; I don't think he ever went to school with my father like he told me. He and the pretty lady, her name was Jessica, were the two crooks who snatched me.

The other two guys who broke the door down were really tough. The huge one was named Bobby,

and the little one was Teddy. I was scared of him
because he had this ice pick he held under Willie's
chin and made him call my dad and tell him to bring
the pills right away if he wanted to see me alive again.
I don't know what kind of pills they were, but I
hoped my father would bring them right away.

So we sat there waiting, and I decided they
were all crooks. I was afraid they would kill me
and my father, because even if he gave them the
pills, I didn't think they'd let us go on account of
they'd know we'd call the police and report them.
I didn't know what to do, and I felt like crying,
but I didn't.

Bobby made the lady bring him and Teddy some
drinks, and she also brought me another Coke.

"Don't worry, Chet," she said to me. "You're
going to be all right. You'll go home with your
dad."

"Sure you will, kid," Bobby said.

But now I didn't believe any of them.

That Teddy, the one wearing glasses, made me
nervous. He never sat down; he just stood holding his ice pick and watching us. If I had a gun,
he wouldn't act so mean, believe me. If he tried
to stick me, I'd just shoot him.

"I've got to go to the bathroom," I said.

"Sure, kid," Bobby said. "And I'll come with
you. I wouldn't like you to take a powder."

I didn't know what he meant by that. But he
went with me to the bathroom, which was at the
back of the house. Bobby inspected it first, and it
didn't have any windows so I guess he figured I
couldn't get out and run away. He waited for me

to come out, and then we went back to the living room.

After we had all been sitting a while, no one talking or anything, we heard a car pull up outside.

"That must be the guy," Bobby said. "Teddy, I'll handle him. You just keep an eye on these two assholes."

My father came in and looked at all of us. He looked a long time at Willie and Jessica, then turned to stare at Bobby and Teddy. And then he motioned to me.

"Go out to the car, Chet," he said quietly. "We're going home."

"Hey, wait a minute," Bobby said. "You the chemist from McWhortle Laboratory?"

Dad nodded.

"You got the ZAP pills?"

"Yes, I have them."

"Then hand them over and we'll talk about what comes next."

"Come on, Chet," my father said. "We're leaving."

Bobby sighed. "Get the pills, Teddy," he said.

The little man moved close to Dad, holding out his ice pick, waving the tip back and forth.

"Let's have them," he said.

Then my father moved so fast I could hardly see what happened. He jerked the glasses off Teddy's face, snapped them in two, dropped them on the floor, and stomped on them hard. I heard the sound of breaking glass.

Teddy jabbed out blindly at where Dad had been standing, but he wasn't there. He had moved to the side, caught Teddy's arm, and twisted it up behind his back. The ice pick fell on the floor. Dad pulled the arm up higher and the little guy screamed when the bone broke. My father released his arm, and it just dangled.

Then, quick as lightning, my dad rushed at Bobby and punched him in his fat belly. Bobby went "Ooof!" and kind of doubled over. Dad grabbed up a big brass table lamp and smashed it down on Bobby's skull. He just fell down and my father started kicking him in the head. He kept kicking until Bobby's face was all bloody and his nose was yucky.

Then he went back to Teddy who was flat on the floor, groaning and holding his broken arm. Dad started jumping up and down on him, his chest and his stomach. He'd just leap in the air, come down hard, and then do it again. I think the little guy passed out.

Then my father stopped and took a deep breath. He looked at Willie and Jessica. While he had been destroying the two guys, they just sat there, really stunned.

"Chet and I are going home now," my father said sternly. "Any objections?"

Willie cleared his throat. "None whatsoever," he said.

"Let's go, Son."

We went out to our car together. I took his hand.

"Dad," I said, "you were awesome."

After Mabel Barrow left the motel, I stayed for almost an hour, sipping diet root beer and reflecting on what an intimate and *nurturing* encounter ours had been. I felt that I had, perhaps for the first time in my life, been totally open and honest with another human being. I had *shared* myself, my inner self, with Mabel, and the experience gave me a glow of happiness.

I returned to my office, and Goldie told me that my daughter and wife had phoned several times, sounding frantic. I called home immediately and learned that Chester Barrow had been kidnapped and his father had gone to rescue him. In addition, Tania and Chet had been planning to run away. Also, my brother Chas had phoned and wanted me to call him as soon as possible.

"Courage, dear," I said to Marleen. "I'll come home at once and provide all the support I can."

By the time I arrived at Rustling Palms Estates, Greg Barrow had returned home with Chester, and that family was reunited and happily bonding with one another. Marleen, Tania, and I gathered in our own kitchen, and I urged Tania to tell us honestly why she had intended to run away.

She offered many critical comments on my past behavior. I assured her that the censure was warranted, and the blame was completely mine. I promised to abandon my bad habits and begin to conduct myself as a loving father should.

"That's another thing, Daddy," Tania said. "Sometimes I think you don't love Mother and me. You never say you do."

After ten minutes of earnest pleading, I believe I convinced both wife and daughter that my love for them was genuine and deep. Henceforth it would be verbalized frequently and reflected in my actions.

"Remember," I told them, "we are a world of three, and it is in our power to be supportive of one another. The important thing is to get in touch with our innermost feelings and share them in a homey atmosphere of warm intimacy."

They eagerly agreed that sharing could revive our family and create the closeness we sought. Then Tania left to learn from Chester Barrow the details of his brief kidnapping. I phoned my brother and related all the events of that afternoon. I also informed him of my resolve to mend my ways and provide the spousing and fathering my dear family deserved.

"Glad to hear it," Chas said. "So Tania isn't going to run away?"

"I think I persuaded her that I am fully aware of her discontent and will do everything in my power to ensure her happiness."

"Good God Almighty!" Chas said, and hung up.

My wife had gone upstairs, and after speaking to my brother I followed her. I went first to the guest bedroom where I freshened up, using more of that cologne Marleen had given me to try. Then I knocked on the door of her bedroom.

"Come on in," she caroled.

We sat close together on the bed, and I spoke again of our love, the need to share our innermost feelings, the importance of compassionate understanding, sympathetic parenting, and mutual nurturing.

Marleen lay back on the bed and held her arms out to me.

"And don't forget quality time!" she cried.

* * *

Jessica phoned me at Hashbeam's Bo-teek, and the moment I heard her voice I knew the whole deal had crashed. Well, what the hell, I knew it was a crapshoot when I got into it.

Jess told me what happened, talking so fast I could hardly keep up.

"Laura," she finished, "Willie and I are taking off. As soon as we can. Before those two gorillas come to."

"They're not dead?"

"Nah. I wish they were, but they'll revive. Both of them are candidates for Intensive Care. But eventually they'll get out, and I don't think we ought to be around when they do."

"You got that right, Jess," I told her. "If you and Willie are lamming, I think I better skedaddle along with you. How soon can I get my car back?"

"We're leaving right now. I'm taking my packed suitcases. I hate to leave so many nice things."

"Don't worry about them," I said. "They're only *things*. Just worry about saving your ass."

"Yeah," she said, "you're right. Survival is what it's all about."

It was Wednesday evening before we got everything organized. We met at my place. Willie had his silver Infiniti packed with all his wardrobe, including evening gowns and wigs. Jessica decided to dump her old clunker and drive with me in the Taurus.

"Drive where?" I asked again.

"How about New Orleans?" Jess suggested again.

"Suits me," Willie said. "I got enough cash to keep us going awhile. If we have to, we could open a small crib until I can set up an information racket again. Is that okay with you ladies?"

I didn't like the idea of getting back in the skin trade, but I didn't want to spend the rest of my life at Hashbeam's either—especially with Big Bobby Gurk on the prowl.

So we all had a final drink before we set out. I had a bottle of champagne in the fridge, left over from my cocktail party, and that's what we had.

"Here's to a glorious future," Willie said, hoisting his glass in a toast.

We all drank to that, and then we got in our cars and headed out. I remember that as we drove along that night Jessica and I sang that old song that goes, "Row, row, row your boat, gently down the stream . . ."

Like she said, survival is the name of the game.

On the drive back home I said to Chet, "I want you to promise me something, Son." And whatever had happened, whatever Mabel had done or hadn't done, he was *my* son.

"Sure, Dad," he said. "Whatever you say."

"When you tell Mother and your friends about your kidnapping, please don't mention anything about the pills. It's a confidential research project I've been working on, and I wouldn't like people to know about it."

"I won't say a word, I promise."

"It'll be our secret," I told him. "Just the two of us."

"Yeah," he said happily. "I can keep a secret."

Mabel was delighted to see us, of course. She wept, embraced both of us, and wanted to hear the story of Chet's rescue over and over as if she could hardly believe our good fortune.

"And you didn't have to pay any ransom!" she marveled.

"Not a cent," Chet assured her. "Dad took care of those crooks. He just mopped up the floor with them. You should have seen him. He was Rambo!"

After dinner—macaroni and cheese—I went into my study and closed the door. I had some heavy thinking to do.

There were ten ZAP pills remaining, and I hid the container in the bottom drawer of my desk. Their potential frightened me because I realized I had been in a murderous frenzy when I attacked those two men. It was only by the grace of God that I refrained from killing them.

Drugs with that effect, I knew, should not be made available, even on a limited basis for what might be considered patriotic reasons.

The question was how to end the ZAP Project. If I told Colonel Henry Knacker I had failed, he'd be sure to take the assignment to other research laboratories, and what I had created, I was certain, would eventually be duplicated by other chemists.

There was also the problem of what might happen when the two criminals I had assaulted were released from the hospital. Surely they would come looking for me again, and I feared they might devise more vicious and successful methods of obtaining the pills.

I finally decided that my best course of action was to make the ZAP Project a matter of public knowledge and depend on public outrage to put an end to the development of testosterone additives.

To accomplish this, I determined to write anonymous letters to *The Miami Herald*, *The New York Times*, and *The Washington Post*, detailing the interest of the U.S. military in producing a "diet enrichment" that would turn our combat soldiers, even temporarily, into conscienceless killers. I was confident that investigative reporters would be assigned to look into my allegations, and I had faith that the resulting outcry by the American people would end the ZAP Project forever. And the publicity would certainly deter the criminals from attempting further mischief.

I realized, of course, that by writing even anonymous letters to the newspapers, I was breaking the vow of secrecy I had signed, and I could be prosecuted. But I didn't care. Marleen Todd had been correct: A psychoactive drug that flouts the norms of society is simply wrong. It is unethical and immoral to develop it and prescribe it. Humanity comes first.

There was a soft knock on my study door, and it was opened.

"I'm going up to bed now, Greg," my wife said. "Chet is already asleep. I guess he was worn out, the poor kid."

"Mabel, we should have spoken to him about why he wanted to run away. He's obviously unhappy."

"*Was*, maybe, but he isn't now. He said that after what happened today he knows we both love him. I told him we certainly did, but we haven't paid as much attention to him as we should have. I said all that is going to change. From now on we're going to do more things together, as a family. Am I right, Greg?"

"You're exactly right. And I'll tell him so myself tomorrow."

"Are you coming up soon?"

"In a few minutes, after I lock up."

"Hurry, honey," she said.

I went through my nightly routine, locking doors and windows, turning off lights. Then I went upstairs. Mabel was waiting for me, naked in bed.

Later she said, "Darling, I've never had so much *fun* in my life!"

I said, "I haven't finished yet. We've got all night."

"Oh lordy, lordy, lordy!" she said joyfully.

"You know, Cherry," Chas said to me, "if I didn't know better, I'd say my brother was stoned. He wasn't drunk, but he was talking like a goof. After he told me the kids had decided not to run away, he started blathering about parenting, sharing his innermost feelings, and nurturing his wife and daughter. You think the idiot has finally flipped his wig?"

"I doubt that," I said, laughing. "I think he's suddenly discovered some basic truths and is trying to express them in the gobbledygook that passes for the language of sociology these days. I don't know where he picked up the jargon, but if he really means what he says, it doesn't make much difference how he expresses it. The important thing is that he seems to have become a paterfamilias again."

"Yeah," Chas said. "Let's hope it lasts."

The problem of the runaways having been solved, we relaxed for the first time that afternoon. There was beer in the fridge, and we each had one, drinking from the can because it seemed the lazy, carefree way of doing things now that the crisis had passed.

"Now about us," Chas said, and stopped.

"Yes?" I prompted him. "What about us?"

He took a deep breath. "How about this? Let's get married."

I stared at him. "You're serious, aren't you?"

He nodded.

"When did you decide?"

"It's been growing," he said. "Germinating. I finally knew I'd have to go off the high board, or it would be the end of me. A purely selfish decision. Half a decision. The other half is yours."

"You know the answer to that," I said. "Yes, yes, and yes."

"Wait a minute," he said. "There's something that has to come first. You game?"

"Yes," I said, "I'm game."

"Don't help me. I can do this myself."

He wheeled himself over to the bed and set the chair's brake. He braced his massive arms, lifted himself up and swung onto the coverlet.

"Over the top, lads," he said. "Follow me, men. Do you bastards want to live forever?"

He began to undress with nervous fingers. I took off my clothes and lay down beside him. He looked at me with a tender smile. He stroked my naked body.

"It all looks so *good*," he said. "I'll have a few slices of white meat, please. And the drumsticks, of course," he added.

"Do you think we'll live happily ever after?" I asked him. "Like Tommy the Termite?"

"Hell, no!" he said. "We'll fight, we'll claw, we'll scream, we'll send each other right up the wall. Occasionally. We're human, aren't we? But I think we'll make it. Don't you?"

"Oh, yes," I said, reaching for him. "We'll make it."

Lawrence SANDERS

Guilty PLEASURES

Putnam